AN
Autumn
KISS

TIMELESS
Victorian
COLLECTION

AN
Autumn
KISS

LAURA ROLLINS

ANNETTE LYON

LISA H. CATMULL

Mirror Press

Copyright © 2022 Mirror Press
Paperback edition
All rights reserved

No part of this book may be reproduced or distributed in any form whatsoever without prior written permission of the publisher, except in the case of brief passages embodied in critical reviews and articles. These novels are works of fiction. The characters, names, incidents, places, and dialog are products of the authors' imaginations and are not to be construed as real.

Interior Design by Cora Johnson
Edited by Meghan Hoesch, Lisa Shepherd, and Lorie Humpherys
Cover design by Rachael Anderson
Cover Photo Credit: Shutterstock #1929757529

Published by Mirror Press, LLC

ISBN: 978-1-952611-30-8

An Autumn Kiss is a Timeless Romance Anthology® book.

Timeless Romance Anthology® is a registered trademark of Mirror Press, LLC.

TABLE OF CONTENTS

The Plucky Miss Ruth by Laura Rollins _____ 1

Mr. Dowling's Remedy by Annette Lyon _____ 69

A Railway Through the Roses by Lisa H. Catmull _____ 165

Timeless Victorian Collections

Summer Holiday
A Grand Tour
The Orient Express
The Queen's Ball
A Note of Change
A Gentlewoman Scholar
An Autumn Kiss

Timeless Regency Collections

Autumn Masquerade
A Midwinter Ball
Spring in Hyde Park
Summer House Party
A Country Christmas
A Season in London
A Holiday in Bath
Falling for a Duke
A Night in Grosvenor Square
Road to Gretna Green
Wedding Wagers
An Evening at Almack's
A Week in Brighton
To Love a Governess
Widows of Somerset
A Christmas Promise
A Seaside Summer
The Inns of Devonshire
To Kiss a Wallflower

The Plucky Miss Ruth

By Laura Rollins

Chapter One

England, 1895

Time, it seemed to Ruth Hughes, had stopped in the gardens at Gildredge Manor.

The autumn leaves hung on brown branches, but never dropped. The muggy weather had cooled, bringing one brisk day after another but never truly turning cold. The pink aster and deep red dianthus peered up at her, rich and bright, but never fewer in number than the day before.

If she didn't know better, Ruth would say she was stuck in a continuous loop.

Such a delightful notion, a continuous loop. She couldn't quite remember where she'd first read that term, but it had stuck with her all the same. To relive a single day, over and over again . . . only breaking free when a lesson was learned, or a goal accomplished. When she'd first come across the term, she'd thought on little else for days.

Walking alongside her cousin, Nettie, Ruth couldn't help but keep an eye out as they turned off the street, walked through the gate, and into the gardens. Here she always found a little bit of calm, a break from the busy Eastbourne. There, just inside the gates was the gardener, Mr. Harrison, same as he always was.

"Good afternoon," Ruth called to him, repeating the words she always said. "The flowers look beautiful today."

"Thank you, miss," he replied. "I can take credit for the fine soil and proper placement." As he spoke, Ruth mouthed along with the words, she'd heard them so many times. "But it's the Good Lord who you ought to give credit to for the brilliant blooms."

They walked over the well paved path, deeper into the gardens. Each bed was perfectly planned, boasting blooms and greenery native to both England and abroad; truly some of the most exquisite blooms Ruth had ever seen. Short yellow violas were planted just in front of a stunning pink clematis variety she'd never seen anywhere else. When she'd asked the gardener about it several days ago, he'd called it Rooguchi clematis.

Beyond that was a vibrant purple butterfly bush and then some stunning white Japanese anemone—again, another name she only knew due to her asking the gardener. She hadn't a mind for botany; she'd much prefer spending her time studying science, new engineering feats, or even the inexplicable, yet wholly familiar, attributes of Time itself.

Still, that didn't mean she couldn't thoroughly enjoy the beauty around her. And these gardens were nothing short of lovely. Colors covered every corner—yellows, pinks, purples, and even blues—all resting against a variety of greens. Reminding her of an artist's palette, it was a rainbow of life and vibrancy. And the smell . . . heavenly. Sometimes light, sometimes heavy. Sometimes floral, sometimes woodsy.

All in all, not a terrible place to be stuck in a continuous loop.

Of course, if this truly *was* a continuous loop, next up they would see—

"Good afternoon," Ruth called out as a nanny walked by them, going the other direction, pushing her charge in a white baby carriage. Miss Gates, right on cue.

Nettie silently nodded her greeting as the woman passed.

The small movement on her cousin's part put Ruth in mind of a summer they'd spent together as young girls. Then, Nettie had been as openly spoken as Ruth; only, when Nettie spoke up it rarely went without censure from one of her parents or her governess. Though Ruth and her parents had visited for over a month that summer, it had only taken Ruth three days to see that her cousin's life was far different than her own, no matter they were of equal standing among society.

They visited Nettie's family again two years later, and Ruth found her cousin quiet and demur, and she'd remained such ever since.

Ruth shook the sad memory away and instead chose to focus on the lovely sights around them.

"This garden is exquisite, is it not?" she asked Nettie.

"Nothing was ever more so," Nettie replied in her soft voice. "I especially love the view of the sea up ahead."

"I must confess, if Mother must banish us from home every afternoon, this is not a bad place to be sentenced to."

Nettie was silent a moment longer than Ruth expected before saying, "I do hope my presence is not a burden."

Ruth pulled her cousin to a stop. "Nonsense, we all love having you." Nettie had lived with them since her parents unexpectedly died nine months previously. Though the circumstances were heartbreaking, having Nettie around had been an absolute joy. "I insist you believe me," Ruth continued, "for I am in earnest."

Though she didn't say anything, Nettie smiled. Seeing her cousin happy again was enough for Ruth and she felt her previous morose memories lifting as they continued in silence.

If this was a continuous loop, then around this next bend would be Mr. Davies, the costermonger. Granted, he wasn't exactly supposed to be in the gardens, but when had that ever stopped a street seller from placing himself right where the hungriest customers were?

As expected, the costermonger's call reached Ruth before they turned the bend.

"Apples, apples, red and ripe!"

"Apples, apples, cheap and bright!"

Ruth smiled and hurried forward. She had no idea where Mr. Davies got his apples, but he wasn't lying when he said they were the best to be had.

"Two apples, please," Ruth said, walking up to him.

Mr. Davies was short, and he wore his hat at such a lopsided angle that a ring of baldness could be seen from beneath one side of the rim. "And how are ye ladies today?" he asked. Near his waist hung a large pallet with short walls, secured to his person with various ropes about his shoulders and midsection. Apples were piled high on it. Ruth rather wondered that the man could walk here every morning without spilling a single piece of fruit.

"Quite well, thank you." She opened her reticule and pulled out a halfpenny which she exchanged for the red apples. "It's a lovely day for a stroll."

"That it is," Mr. Davies said with a smile and a small incline of his head. "That it is."

Ruth and Nettie bid him farewell and turned to continue down the path. But Ruth paused. Suppose she *was* caught in a continuous loop? She had just exchanged the same words she often did with Mr. Davies. Ruth's lips pulled to the side, and she slowly turned and faced the costermonger once more. She could feel, more than see Nettie's confused expression at the change in their never-changing routine.

"Mr. Davies," Ruth called back. "I must say, the buttons along the bottom of your trouser legs are looking exceptionally bright today."

The row of silver buttons which lined the side of a costermonger's trousers were not only often part of their uniform, but Ruth had never known one who didn't consider them a point of personal pride. Mr. Davies was clearly no exception, for his chest puffed out and his lips quirked upward.

"Thank ye, miss, thank ye very much."

Ruth gave him another smile and then turned back toward the path, biting into the smooth apple. It hadn't exactly been a life altering change to the loop, but it had been something all the same. Ruth took another bite, momentarily closing her eyes to savor the sweet and tart juiciness. This afternoon—another one spent at Gildredge gardens at her mother's insistence—would at least differ from all the others in that one small way.

Nettie's hand wrapped around Ruth's arm tightly and pulled her to a sudden stop. Ruth's eyes flew open, only to find her pathway blocked by a man. She would have run directly into him if her cousin hadn't stopped her. Bless Nettie.

"Pardon me, ladies," the man said. Ruth's eyes only came to the man's chest, and a finely togged chest it was too.

Nettie curtsied first, reminding Ruth to do the same.

"Miss Hughes?" the man said, surprise sounding in his voice.

Ruth looked up—and up—until finally her gaze found his face. It took the briefest of seconds, but then her memory caught up. "Lord Lambert." She curtsied again, though she wasn't exactly sure why. "I did not know you were in the neighborhood." She'd met him this past year in London, but had only spoken to him once or twice.

His light hair had a slight curl to it and was kept short, several waves resting against his forehead. He had no mustache, despite the facial hair becoming ever more popular, but his chin was firm and his eyes a vibrant blue which seemed to pull its color directly from the sky.

"I left London only last week," he said with a smile, one that made Ruth's stomach flutter.

She pressed a hand to it, willing it to calm. Lord Lambert was handsome, breathtakingly so, but he had also been the most sought-after bachelor this past Season. And men who frequently had dozens of ladies falling over him never cared for the company of booklovers such as Ruth. Therefore, no matter his well-cut coat or his smile or his gorgeous blue eyes, Ruth willed her heart to ignore what she saw.

Nettie tugged slightly on Ruth's arm.

"Oh," Ruth hurried to say, "I don't believe you've met my cousin, Miss Wright."

"No," Lord Lambert said turning toward Nettie, "I don't believe I have."

Introductions were quick, and after that, much to Ruth's surprise, Lord Lambert did not excuse himself right away, but instead fell into step beside Ruth and Nettie.

"Tell me," Ruth said, feeling the need to have some conversation, "how does your mother fare?"

"Ah, polite conversation is it now?"

Ruth had to twist her head so far to see up to Lord Lambert's face, that she nearly missed her next step. "Pardon me, my lord?" She could only hope he wasn't referring to some misspoken word on her part—her mouth did have a tendency to run away from her at times.

"Only, while we were in London, I came to believe you

cared little for boring topics of health and the weather. Were you not rather more inclined to discuss news articles on archaeological finds in Egypt, or a recent scientific discovery you'd just heard of?"

Ruth's face heated. This wouldn't be the first time her proclivities proved unwanted among the *ton*. "One would rather wonder at your willingness to be seen in my company, if your report of how I handled myself in London were true."

He glanced her way, a look of incredulity across his face, albeit one that had a smile barely hidden beneath. "Are you denying your love of science, Miss Hughes?"

It did not signify what he thought of her; Ruth didn't care to pretend to be something she wasn't. "That I could never do." The words came out with a bit more bite than she'd intended, but ever since she'd been called an "uppity bluestocking" two years ago she'd grown a touch sensitive.

"Good," he stated with finality, and sharing with her another of his handsome smiles. "Because I must confess, if I thought you were going to stick to topics of health and the weather, I would be quite disappointed."

Well . . . it would seem she had gotten her guard up quite unnecessarily. Ruth shared a quick look with Nettie, who was characteristically content to remain quiet. Later they would discuss this conversation, but for now Ruth was left wondering how much of Lord Lambert's character she'd completely misread.

"Have you been following the latest on the railroads?" he asked.

"I have," Ruth confessed.

"There was an interesting article in yesterday's paper."

"About the Barry Railway?"

"The very one."

For the next several minutes they discussed the various

railroad companies, and who was vying to build where. Ruth found the conversation easy and comfortable. She'd not seen this side of Lord Lambert while they'd been in London. Then again, she'd hardly done more than notice him a time or two from across the room. She hadn't had the opportunity to have more than a two-sentence conversation with him before now.

Once, even, Nettie spoke up and Lord Lambert—proving yet again to be different than most of the lords and ladies Ruth had met in London—stopped to listen to her and encourage her in the conversation.

After a time, he bid them goodbye, even going so far as to bow over Ruth's hand, making her stomach flutter once more, and this time she could have sworn her heart encouraged the notion.

With the tip of his hat, Lord Lambert strode back the way they'd just come.

"Well," Nettie breathed softly, "what an unexpected meeting."

"Unexpected in more ways than one." She'd not been expecting to meet a previous acquaintance, neither was she expecting him to prove quite different than she previously judged him to be. Ruth could not help but glance back over her shoulder at him.

Lord Lambert certainly cut a fine figure, even if he was so absurdly tall. He puzzled her. Certainly, it was something she would have to dwell on, but later. For, with her next step a new thought struck.

By stopping to speak with the viscount, she and Nettie were traversing the path a good half hour later than they normally did. What would that mean for her continuous loop?

The path continued straight for a few strides, and then bent to the left, curving sharply. As the pathway stretched out straight before them once more, Ruth could feel the sun dropping in the sky. They would need to leave soon.

A man with his back to Ruth and Nettie pushed an elderly woman in a chair with wheels. He stopped the white-haired woman before a bunch of scarlet red celosia. She spoke to him, and he walked around to the front of her chair, probably to better hear. As he did so, Ruth caught sight of his face for the first time.

Her heart flew up into her throat—it was none other than Mr. Parker.

Mr. Bert Parker.

Ruth took hold of Nettie's arm and spun her cousin around. "Gracious, I just noticed the time," she said quickly.

"Oh?" Nettie said, her voice its typical soft tone. "I am sure we won't be missed if we walk a few more minutes."

Ruth slowed, looking carefully at her cousin. Should she say something? After all, it had been Nettie's heart that had been hurt, not her own. Ruth opened her mouth, but hesitated. Were there not some things best kept unsaid?

Ruth loved Nettie like a sister and would not, could not, do anything to hurt her.

"I am sure my mother will wish us back home soon," was all Ruth said.

Nettie, who had not the temperament to argue, nodded. "I suppose speaking with Lord Lambert did put us rather behind our usual schedule."

Unfortunately, he had. Far enough behind schedule that the entire continuous loop had just been placed on its proverbial head. Ruth resisted the urge to look behind her this time. She didn't need a second glance to know that Nettie's one-time fiancé was speaking with his grandmother not more than fifty yards behind them.

Judging by Nettie's calm demeanor, she hadn't seen him. That was a relief. Ruth could only imagine the vexation seeing Mr. Parker again would cause her cousin. Ruth hadn't known the particulars at the time, but since Nettie had come to live with them nine months ago, Ruth had pieced together enough to know that Nettie and Mr. Parker had been deeply in love, but had been forced to break things off when Nettie's parents found out he was a banker and had not a single title in his family to boast of.

Ruth didn't allow their pace to ease until they were passing between the gates and leaving the gardens completely. Nettie had suffered enough heartache in the past year; Ruth certainly wasn't going to be the one to inflict more on her.

And yet, as they walked home, Ruth couldn't put Mr. Parker from her mind. Nettie had truly loved the man, and it hadn't been all that long ago. Ruth believed Nettie was happy living with her and her parents, but she wouldn't wish to keep such a life forever. And, although it was an extremely unchristian thought, Ruth had to acknowledge that the two sole obstacles to Nettie marrying the man she loved had both passed on and could do nothing to stop her.

As they reached the townhouse, Ruth let Nettie go in first. "I want to watch the sunset for just a minute."

Nettie nodded. "I'll let Aunt know where you are in case she needs you."

Ruth waited until her cousin was inside and then turned and, instead of facing the sunset, looked toward the direction of the gardens.

Ruth placed her hands on the stair railing and leaned against it. What was it she'd often heard regarding continuous loops? They were only broken when someone solved a problem or satisfied a need. Perhaps this was hers—Ruth needed to give Nettie and Mr. Parker a second chance.

It wouldn't be easy. It would have to appear natural. It would need to happen on a day when Nettie was feeling in fine spirits.

A smile tugged on Ruth's lips.

But, if she played things just right, this could be exactly what her cousin needed to secure happiness. Nettie was quiet and shy, but no sweeter heart had ever walked the earth. Ruth knew of no other woman who deserved happiness and love more.

With her smile growing and an excitement that filled her entire being pulsing inside her, Ruth finally entered the townhouse.

She had a lot of planning to do tonight.

Tomorrow, she would face another loop, but this time she'd go in prepared and with a plan.

Chapter Two

"The flowers look beautiful today," Ruth called to the gardener.

"Thank you, my lady," he called back. "I can take credit for the fine soil and proper placement. But it's the Good Lord who you ought to give credit to for the brilliant blooms."

And just like that, they had entered the continuous loop yet again. Ruth kept a watchful eye out for Mr. Parker. Just because he'd been on the far side of the gardens yesterday, didn't mean he'd be there today. He could just as easily be on *this* side of the gardens, or just around the first bend, or not here at all.

The nanny drew near, pushing the young child the opposite direction Ruth and Nettie were walking.

"Good afternoon," Ruth said.

She looked a little less worn thin—perhaps the child was behaving today. Ruth turned to Nettie after the nanny had moved out of ear shot to say as much, but paused. Nettie's face was drawn and her brow was low.

Was Mr. Parker here then? Had Nettie seen him?

But a quick look around proved that Mr. Parker wasn't about at all.

Then, this blue devilment had nothing to do with him. And if Nettie wasn't upset about Mr. Parker, then there was probably only one other thing making her this pale.

Ruth could not pretend to know what it was like to lose both parents, unexpectedly. But she did know that grief could hit at random times, and it was like one was drowning in it all over again. Ruth didn't say anything, but slipped her arm around her cousin's.

Since Nettie had come to live with Ruth and her family immediately after the tragedy, Ruth had seen her sorrow from the beginning. Heard Nettie cry night after night. Seen her arrive at breakfast pale and pink eyed. Watched as she slowly began to smile again. Stood by her whenever grief hit once more. Ruth had learned, through it all, that often her cousin didn't care to talk about it, but she did greatly appreciate not being left alone during those awful times of sadness.

"Do you know what I was just thinking of?" Ruth asked. She couldn't take the grief away from her cousin, but perhaps today she could distract Nettie away from it, at least a little.

Nettie didn't respond, but Ruth knew she'd heard all the same.

"I was just thinking of that time," Ruth continued, "when we were five, I believe. You and I snuck into the kitchen and took those lemon-raspberry tarts. Gracious, but they were delicious." All these years later, Ruth could still almost taste the sour-and-sweet treats whenever she thought of them.

"We shouldn't have done that," was all Nettie said.

Bother. No doubt, instead of distracting Nettie, she'd only brought to mind one of the many times Nettie's mother had chastised her.

Ruth pursed her lips—there had to be something she could say that would help. But one thing was for certain— Ruth couldn't very well force Nettie to meet Mr. Parker in her current condition. Ruth had never considered herself particularly adept at understanding another person's emotions, or at feeling what another might feel. No doubt, that was the reason she'd picked the wrong memory to bring up just now. Ruth's strengths lay more in understanding scientific journals and in never growing tired of reading or learning.

Still, even she knew now was not a good time for a reunion.

They walked on, perhaps a bit slower than usual, and Ruth's lips pursed. No, Nettie wasn't ready to see Mr. Parker yet. But could not Ruth find a way to ascertain if he was even in the gardens? If he'd only intended to come the one time, yesterday, then she would have to throw out every note she'd written last night and start afresh. If he came here again today, she might be able to reasonably assume he'd come again another day, and that might be a better time to have herself and Nettie "happen" across him.

"Apparently," a deep voice came from Ruth's right, "I am not the only one who decided a single stroll through the gardens was not enough."

Ruth turned and found Lord Lambert walking up to her.

"No," she called to him, "a single stroll is certainly not enough."

He fell into step beside her, and Ruth couldn't deny that she found herself happy over the notion of seeing him again. Still, she didn't miss that Nettie moved away slightly. Ruth wasn't surprised that her cousin chose to discretely remove herself from the conversation, especially considering Nettie's current mood, but it saddened her all the same.

"Have you seen the view of the sea from the terrace?" Lord Lambert asked them.

"Nettie and I walked that way the first day we'd come." Ruth glanced at her cousin, but Nettie only nodded wordlessly.

"I found it quite impressive," Lord Lambert said.

A woman adorned in more ruffles and pearls than Ruth had ever seen outside a ballroom walked past them. Lord Lambert bid the woman a good afternoon, tipping his hat her direction, but continued on with Ruth, saying no more to the woman than that.

"We met at Queen's Hall last month," Lord Lambert said by way of explanation.

He knew that elegant woman, yet chose to walk with them? Ruth tried telling herself it was nothing. He didn't want to appear rude by excusing himself so soon after striking up a conversation. It was only an act of politeness and nothing more.

But she sincerely doubted her heart believed any of it.

"Did you attend the promenade concert while at Queen's Hall?" she asked, even while repeating all the reasons he chose to talk with her to herself.

"I did, and I found it immensely enjoyable. Were you in attendance?"

"I was. It was one of the last gatherings we attended before leaving London." For some reason, it surprised her that a man whom she'd assumed cared quite a lot about his appearance among society would enjoy a performance aimed at making music available to all, even the most lowly.

Here again, she seemed to have misjudged him. "Do you suppose they will have the concert again next year?" she asked.

"The newspapers all say they will." His smile brightened. "I certainly *hope* they will."

Ruth's stomach began fluttering once more, and this time she could have sworn her heart encouraged the notion. Her head, however, was not so easily swayed. What did it signify if he enjoyed good music in a modern concert hall?

Still, as they spoke on about the various activities they'd enjoyed in London, Ruth couldn't help but wonder at who

Lord Lambert truly was. Yes, they'd spoken a few times before today, but never for this long, and never with such ease.

"Apples, apples, red and ripe!

"Apples, apples, cheap and bright!"

"Care for an apple again today?" Lord Lambert asked her.

"Only if it's one from Mr. Davies," Ruth said, grateful for the change in topics. "His are the best to be had." She didn't generally like being the center of attention. Science or news from the Orient she could discuss all day, but she didn't like to talk about herself. It left her feeling on edge and under scrutiny.

However, as Lord Lambert purchased three large apples, she couldn't help but acknowledge that just now, with Lord Lambert, had felt different. His teasing didn't leave her feeling like a bug under a microscope. He returned with the apples, handing one to Ruth and one to Nettie while keeping one for himself.

"Thank you," Ruth said, taking hers and breathing in the sweet smell.

"That is very kind of you," Nettie said, taking hers. "However, if you two don't mind, I think I'd prefer to sit a spell. You two may continue on without me."

Not giving either of them time to argue with her, Nettie walked away and sat on a bench nestled among some pink echinacea. Without glancing back at them, Nettie rested her apple in her lap, instead of biting into it.

"Shall we?" Lord Lambert asked, quite as though they hadn't just been left unceremoniously alone.

Ruth felt a moment's pang of sadness for her cousin. Nonetheless, she couldn't deny that she rather liked the idea of being left to walk with the tall, handsome man. For, with each conversation, he was proving himself not to be whom she'd originally assumed.

Did that make her a terrible cousin? She could only pray it didn't. Perhaps she could find a way to cheer up Nettie once they returned home.

"Are Mr. Davies's apples always this good?" Lord Lambert asked as they strolled and ate.

"He never fails to sell only the best."

"How often do you two come here?"

"Every day. My mother claims it's good for a young woman's health to take a turn out of doors in the afternoon. Though, there was this one time, when I was thirteen, I brought *The Count of Monte Cristo* out with me."

"That sounds enjoyable."

"It was . . . until I lost track of time and came back into the house red as one of Mr. Davies's apples."

"Did you not choose a spot in the shade?"

"Who has time to search out such a thing when Edmond Dantès is digging his way out of the infamous Château d'If?"

Lord Lambert laughed. "I suppose shade is rather immaterial when seen in that light." After sharing another laugh over the matter, he glanced behind them and toward Nettie. "Is your cousin well today?"

Ruth sighed. "Her parents passed about nine months ago. Most days she is fine, but there are times when it hits her again."

Lord Lambert nodded. "I lost my father a little over five years ago. I can understand what she's going through, at least in some ways."

"I am sorry for your loss."

"Thank you. My mother and three sisters still live nearby, and I see them frequently. It helps." His gaze drifted back toward Nettie. "Is there something we might do to cheer her up?"

He cared enough to be willing to do something for a

woman he barely knew? Ruth's heart warmed this time, instead of her face. "Well . . . " her voice trailed off. How much did she dare confide in Lord Lambert?

At length, he bent down, bringing his mouth closer to her ear. "You, dear lady, are exhibiting all the signs of a woman deep in conspiracy."

Ruth pressed her lips firmly together to keep from smiling so large she appeared the fool. "Perhaps I am."

He straightened, a flash of surprise appearing in his expression. "She doesn't even try to deny it."

Ruth shrugged. "Why should I?"

"What, then," he said, his voice dropping low once more, "does it take to get invited to take part in the conspiracy?"

Ruth turned, facing him fully and truly studying him. "Have you read H. G. Wells's *The Time Machine*?"

"I confess I have not." He suddenly looked a little less confident. "Is that necessary to join?"

Well, it was a rather new book. "What of Edward Bellamy's *Looking Backward*?"

He slowly shook his head.

"Surely you've read *Rip Van Winkle* then?" He still looked at her with a blank expression. "By Washington Irving." She'd spent hours the previous night looking through those three stories for any clue regarding how best to approach a continuous loop.

His lips twisted to the side. "I see I have some work in front of me."

At least he wasn't running away, decrying her mad. She enjoyed that realization far more than was reasonable. "Well, I suppose those readings aren't exactly necessary for today's objective. But you ought to read them as soon as you are able." Could one truly consider himself knowledgeable in today's society and not have read a single book regarding travel through time? Ruth didn't believe so.

"Not for today?" His face lit up. "Then we are not here simply to conjecture and speculate."

"Oh no, I did most of that last night." Ruth said, matter of factly.

Lord Lambert laughed out loud—and the sound made its way directly into her chest, resonating there and drawing a matching laugh from her.

"Then, by all means, Miss Hughes, tell me what I am to do."

Chapter Three

"Good evening," Ruth said to Miss Gates as they crossed paths.

"Good evening to you ladies as well," the tired-looking woman replied before walking past Ruth and Nettie.

Ruth hesitated slightly, turning to her cousin after the nanny was well out of ear shot. "I think that's the first time I've ever heard her voice."

Nettie, who was in slightly better spirits today, glanced back over her shoulder. "Some people just take longer to get to know, I suppose."

Ruth nodded—Nettie would know, she was such a person.

"You know," Nettie continued, again glancing over her shoulder toward the nanny, "I always thought that would be my future."

Of a truth? "Surely not," Ruth said, looping her arm through her cousin's. "I predict far more exciting adventures in your future."

Nettie smiled gently. "A year ago, I would have argued against that. But now . . . " She shrugged. "Perhaps you are right."

"Oh?" Was her cousin dreaming up new plans for her life? Was she finally seeing past the limited scope of what her parents had always insisted she be? Ruth certainly hoped so. She missed that little girl Nettie had been when they were both five years old, carefree, and unhampered by society's expectations.

Just then, Lord Lambert walked up. "Good evening, ladies."

Ruth and Nettie curtsied and bid him hello. Similar to yesterday, Nettie moved off a ways, giving Ruth and Lord Lambert plenty of space to speak. Ruth hadn't expected Nettie's response, seeing as her cousin seemed happy again today. Still, she couldn't deny that it made asking her questions all the easier.

"How did the oak trees appear to you yesterday?" she asked, using the code phrase for Mr. Parker they'd chosen the day before, at Lord Lambert's insistence.

"Quite well," he said enthusiastically. "And, I believe the oak tree will be found in this garden quite frequently."

Ruth squeezed his arm tightly in her excitement before realizing what she was about and forcing her hand to relax once more. "That is good news," she said politely. Only, it was so easy to speak with Lord Lambert.

Ruth hadn't been sure at first how much to tell him. But as she'd begun explaining her cousin's situation yesterday, she'd found all his responses to be sympathetic and kind. In the end, she'd told him the whole of it, and he'd readily agreed to help. He hadn't even lifted a brow at her telling him about her continuous loop theory—or that giving Nettie and Mr. Parker a second chance at love was what she needed to do to break the loop.

His help proved providential. Ruth obviously couldn't both take Nettie home *and* continue to stroll the gardens in the hopes of finding Mr. Parker. So, he'd gone after Mr. Parker yesterday leaving her to see to her cousin.

"And how are the roses?" he asked. It was code for how was Nettie.

"The roses," Ruth began slowly, "are looking brighter today."

He must have heard her hesitancy, for Lord Lambert asked, "But?"

She shot her cousin a quick glance. Nettie was standing beside a long row of boxwood bushes, softly fingering one of the brilliant green leaves. It may have only been the lighting, but she appeared a bit pale.

"But," Ruth said, "I believe one cannot undervalue research."

He bent in toward her and whispered. "So . . . you're saying not today? That we need to . . . research more or something?"

She lightly bumped her shoulder against his. Well, it was actually her shoulder against his arm since he was so much taller. "A code doesn't work if you can't follow what I'm saying when I use it."

He lifted a hand up in surrender. "I never said I was an expert at speaking code."

"But you were the one who insisted we use it."

"You can't run a clandestine enterprise without using code. Even an unread buffoon like myself knows that."

"Then do try to keep up," Ruth said with mock solemnity.

"Yes, of course." He straightened once more. "What then, do you plan to research today?"

Ruth bit down softly on her lower lip. She hadn't entered the gardens that morning feeling confident in what the next step ought to be. Only, she worried, despite Nettie's brighter outlook on life, that today wasn't the right day for the two to meet.

"Perhaps," she began, "I will see to the roses and you might check on the oak tree again?"

"Again?" he echoed. "I'm afraid people might think it strange if I check on the oak tree for a second day."

"I don't see why that should be."

"I have never seen that particular oak tree before yesterday. To seek it out again . . ." his voice trailed off and he shrugged.

Ruth shook her head. "We have shared no more than a passing acquaintance before two days ago, yet you found it perfectly natural to start a conversation with me."

"Were we only passing acquaintances?" His eyes lit with some memory or another. "I remember several shared conversations over this past London Season."

"I suppose we did speak at more than one ball."

"And there was Sutby's musicale."

She did recall that.

"And a picnic or two," he continued.

That was true.

"And that one time you tripped—"

"I recall," Ruth interjected. She didn't need to be reminded of *that* particular moment, and what a fool she'd appeared all covered in hay and manure.

Though Lord Lambert did stop his well-remembered list, his smile didn't dampen.

"Ruth?" Nettie moved up beside her. "Forgive my interruption, but, might we return home a little early today?"

Now that Ruth looked again, it became clear that it hadn't been the lighting before. Nettie truly was a bit pale.

"Of course," Ruth said. "We could return this very minute if you wish it."

Nettie gave her a small smile of gratitude. "Thank you. I'm afraid I've rather a nasty headache coming on."

Ruth's instincts, then, that today was *not* the day had been spot on. She turned to Lord Lambert, but before she could say anything, he bowed over her hand.

"Then this is where I bid you ladies goodbye for now."

Ruth hesitated—what would he say if she invited him to walk them back? She quite suddenly had no desire to leave his company.

However, as Lord Lambert stood up straight once more he gave her a particular smile. "If you will excuse me, there is an oak tree on the other side of the gardens I wish to see again before I leave today." With a wink aimed Ruth's direction, he turned and strode away.

Ruth pulled her lips to one side, in the hopes that it would help hide some of her smile. Having an accomplice in her scheme was making this whole thing far more diverting.

"He seems a nice gentleman," Nettie said as she and Ruth began their walk home.

"Yes, quite," was all she could say, though Ruth's mind was certainly filled with Lord Lambert's smiles, laughs, and that last wink.

"Perhaps a bit taken with you?"

"What?" Ruth stopped in her tracks and whirled around.

Nettie laughed. "And maybe you are taken with him as well?"

Ruth pursed her lips. "Don't be ridiculous."

"You two are a handsome couple."

That was all nonsense. "He was happy to have found someone he knows, that is all." Ruth took Nettie's arm and started them toward home again.

"Are you sure that's all?"

For a woman who disliked speaking of her own previous *amors*, she certainly took interest in Ruth's. "Lord Lambert may be charming—"

"Oh, then you admit he's charming."

"—but," Ruth continued, adamantly, "he would never be interested in a woman like me."

"Why not?"

How did she say this without sounding offensive, or worse, defensive? "He cares for society and parties, and I care..."

"For books and solitude?"

"Precisely."

"Then, is that why he may acknowledge other women we walk by, but he never seems to care to stroll with them?"

"Miss Nettie Wright," Ruth said, pretending to be aghast.

Nettie shook her head and smiled, despite clearly not feeling well. "Perhaps you are right and it is nothing. Either way, I'm glad you enjoyed his company this afternoon. I'm afraid I wasn't much for conversation."

Ruth patted her cousin's arm. "Never mind that. You aren't feeling well. We'll get you home and comfortable and you'll be feeling right again soon enough."

Ruth entered the gardens, an eager smile on her face and Nettie at her side. Today was the day; she could feel it. Nettie had retired early that night, leaving both Ruth and her mother a bit concerned. The next morning, which had been yesterday, she'd awoken still drawn. Though she and Ruth had walked the gardens with Lord Lambert that day, they hadn't attempted any reuniting. Instead, Ruth and Lord Lambert had been left to speak on topics other than their goal.

They'd discussed the works by H. G. Wells, whose newest book Lord Lambert had indeed begun reading at Ruth's suggestion. They discussed the newest lines being laid for the ever-expanding railroad, and were in agreement that the new railways were a boon to England. All in all, it had been a stimulating conversation, if not exactly the one she'd been hoping for Nettie to have.

But that had been yesterday. Today, Nettie had awoken in fine fettle.

Today, the autumn air seemed welcoming. Almost enchanting.

Today, the flowers seemed extra brilliant.

Certainly today would be the day.

Just as they entered, Ruth and Nettie found the gardener standing almost perfectly still, looking out over the blooms and vines around him.

"Your hydrangea continues to amaze us all," Ruth called out. With one clump sporting azure blue and another bunch covered in pink petals, much of Eastbourne was talking about the flowers. Ruth was no expert but understood the acidity of the soil was responsible for the flower's color. How the gardener managed to get both colors in beds so close to one another was a testament to his skill.

"The sole purpose of a gardener is only to provide what is needed; the Good Lord and the plants do the rest." He bid them good day with the tip of his well-worn hat and moved back to work.

Ruth ran her gloved hand over the green leaf of a wild rose bush as they walked by it. The pink flowers were striking. She supposed people were much like plants. When given what was needed and left to grow, they bloomed into the best versions of themselves. With any luck, this garden would prove the perfect place for Nettie to bloom into the woman she was always meant to be.

"Good afternoon, Miss Hughes, Miss Wright," Lord Lambert said, reaching them at the same place in the path he had for the past several days now.

A zip of pure energy shot through Ruth at seeing him. What a change a handful of days could make. Not long ago, she considered Lord Lambert no more than a passing acquaintance. Now, he was quickly becoming a dearest friend.

"Good afternoon," both Ruth and Nettie intoned.

An easy conversation started up between them. For as often as Ruth had seen Lord Lambert command a crowd during the Season, she had to confess to being a bit surprised that she always felt he cared about what she had to say. Her experience with others who enjoyed large crowds had not always been so pleasant.

But when she walked with Lord Lambert, she felt completely comfortable being herself. Her thoughts, her ideas, they were all welcomed and valued.

"Apples, apples, red and ripe!" the costermonger's call echoed from around the bend. "Apples, apples, cheap and bright!"

Lord Lambert purchased an apple for each of them, but as he and Ruth moved away, Nettie stayed back a little to ask after the man's wife and family.

The moment Nettie was out of earshot, Ruth took hold of Lord Lambert's arm. "I think today is the day to have our stroll take us by Mr. Parker."

He took a bite of apple and chewed slowly. "Excuse me," he said, all fake confusion, "of whom are you speaking?"

Ruth shot him an irritated look, while trying to hide her smile. "I mean, I think today is the day we ought to walk by the *oak tree.*"

"Ah," Lord Lambert drew the word out. "Now I understand you."

Ruth shook her head at him and his ridiculous need for their code.

As she did, her gaze flitted over to her cousin. "Do you

not think she seems quite cheerful?" Ruth asked. "I think it would be far better she 'happen' across the oak tree on a day when she's feeling herself rather than not."

"I think you both appear exceptionally happy today," he said.

Ruth turned at his words and caught him looking down at her most pointedly. A heat spread through her. "If I do appear exceptionally happy today it is because . . ." Ruth dropped her voice softer as her cousin neared them once more ". . . I hope to walk by the oak tree."

"The oak tree?" Nettie said reaching them, the brilliant red apple half eaten in her hand.

Perhaps Lord Lambert's code was not so ridiculous after all. "Yes," Ruth said, forcing what she hoped looked like an easy smile. "The one Lord Lambert mentioned the other day. We thought we might walk by it just now."

"Sounds delightful," Nettie said, and she moved to walk beside them.

"If you could travel forward in time," Lord Lambert asked them both, "which year would you choose to travel to?"

Nettie's brow creased. "Travel forward in time?"

"We were discussing H. G. Wells's *The Time Machine* just now," Ruth explained.

Actually, they'd been speaking of it yesterday, but they needed some excuse, and when it came to planning and scheming with Lord Lambert, it was surprisingly easy. Working with him rather put her in mind of two gears—one would turn and the other fell easily into step with it.

As they discussed the various times they might travel to if ever such science were to exist, Ruth kept a watchful eye out. If she wasn't mistaken, Lord Lambert did as well.

In the end, it was decided that The Time Traveler, as the main character was called in H. G. Wells's book, set his sights too far in the future. He would have learned far more valuable information if he'd only traveled a thousand or so years forward.

"At first, I was enamored with the idea of traveling so far ahead," Ruth said. "But the more I think on it, the more it seems illogical."

"How so?" Lord Lambert asked.

"It's like trying to better understand a flower by studying a tree. To travel eight hundred-thousand years into the future, would be to go to a place so wholly removed from our current day that I don't think one could compare it at all."

"Wasn't he just traveling forward to prove he could?" Nettie questioned.

"No," Ruth said, "I feel certain H. G. Wells is trying to show us that we must be careful, or our future will not be a good one. But, truthfully, how can one take in a degraded society and think it's because of the choices of those made eight hundred-thousand years ago? Why not those choices made one hundred-thousand years ago? Or even made fifty years ago?"

"Or nine hundred-thousand years ago?" Lord Lambert offered. "We may already be too late to stop such a future."

"Precisely," Ruth said, probably louder than she should have in her enthusiasm, for a few people passing them shot her disapproving glances.

Nettie laughed softly. "I wonder what H. G. Wells would say if he heard you speak so."

"Since I'm not likely to ever meet the man, I suppose we'll never know," Ruth said with a shrug.

Lord Lambert's step slowed, and Ruth glanced up at him. His brow creased. He met her gaze for a brief moment, before running a hand over his chin. "I could have sworn this is where that oak tree would be."

The pleasure at their previous conversation melted faster than ices in the summer sun. Ruth's mouth pressed to the side. "Are you certain this is where you saw it before?"

Lord Lambert nodded. "I am certain of it."

That didn't bode well. Ruth searched each face around them. There weren't many people enjoying this part of the gardens, but there were a few. An elderly lady and two very excited grandsons. A young girl and a man who appeared to be her father. Three young women who kept trying to catch Lord Lambert's eye as they walked by, then giggled after they'd passed.

But no Mr. Parker pushing his aged grandmother in a chair.

The first day that Nettie was doing well enough to face someone of great importance from her past, and the man couldn't be bothered to show? What good was it being trapped inside a continuous loop if the one person they needed wouldn't be here on schedule?

Lord Lambert placed a hand softly against the small of her back. "Perhaps the oak is just down the walk a bit further."

Ruth nodded, but she didn't feel particularly hopeful. As they walked, the conversation moved to one of trees—oaks and beech and ash—though it was mainly Nettie who carried the conversation. She apparently had warmed to the idea of having Lord Lambert join their daily walks.

But why couldn't she be spending the time warming up to the idea of speaking with Mr. Parker again? Why today, of all days, did the man not come to the gardens?

Ruth did not give up immediately, however, encouraging both Nettie and Lord Lambert to continue walking longer with her than they usually did.

They spoke of their individual families. Ruth's parents had always supported her desire for books. It had, in fact, been a shock to Ruth when she started going out into society to learn that most women her age were not granted so much say in their own education.

Nettie brought up how she used to listen to her mother play the piano with such feeling she'd often been moved to tears as a girl. Ruth smiled at the story—it was nice to know that not all of Nettie's childhood memories were sad.

Lord Lambert confessed to indulging his sisters and their love of chocolate fudge. His mother claimed not to care for the American confection, but he'd caught her sneaking a pinch more than once. Both Ruth and Nettie laughed at the way Lord Lambert lovingly re-enacted his mother hurriedly wiping chocolate away from her mouth while pretending she hadn't just eaten the sweet.

As the sun dipped toward the horizon, and it became clear she and Nettie must leave, Ruth couldn't stave off her deep disappointment as they bid Lord Lambert goodbye.

"Perhaps tomorrow we shall find the oak tree?" he asked in farewell.

Ruth nodded. "Perhaps tomorrow."

But when tomorrow came, the sky was dark and a soft rain fell. Still, Ruth asked Nettie if she cared to walk the gardens again.

"Oh, I think not today," Nettie said with a shiver.

"It isn't so heavy a rain as all that," Ruth countered, knowing her argument sounded weak.

"But it is still raining."

"I don't know about that," Ruth said, glancing out a rain-speckled window. "It's more a very thick humidity."

Nettie laughed. "You remind yourself of that when you catch cold from being out in it."

Even after several other attempts, Ruth could not convince Nettie, and so she left home, umbrella in hand, alone.

The disappointment from yesterday still weighed on her. But Ruth was not fickle. Any scientist worth her salt understood that sometimes one must face setbacks. The best thing to do in such situations, was to get right at it once more. Figure out what went wrong and try again as soon as possible.

So, head held high, Ruth walked quickly toward the gardens, ignoring the light drizzle; and when she arrived, there was the gardener, same as always.

Ruth took a deep breath and once more entered the continuous loop.

Chapter Four

"I'm glad you've come," Lord Lambert said, striding over to Ruth.

The gardens were more empty than usual, undoubtedly due to the rain. Still, the apple costermonger was present, his cry as loud as ever.

"And I you. Unfortunately, I could not convince Nettie to join me in the rain." It was coming down even lighter now than when Ruth had left the house. Nettie should have just come. Ruth was perfectly comfortable with her umbrella and Norfolk jacket.

"Strolling through the rain, *alone*, are you?" he asked, waggling his eyebrows.

Ruth lifted her chin. "My parents trust me."

Lord Lambert shook his head, though it was clear he was only in jest. "My grandmother is rolling in her grave."

"Besides, if I do run into trouble, I always have my hat pin." Ruth pulled out the six-inch, thin pin.

His eyes widened, though his smile didn't falter. "You came armed."

Ruth replaced the pin. "Why do you think my parents trust me?"

He laughed, even as the nanny and her charge hurried by, drawing her eye to them. A heavy blanket hung over the top of the carriage protecting the baby inside from the rainfall. Ruth hoped the baby was well wrapped up beneath.

"While I am glad to know you are well prepared to walk through the gardens," Lord Lambert continued, "I was hoping your cousin would be joining you today."

"Finally tired of conversing on steam engines and ruins in Egypt?"

"Not in the least."

His sincerity surprised her somewhat. Everyone she knew eventually got tired of her constant excitement over science and advancements. That he continued to encourage such conversations made her smile.

"However," he continued, "I did just see Mr. Parker enter the gardens not more than five minutes before I came across you."

Ruth shut her eyes, wrapping a hand over them. "Of course you did."

Perhaps she should be thankful to be caught in a continuous loop. Apparently, she would need *many* tries to get Nettie and Mr. Parker back together again.

"Forgive my ignorance," Lord Lambert said slowly, "but, since you know Mr. Parker is residing in the neighborhood, why not simply invite him over for dinner some evening?"

Ruth began walking once more and Lord Lambert fell in beside her. "I wish I could. But Nettie called off their engagement at the express urging of her parents. I think both she and my parents would consider it bad form to have the man over just because my aunt and uncle are in the ground now."

"But it's not bad form for you to meddle by arranging a meeting in a garden?"

"A lady does not stoop to meddling in her cousin's life, Lord Lambert. She . . . investigates possibilities."

He laughed, the rich tone warming every bit of her despite the autumn chill. "Well then," he said, moving slightly closer to her—but then their umbrellas bumped, and he was forced to step away again. "Excuse me," he said with another laugh. "I'd forgotten what a nuisance these things are."

"But they're a perfect example of how a few levers and some fabric can become something exceptionally useful. Not every problem requires a complicated solution."

"My trousers may disagree."

She glanced down to find the fabric about his ankles dark with rainwater. Perhaps he did have a point.

"That isn't even the worst of it," he added, "for it prevents me offering you my arm as we stroll."

The heat she'd felt at his laugh doubled, and there was no stopping the smile it brought out either.

"Well," Ruth said, closing her umbrella. "That doesn't require a complicated solution either." She stepped up close, placing her hand atop the arm holding his umbrella, while simultaneously closing her own.

"A reader and a problem-solver," Lord Lambert said with a smile, even as he reached for her umbrella with his free hand. "May I?"

She handed it over to him, grateful to not have to worry about the way it would undoubtedly hit against her skirts.

"Now, tell me, Miss Hughes, what are we to do about our rose and oak tree?"

"I must confess," she said, "I am unsure if we can make any meaningful progress today."

"We could greet Mr. Parker ourselves. Then, see if he

could meet us here again tomorrow, when your cousin could join us."

"But what if, in learning that we are residing in the neighborhood, Mr. Parker decides to remove himself from it?"

"Was his and your cousin's falling out so bad as all that?"

Ruth's lips pulled into a tight line. "It was awful."

"Perhaps you should tell me the whole of it, so that we may sort out our next move."

"I am not sure how they met," Ruth began, her gaze on the rain as it hit leaves and blooms, only to run off and onto the ground below. "But they were madly in love before my aunt and uncle found out. When they did find out, however, they were furious. Mr. Parker is a banker, not a man of title or great wealth. In their eyes, that made him unequal to my cousin, no matter that he is highly respected by all his peers and clearly doted on Nettie." Ruth shook her head. "One would have thought such notions would have died with our grandparents. What good are the steam engine and the electric light bulb if we still refuse to see each other for who we truly are?"

Lord Lambert placed a hand over her own. "Unfortunately, prejudice against other classes continues in the hearts of far too many."

"I'm glad you understand. Nettie's parents did not. It didn't matter what she said to them, or how often Mr. Parker sincerely pled his case. In the end, Nettie couldn't find it in herself to go against her parents' wishes, and she called off the engagement."

"That could not have gone well for her among society."

"Fortunately, she escaped scandal. My uncle and aunt were so furious that not only had Nettie accepted Mr. Parker, but that he proposed without asking my uncle's permission first, they refused to speak of it to anyone. The family knew, but that was all."

"So Miss Wright's parents effectively forced the two apart."

Ruth could so easily remember how inconsolable Nettie had been. "Though she broke things off, Nettie was still miserable without him. Completely heartbroken."

"You were right when you told me it was a mournful tale." His tone held the regret and sadness her heart felt. "Unfortunately well-suited to a rainy day."

They took several more strides in silence, both wordlessly sharing in the miserableness of such events.

"Do you think it is wrong of me to push them together once more?" Ruth asked after a time. "I know they truly loved one another, but sometimes I start to worry that my aunt and uncle will curse me from the grave for what I am trying to do."

"Or," he countered, "perhaps now they are sorry for what they did to their daughter and it is they who have led you to this very opportunity in the hopes of making amends now."

"I hadn't thought of that." Continuous loops were often caused by either strange scientific anomalies, or by paranormal influences. At least, that was the case in books. This was Ruth's first experience dealing with such matters outside of stories and lore.

"That being said," Lord Lambert's words were drawn out, "there is the option of telling your cousin that you've seen Mr. Parker about in the gardens and seeing how she feels about meeting him again."

Ruth's nose scrunched up. "You know, the first time I saw him, I almost did. But then Nettie and I were walking back home, and the moment never really presented itself."

"And now?"

"Now I'm convinced telling Nettie first isn't the right thing. She's a dear, but sometimes a little too worried about what others will think of her, or about doing what is expected and proper. If I tell her, she may refuse to meet him at all."

Despite not knowing the true reason behind the current continuous loop—Nettie's deceased parents or some other scientific anomaly—her resolve solidified. "No, I think it is best we arrange the meeting and then allow them to take it from there." The more she thought on it, the more certain she was.

"So, our aim is to visit with Mr. Parker today so that we might convince him to return to the gardens again tomorrow when your cousin can also be persuaded to come."

"Precisely. Truly, all we are doing is returning to them the opportunity that was taken before."

"Because no one should choose for another what will make them happy," Lord Lambert agreed.

"That is the moral of the story, I believe."

This time it was Lord Lambert who slowed their step. "Is that the message you heard?"

"Well, yes. My aunt and uncle's interference in Nettie's life did not help her avoid misery, as they were certain it would, but only brought that very thing into her daily life."

"Interesting." He stopped and faced her fully, his sky-blue eyes coming to rest on her. "That wasn't quite what I heard."

The expression which crossed his features was one Ruth found herself ill equipped to interpret. He was smiling, yet his eyes seemed to suddenly be alight with a spark she couldn't seem to accurately label.

He bent down, bringing his mouth close to her ear. The spark in his eyes seemed to leap to her, igniting the same fire inside her chest.

"I'd rather thought the lesson to learn was, once a person finds someone to care for, he should never let go."

"Is that so?" she whispered.

"I feel certain such is true."

The heat he shared with her seemed to flicker across her skin. "I suppose it is every individual's right to learn whatever lesson they so choose."

He chuckled softly, pulling back as he did so, and they began forward once more. Though, Ruth found herself walking closer to him than she had been before. She'd often gone out walking with this gentleman or that during her Season, but none of those experiences felt like this one. None of them had left her head feeling light and her heart pounding. None of those had left her wishing the moment could stretch forever no matter the rain and dreary weather.

"I do have one question for you, though," Lord Lambert said.

He glanced over at her, his eyes quickly moving away once again. Why—he seemed almost nervous. He still walked with head high and shoulders back, which only emphasized his incredible height. Yet there was an uncertainty evident in the way he wasn't smiling now. Not that she minded that his lips rested in a line instead of tipping upward. Truth was, now that she thought on it, she couldn't remember an expression crossing his face in which she didn't like the turn of his lips.

Which was probably a ridiculous thought and one not at all worthy of a woman who stayed up to date on all the latest scientific discoveries and advancements.

And yet . . . she found she couldn't *stop* thinking of his lips.

And what it would be like if he kissed her.

Lord Lambert glanced her way once more. "Do you mind if I ask you a question?"

Ruth shook herself. "Of course not. Ask anything you'd like." She was being rude letting her mind wander so—thank the heavens no one had yet discovered how to ascertain what was going through the mind of one's companion.

"I was hoping," he said slowly, and his tone only further emphasized his uncertainty, "you might grant me permission to call you by your Christian name, Ruth?"

He knew her name? Ruth glanced away before he caught sight of the grin which she couldn't keep from spreading over her face. Granted, it wouldn't have been hard for him to learn her name, but that he cared enough to seek it out and remember it when someone told him . . . well, it turned the heated sparks inside her into a roaring fire.

"Yes," she finally managed to say without sounding like a bumbling fool. "That would be quite fine."

His smile was back, as was the spark in his eye. "Then you should call me Harvey."

"Very well, Harvey." She drew his name out long and slow, trying it out on her tongue and loving the way it felt. "Shall we go speak with Mr. Parker?"

They lengthened their stride and soon reached the bend in the path and there, only a dozen strides ahead of them, walked Mr. Parker. He was alone today. Apparently his grandmother preferred clear skies as did most the rest of the neighborhood. Still, he had come. Mr. Parker walked with his back toward Ruth and Lord Lambert, but after seeing him so many times from this distance over the past few weeks, she recognized him all the same. And was it just her, or was Mr. Parker walking with a stoop to his shoulders?

"Mr. Parker?" Ruth called out as soon they were close enough to politely do so. "Is that you?"

She caught Harvey—heavens, but she did truly like that name—snickering at her attempt to sound as though their meeting with Mr. Parker hadn't been a plan of hers for weeks now. Ruth elbowed him slightly in response.

Mr. Parker turned, a look of surprise quickly overtaking his face. That was, a surprise that caused his jaw to tighten and his shoulders to go stiff.

"Miss Hughes..." Mr. Parker's gaze jumped from her, to Harvey, and immediately away again. He rather reminded her of a cornered animal, searching out which direction would provide him the safest escape. "What a pleasant surprise."

She'd forgotten how handsome Mr. Parker was. Though his smile now was clearly stiff and forced, she could imagine that, when sincere, his smile could captivate any woman. His dark brown hair was well-combed and had just the right amount of wave to be fashionable and look sharp. He wore small, oval shaped glasses which seemed to grant him an air of intelligence. Nettie had once told Ruth that Mr. Parker was the smartest man she'd ever met, so perhaps the air of intelligence wasn't only due to his glasses.

Ruth's heart squeezed painfully at the thought of all her cousin had lost when her parents had forced these two apart.

"I had no idea you were visiting Eastbourne," Ruth said. It wasn't an exact lie—she *hadn't* known he was here, until a couple weeks ago. And in a place where time seemed to have little meaning, that made her statement basically the same thing as a truth, didn't it?

"Ah, yes," Mr. Parker said, once more glancing about as though wishing for a means of escape. "My grandmother's health is not what it once was, so I decided to take a holiday and bring her here in the hopes that the warmer climate would help ease some of her discomfort."

"How thoughtful of you."

Beside her, Harvey coughed slightly.

Gracious, here she'd been so caught up in reconnecting with Mr. Parker she'd completely forgotten her manners.

"Forgive me," she hurried to say, and quickly introduced the men.

At hearing Harvey's title, Mr. Parker's posture grew even more stiff, which Ruth had not known was possible. It seemed Mr. Parker's experience with Nettie's family had made an unfortunate and lasting impact on his impression of all titled men. However, Harvey's greeting was as friendly as ever. Ruth could only hope that would ease some of Mr. Parker's resentment.

"I know my parents would enjoy seeing you again," Ruth said after the introductions were finished. "Perhaps you could stop by the house sometime?"

Much to Ruth's surprise, and relief, he didn't turn the notion down immediately. Instead, Mr. Parker hesitated, his head rocking back and forth slightly as though he were rolling the idea around inside.

In the brief moment of silence, another sound reached them,—a woman's voice. Ruth recognized it immediately, and judging by the way Mr. Parker grew instantly still, she could only guess that he did too.

Nettie turned the corner the next minute, the tap of her boots against the water-covered stone walkway quick and sharp.

"There you are, Ruth. You've been gone so long and in such bad weather, your mother sent me—"

Her words cut off suddenly, her gaze on Mr. Parker, and him alone.

"Nettie," Ruth said, trying to infuse her tone with casual cheerfulness. "Look who we happened upon during our walk."

The tense stillness between Nettie and Mr. Parker was so strong that it filled the space around Ruth and Harvey as well. The very air itself seemed to pulsate with the intense emotions rolling off Nettie and Mr. Parker. Though the rain fell, it alone dared move. The patter of drops hitting the ground was the only noise to be had.

If Ruth had felt as though time had stopped in the gardens before, it now felt frozen around them. Almost a palpable gel that was growing ever firmer the longer it was allowed to set.

Breaking through suddenly, Nettie took hold of Ruth's arm and forcibly dragged her away from both men. The minute Ruth left the shelter of Harvey's umbrella, rain pelted down against her face and arms.

Nettie, her back now toward both men, said nothing as she continued to tug Ruth further and further away.

Ruth opened her mouth to protest, but staying upright and processing what had just happened took too much concentration; there was nothing left to formulate actual words.

Ruth glanced over her shoulder. Mr. Parker was stalking away, moving the opposite direction and every bit as fast as Nettie.

What a disaster. Ruth shook her head at herself. All her careful planning—all her hopes to slowly draw her cousin and the man she once loved together again—all of it obliterated.

Chapter Five

"Please, Nettie, may I come in?"

It was the same plea Ruth had made over a dozen times since returning home with her cousin, and still Nettie's bedchamber door remained locked.

Ruth's shoulders slumped, and she rested her forehead against the door. What had she done? If she explained to Nettie that she'd only wanted to give her a second chance, would she understand? Or would her cousin be furious at her forever?

The sounds of Nettie crying reached Ruth. Her heart twisted, sending a sharp pain radiating through Ruth. She'd never meant to cause her cousin yet more grief. She'd only wanted to help.

When dinner was served that night, Nettie didn't come down, and Ruth found she had no appetite. Mother and Father asked what had happened, but when they found Ruth unwilling to tell the whole story, they granted her space and solitude.

She would have to tell them eventually, but tonight she needed to focus on comforting Nettie.

Even after dinner, Nettie refused to leave her room and refused entrance to anyone, even her lady's maid.

Ruth waited by the door for over half an hour before trudging down to the parlor and plopping down into the oversized wingback. She stared at the dying fire in the hearth. She'd seen her cousin grieve before. It was Nettie's nature to pull inward, to wish to be left alone in her sadness. But it had never been this bad. Not when Uncle and Aunt first forced Nettie and Mr. Parker apart, and not even when Nettie's parents had died unexpectedly.

This was different. In the past, Nettie may have pulled inward, but when Ruth reached out to her—in the form of a hug, or by reading to her—at least Nettie hadn't shut her out.

Did Nettie's current actions indicate she blamed Ruth? That she no longer trusted Ruth or saw her as a friend?

What a horrid idea.

Ruth had to explain. Surely if she told her cousin everything, Nettie would see that Ruth only wanted what was best for her.

Wouldn't she?

A footman stepped into the room. "Lord Lambert to see you, miss."

Ruth ran a hand over her face, wiping away the few tears that had fallen. If only she could wipe away her uncertainty as easily.

Harvey walked in. Only then did Ruth realize how dark the parlor had gotten. With the sun having set and only embers left in the hearth, the room was almost completely without light. It suited her mood.

Harvey walked up to her, holding out her umbrella. "I thought I'd best return this."

She took the umbrella. It was dry, but felt unusually heavy. Strange how sorrow could affect all of the senses.

Harvey rested his hands atop her shoulders, drawing her gaze back up to him.

"Are you all right?" he asked.

Ruth nodded that she was, but tears began to flow once more. Harvey thumbed away one, then a second.

"I never meant to hurt her," Ruth said between the tears.

"I know," he said. "She will too, given time."

Ruth squeezed her eyes shut, forcing more hot tears to roll down her cheeks. She sincerely hoped he was right.

Harvey took the umbrella from her once more and rested it near the fireplace. Then he took her hand, led her to the settee, and helped her to sit. He sat beside her, perhaps a bit closer than was strictly proper, but she was grateful for it all the same.

It felt right, being close to Harvey like this. The comfort his presence gave, the non-judgmental calm he instilled, it was exactly what she needed.

"You shouldn't feel guilty," he said at length, taking hold of her hand in his.

"Are you a mind reader now?" Ruth said, smiling despite herself.

"I have three sisters, remember?"

"Wouldn't they have felt guilty as well, knowing they'd caused a beloved cousin pain?"

He slowly traced circles along the back of her hand. "You didn't mean to cause her pain."

"But I did cause it. I did know that seeing Mr. Parker again might be hard for her, and I forced it anyways."

"You didn't intend for them to meet today, nor in that way."

She sagged against the cushions slightly, her head coming to rest against his shoulder. "I still feel guilty."

He gave her hand a gentle squeeze. "I know."

They sat in silence for a minute. Ruth closed her eyes, allowing his presence to warm her.

"If we look at today another way," Harvey said slowly, "both your cousin's and Mr. Parker's reactions prove they aren't impartial toward one another."

Ruth opened her eyes once more, but didn't pull away. She needed his nearness too much still. "Do you believe so?"

"Absolutely. If they both had come to terms with being apart, they would have met as disinterested friends."

"I never expected them to see one another and treat the other indifferently, but they did respond far more dramatically than I anticipated."

"Exactly. Feelings are still there, between them, strong and undeniable."

The realization provided a strange sort of comfort.

"The real question," Harvey said, "is what do we do about it now?"

"For tonight, we let Nettie be. I've seen her go through hard things before. She turns inward for a time, but she always comes around eventually." Just saying the words aloud was soothing. Ruth knew Nettie well enough to know tonight's grief was temporary. It had seemed far more overwhelming before Harvey arrived, but now Ruth could see it for what it was. "She just needs some time alone right now."

"And then? Are you still hoping we can get them to cross paths again in the gardens?"

"No," Ruth picked her head up off his shoulder, facing him. "This time we do it right. I will talk to Nettie and find out if she cares to see Mr. Parker again. Will you do the same for him?"

"We were only introduced for the first time this afternoon, yet you want me to ask him about a woman he once proposed to and was then rejected by."

Ruth scrunched her nose; it was a pretty big thing to ask of Harvey. Still, what other option was there? "Would you, please? This is their life, and they have a right to decide what to do." Wasn't that the whole point all along? Nettie's parents decided for them last time—now Ruth had taken it upon herself to decide for them this time.

But not again. Now, it was truly Nettie and Mr. Parker's time to decide for themselves.

"For you, I'll do it," Harvey said with a smile.

"Thank you." In a moment of what might have been insanity brought on by relief and hope, Ruth leaned over and placed a kiss on Harvey's cheek.

Then, she found it hard to pull away. Her hand rested against his chest, though when she'd placed it there she couldn't say. He smelled of sandalwood soap and rain. He turned in toward her, their noses brushing by one another. Heat spread like a wildfire though her.

They sat, only a breath between them. Would he kiss her? Did she want him to?

The moment she thought the question, her entire being answered.

Yes, she most certainly wanted Harvey to kiss her.

But instead, he simply sat there, so close it wouldn't be hard to kiss him at all. The air buzzed as though charged by one hundred electric lights. He leaned in.

Closer.

Closer.

When his lips met hers, it was soft, like a question. She was aware of every inch of herself and how close they sat—her arms pressed against his chest, the way he had to lean in to kiss her, the gentleness of his caress.

Far too soon, he pulled back.

"I think it is best if I bid you a good evening, Ruth," he

said, his voice low. He stood and strode toward the parlor door without another word, leaving her sitting atop the settee, her skin all tingling.

Just before leaving, however, he glanced back at her. The look he gave her was the same expression he'd given her earlier that day, one where he smiled, yet his eyes were alight with a spark she couldn't ignore. She hadn't felt capable of understanding it then, but now she had a pretty good idea what it meant after all.

Chapter Six

"Well, what do you think?" Ruth asked, her shoulder pressed against a bedpost as she leaned on it.

Nettie, who was sitting up in bed and dressed in a morning gown, pursed her lips and glanced toward the window. She looked drawn, with bags under her eyes and her hair sticking out oddly from her low chignon. Nettie may have gotten up this morning, dressed, and even been willing to let her lady's maid do her hair, but clearly she'd lain back down afterward and messed up most of the effort.

"I don't know," Nettie said with a breath of frustration. She turned to Ruth suddenly, spearing her with a firm glare. "*He'll* be there, won't he."

Ruth slowly nodded. "I asked Har—Lord Lambert to speak with him."

Nettie's brow dropped. "To ask him not to see the gardens again? I'd hate to be the reason he—"

"No," Ruth interrupted, "to ask him if he *would* come to the gardens again . . . to see you."

"Oh." Nettie's face visibly paled.

Ruth pushed off the bedpost and sat next to her cousin.

In a few sentences she quickly explained the day she'd first seen Mr. Parker, her plans to reunite them, and all that had happened yesterday in the rain.

When she finished, Nettie sat silently, her hands in her lap.

"Are you mad at me?" Ruth asked.

"No," Nettie said, her voice soft as a mouse. Her gaze jumped to Ruth and then back to her hands. "And yes."

"I'm so sorry." Ruth laid her head down on Nettie's shoulder. "I should have just told you that first day I saw Mr. Parker. You're a grown woman, and I should have let you make your own decisions instead of presuming."

Nettie didn't respond.

Ruth waited and waited—for an indication that Nettie truly had no desire to see Mr. Parker again, or for a hint that she might just be willing. But neither came and the minutes ticked by.

Ruth could stand it no longer. "He was rather handsome in that brown suit, was he not?" Stating her own opinions was not presuming—it was simply . . . well, an opinion.

"Yes he was," Nettie agreed. "As handsome as ever."

Ruth sat up straight and faced her cousin. "Then why not meet him today? Just talk to him."

"My parents would roll in their grave."

"Or . . . maybe now, with some heavenly perspective, they are sorry for what they've done, and it was actually they who have brought you two together again."

Nettie's brow dropped and she appeared pensive. "Do you think it might be?"

Ruth shrugged—and offered up a silent prayer of gratitude for Harvey's input on the matter.

Nettie's lips pulled to the side. "But what if he hates me?"

"I won't presume to know him well," Ruth was done with

all presumptions. "But I would *guess* he doesn't hate you at all."

"How could he not? I ended our engagement."

"Yes, because your parents forced you to."

Apparently, even Nettie could not deny this for all she did was look back toward the window and nod. "It is a lovely day for a stroll."

Ruth's heart leapt inside her. If Nettie would only *speak* with Mr. Parker, Ruth felt certain they'd find they both still cared too much for the other to walk away from a second chance. Still, she held her tongue. Ruth even went so far as to roll her lips inward to keep from pushing Nettie into anything inadvertently.

"Would it not be better," Ruth said at length, "to go and find out—either way—than to wonder for the rest of your life what might have happened had you gone?"

"If I go and he's not there, or he refuses to speak with me, I don't know how I'll handle it."

"I'll be right there with you. We've gone through a lot together and no matter what, you aren't losing me."

Nettie leaned forward and took hold of Ruth's hand. "I don't have as much confidence as you do that this will end well. However, I do know that I have regretted ending our engagement every minute of every day since it happened. I don't want to live regretting not going to the gardens today, as well."

Ruth smiled, squeezing her cousin's hand tightly. "Then let's get our jackets."

The gardens at Gildredge Manor looked like they always had. Autumn was evident in the leaves and foliage. The weather was cool today, despite the sun shining bright. Flowers bloomed in nearly every corner—orange coneflower, purple pincushions, and vibrant red phlox—hailing the last of the fine weather.

Ruth stepped into the gardens and greeted Mr. Harrison. "The flowers look beautiful today."

"I can take credit for the fine soil and proper placement," he said with the dip of his cap. "But it's the Good Lord who you ought to give credit to for the brilliant blooms."

This was it; Ruth could feel it in her bones—their last trip through the continuous loop.

Oh, she might come and see the gardens again. She might greet Mr. Harrison and buy apples from the costermonger. But never again would she dance between Nettie and Mr. Parker, willing them to "happen" upon one another, all while appearing innocent herself.

Miss Gates came into view, pushing the same buggy she always did. As they passed one another, Ruth smiled at the woman and she smiled back. The baby in the carriage let out a small cry, drawing the nanny's attention immediately back to the little one. As they walked on, the sound of the very young baby's giggling gurgles continued to reach Ruth. She'd never heard the baby make such a happy sound before. Perhaps the little one felt the continuous loop coming to an end just as Ruth did and was ready to move on to the next adventure.

"Apples, apples, red and ripe!

"Apples, apples, cheap and bright!"

Ruth smiled at the costermonger's call. "Do you want one?" she asked her cousin.

"Not today," Nettie said. She appeared far more poised and collected than Ruth felt. But Ruth knew her cousin well enough to know she was probably just keeping all the nerves and anxiety inside.

Both Ruth and Nettie waved at Mr. Davies as they passed him, but didn't stop to purchase any apples.

On they walked, and soon they reached the turn in the path. Ruth felt Nettie stiffen beside her, though she continued on without slowing her step in the least. Neither woman said anything. What was there to say?

Either Mr. Parker was there, waiting around the bend, or he wasn't.

If he was, there was still no guarantee he would welcome a connection with Nettie again.

Ruth was proud of her cousin for facing this second chance head on. She might be a quiet, shy woman, but she had a silent strength in her that few ever got to see. Hopefully, Mr. Parker would recognize that and cherish her all the more for it.

The well-paved path finally straightened and there stood Harvey.

Beside him was Mr. Parker.

Ruth's stomach flipped. It wasn't even her own one-time fiancé they were meeting, and yet she was filled from head to toe with anticipation and worry. What must Nettie be feeling now?

For her part, Nettie continued on, not a hiccup in her step. She walked directly up to Mr. Parker, her gaze never leaving him.

"Hello, Bert," she said softly.

Even with all Ruth had learned these past several weeks, she still didn't consider herself an excellent reader of people. Yet, if she had to judge, she'd say Nettie's voice held as much hope as it did trepidation.

Mr. Parker doffed his hat, and immediately took to shifting it between his two hands. "Hello, Nettie."

Mr. Parker swallowed hard then extended his elbow to

Nettie. She took it with both hands, falling into close step beside him. They turned as one, walking down the path and away from Ruth and Harvey. Only after several steps did Ruth hear the soft sounds of them speaking.

"I may be wrong," Harvey said, moving to stand shoulder to shoulder with Ruth, "but I'd say that has all the signs of a good future."

Ruth couldn't hide her smile. "I certainly hope so."

Harvey extended his elbow to her. "Shall we promenade as well?"

She took his arm and, feeling so light and happy, she laughed softly. "Yes, but at a respectable distance from Nettie and Mr. Parker."

"Of course, of course," Harvey said, as they began walking. "We must give the young couple some privacy."

Ruth giggled again. Oh, how she hoped things would go well between Nettie and Mr. Parker. Her cousin had known such sadness this past year. She deserved all the happiness in the world.

After a few steps, Harvey placed a hand over the top of hers. "Ruth."

She glanced up at him, her mind flitting back to the first time they crossed paths here in the garden several days ago. His height was nearly all she could think about then, and the fine suit he'd been wearing. Now, though, she saw his smile, his willingness to help, how he never mocked her fanciful ideas, or judged her for reading scientific journals or adventure novels.

"Yes?" she finally asked when he didn't continue.

Still he hesitated before saying, "I didn't overstep yesterday, did I?"

Ah, their kiss. Heat rushed to her cheeks.

Harvey hurried on, as though, now that the words had

begun, he couldn't stop them. "It was only that, afterward, you just sat there. I suppose I should have asked first. Or maybe not rushed off afterward. Or maybe not even used bringing your umbrella back as an excuse to see you?" His tone was growing more desperate by the sentence. "I *thought* it would be welcome, but if it wasn't, I sincerely apologize. Sometimes—"

"Harvey." She squeezed his arm. "It was welcomed."

"Oh good," he heaved out a sigh, followed by an embarrassed laugh. "For all the time we've spent together, I wasn't fully sure."

"That is partially my fault," Ruth confessed. "I've very much enjoyed our time together, but I confess to presuming you would never find any true interest in me."

The path took them beneath a tree and while Ruth passed under it without a problem, Harvey had to move a branch up and out of the way. "Not interested? What man wouldn't be?"

Plenty of men, in her experience. But she shook that thought aside; it was just as well because she hadn't been interested in them either. "It's only that, this past London Season, you struck me as one who prefers large gatherings while I prefer solitude. You crave conversation and I'd rather enjoy a good book."

"I am tall and you are short."

Ruth bumped into him with her shoulder. "I'm only short when compared to you."

He laughed. "Very well, I see what you are saying. And you're right," his tone turned pensive, "I do enjoy social gatherings and maybe I don't read as much as you do. But I do love discussing with you what you've read, I do love plotting and planning with you, I love it when the two of us walk side by side and talk about anything and everything."

The same fire that he lit in her last evening burned hot once more.

"So," Harvey said slowly, "perhaps that is enough?"

"Enough for what?"

"Enough that I might call on you sometime. No—" Harvey pulled to an abrupt stop. Turning, he faced Ruth fully, taking both her hands in his own. "Ruth Hughes, I would like to *court* you. The whole thing. I want to call on you frequently. I want to sit beside you at church. I want to take you on outings. When the snow starts to fall, I want us to sit beside a warm fire together. I want to meet your parents, and I want rumors to start all around the neighborhood that we are constantly being seen together."

"You mean, if they haven't started already?"

His smile grew, and heaven help her if he wasn't the most handsome man she'd ever known. "I mean, if they haven't started already."

Ruth laughed lightly even as her head swam with all he'd said. But when she searched her heart, she only found that she sincerely wanted the same. "I would like that very much." She took a half step closer to him. "And, so that neither of us are left to presuming anything, I will openly confess that another kiss would be welcome right now."

He leaned in. "I was hoping it would be." He pulled her from the main path, over a few cobblestones, and tucked them into a secluded arbor Ruth hadn't seen before. White flowers dangled from the vines surrounding them. However, she didn't have time enough to ascertain exactly the variety, for Harvey's lips met hers even as their soft scent floated about them.

This kiss was even more spectacular. While yesterday's had been questioning and unsure, today's was a declaration. A confident expression of all they had grown to mean to one another. A heated hope for more still to come.

Behind Ruth, someone coughed loudly.

She and Harvey broke apart. Turning to look over her shoulder, Ruth found Nettie and Mr. Parker standing just behind her, a few paces off the main path, watching them with bemused smiles.

"Apparently," Ruth muttered beneath her breath to Harvey, "I need to add 'don't presume we are alone' to the list."

He laughed, a warm sound that left her feeling light. "Well, Mr. Parker, what do you say we walk these two fine ladies back home?"

"A fine idea," he replied, and Ruth was happy to see him smiling as well. He didn't seem as weighed down as he had before, and his shoulders no longer slumped.

"I vote we take the long way," Ruth said.

"I second the motion," Nettie added, her cheeks turning pink as she glanced over at Mr. Parker.

The four of them hurried back to the main path. Their walk back towards the garden gates included some talking among all four of them and some breaking apart into pairs. But as they strolled, Ruth couldn't help but notice the garden was finally giving way to colder weather. Mr. Davies was no longer at his spot calling out for passersby to purchase fresh apples. The flowers all seemed to droop a bit, the last days of their brilliance behind them.

A brisk wind blew, and several leaves fell from the surrounding trees. Even the wind seemed to whisper that winter was quickly coming their way. As they reached the gate, Ruth stopped, muttering a quick word to her cousin and Mr. Parker to continue on.

"Is everything all right?" Harvey asked her.

"I just needed to look over the trees and flower beds one last time."

"A lot has happened in this garden."

Ruth nodded, soaking in the sight before her. "We achieved our goal and we learned something along the way. Or, at least, I did." Nettie and Mr. Parker had been reunited and Ruth knew, for all her book learning, she needed to do a little less presuming and a little more asking questions of people.

"I'm going to miss our time here," she said softly.

"We'll just have to find somewhere else to plan out adventures and find other unsuspecting individuals to help."

"I suppose we will."

Looping her arm around his, they started forward once more. The wind picked up and a curtain of leaves lightly skipped over the paved walkway, passing them and dancing over the street beyond, as though beckoning her toward whatever awaited her next.

That had never happened before. Ruth sighed.

The continuous loop had ended.

Epilogue

ALL WENT QUITE AS HARVEY had suggested. After leaving the gardens on what turned out to be the last warm autumn day, Harvey and Mr. Parker stayed for dinner. Ruth's parents found both men delightful.

After that there were frequent calls and outings. Mr. Parker soon began insisting everyone call him Bert. They attended church together. They once made the trip into London for the opera—only to get snowed in and having to scramble with nearly half the other patrons to find a room for the night. Christmas had been especially magical with more carols, more smiles, and more mistletoe kisses than Ruth could have imagined could fit into the holiday.

Nettie and Bert's grandmother became especially close, despite Bert's mother acting cold toward Nettie. It seemed the woman worried her son would be rejected again; but as the winter slowly thawed and gave way to warming days, she also started welcoming Nettie into their life.

As for Ruth, she found Harvey's sisters charming and, his youngest sister in particular, as interested in science and books as she was. There were a few afternoons that Ruth and

Harvey's sisters locked him out entirely so they might discuss the newest adventure novels without interruption.

As snowfall and frosty mornings came to an end, and the first daffodils and crocuses began bringing color back to the world, Harvey made it a point to bring Ruth flowers as often as possible. He said the bouquets always reminded him of those first days, searching her out among the flowers.

Then, one day, nestled among the pinks and greens, Ruth found a ring. When she looked up, Harvey was on one knee.

Two weeks later—and possibly at the encouragement of Ruth—Mr. Parker also proposed, and it was quickly decided that a double wedding was in order.

The morning dawned bright on Ruth's—and Nettie's—wedding day. She and Nettie had previously decided to get ready together. And so, as the morning light streamed through the windows and between the open lace curtains, Ruth and Nettie stood before the mirror. Both were dressed in white. They'd chosen to wear dresses made from different patterns but with the same fabrics—it made them appear to match while not being exactly the same.

Nettie's dress had puffed sleeves, a heart-shaped neckline, lace about her throat, and two strips of wide lace about the skirt. Ruth's dress came off the shoulder, and though her sleeves were not puffed they included three layers of lace. Her skirt flounced with every step thanks to the many gathers and tucks.

"You two look like angels," Mother said as she walked around them both, tugging a bit of fabric into place here, straightening a touch of lace there.

"Thank you, Mama," Ruth said. She felt as light as an angel. She was so filled with excitement and happiness, she thought she very well might float right off the floor. Judging by the smile on Nettie's face, she felt the same.

"By now the carriage should be out front," her mother said, moving toward the bedchamber door. "We ought to hurry to the church. It wouldn't do to be late on your own wedding day."

"We'll be right there," Ruth said.

Mother stepped out, as did the many maids and the housekeeper, leaving Nettie and Ruth alone.

"Are you ready?" Ruth asked her cousin.

Nettie blinked quickly a few times but didn't answer.

Ruth wrapped an arm around her. "Don't start crying. We haven't even left the house yet."

Nettie laughed. "I'm so very ready, is all."

Ruth gave her a squeeze. "I know. You've been waiting longer than I have." Despite Mr. Parker proposing after Harvey, Ruth suspected that, in her heart of hearts, Nettie had been waiting for this day since the *first* time Mr. Parker proposed.

Nettie glanced down at her hands. "I think you're right."

"Naturally."

Nettie shook her head. "I meant about my parents."

Ruth sobered. "Oh?"

"I think they both approve of this wedding. I can feel it." Nettie paused, placing a hand against her heart. "In here."

Ruth gave her another squeeze. Finally, after so long a time, it was only right Nettie found peace and happiness.

Nettie laughed again. "I suppose that sounds ridiculous."

"Not at all." Certainly no more ridiculous than Ruth fancying them caught in a continuous loop last autumn.

Nettie pulled away and took Ruth's hands. "I know I wasn't very appreciative of your meddling last year."

"You had every right to be put out with me."

"Still, does it sound hypocritical if I say that now I'm grateful?"

This time it was Ruth's turn to laugh. "Only a little. But it's all right, because I promise, if ever I feel you need my meddling ways again, I will disclose everything to you first."

"I suppose there's no reason to hope you won't find a need to meddle again?" Nettie asked.

Ruth twisted her lips to the side. "I sincerely doubt it."

They hugged one another fiercely.

"I shall miss you," Nettie whispered.

"We won't be far," Ruth responded. "And we shall see one another nearly every day."

"Good," Nettie said. "I've needed you so much this past year, and I don't think that will change after today."

"I've needed you too," Ruth confessed. She may not have lost her fiancé and then her parents. She may not have gone through the same grief and heartache. But she had needed her cousin all the same, to help her see past her books and scientific journals.

"Now," Ruth said, pulling back and not letting her cousin go. "I think Mother's right. There are two gentlemen waiting at the church for us, and we've kept them waiting long enough."

With a few more laughs and giggles, they both made their way to the carriage and then to the church house.

The wedding was perfect. Ruth was certain she'd never forget the way Harvey watched her, with so much love in his eyes, as she walked down the aisle to meet him. Nor would she forget the smell of fresh flowers wafting up from her bouquet—one she'd arranged herself with help from Mr. Harrison.

Sitting near the front of the church house was Miss Gates, the little baby, now nearly old enough to walk, sitting on her lap.

When the time came for her and Harvey to join hands, a

zip of pure energy shot through her at the touch. Over the preceding few weeks, Ruth had wished countless times for H. G. Wells's time machine so she might fly herself to this very moment. How she'd managed to wait so long for this day, she would never know.

Yet, she was here now, and it was every bit as glorious as she'd hoped for.

The ceremony was short, and soon they were all walking out of the church house. As Ruth stepped out into the sunshine, a call reached her.

"Strawberries, strawberries red and ripe!

"Strawberries, strawberries cheap and bright!"

With a laugh, Ruth took hold of Harvey's hand and hurried forward, coming up just behind Mr. Davies. "Excuse me, sir, but I think I've heard that rhyme before."

The costermonger turned toward her, a momentary look of surprise quickly changing into a broad smile. "Miss Hughes, what a delight."

She stretched her hand out, her new ring glinting in the sun. "It's Lady Lambert now."

Mr. Davies took a half-step back, taking in her wedding dress and Harvey's fine suit for the first time. "Congratulations. Congratulations."

They spoke for a brief moment, Mr. Davies saying over and over again how happy he was for them all, and then gifted Ruth and Harvey, as well as Nettie and Bert, several handfuls of fresh strawberries by way of a wedding gift.

Once home, the celebration continued with family and friends over a lovely breakfast. The cake was cut, well wishes made, and hugs and drinks flowed equally.

As the morning slipped toward afternoon, Harvey took Ruth's hand and pulled her away from the crowd and into a little-used corridor.

"Have I told you how enchanting you look today?" he whispered.

"Perhaps, but it wouldn't hurt to tell me again."

He kissed her softly. "Tell me," he said, "is there a way to make a continuous loop? Because I wouldn't mind reliving this day over and over again."

Ruth let her hands fall to his chest. "Well, if there isn't a continuous loop conveniently about, you may have to make pulling me into a corridor a daily occurrence."

"Well then"—he gave her another kiss—"I suppose I might just have to."

The kiss that followed was anything but short. It was the kind that set Ruth tingling with awareness and filled her with heated desire. It was the kind that promised forever and always—of days and weeks, months and years filled with planning together, standing beside one another, and, of course, many corridor kisses.

And if a few of those kisses happened to take place in an autumn garden, well, so much the better.

Note From the Author

Gildredge Manor and gardens is a real place in Eastbourne, East Sussex, England. The manor was originally built by Reverend Dr. Henry Lushington, who happened to be the vicar of Eastbourne. The house passed from one generation to another and was highly spoken of by those who visited. It seems the gardens and views of both the land and sea were especially appreciated.

Though I could find no proof that the gardens were open to the public during the autumn of 1895, I felt it was the perfect place to stage this story. I hope you will forgive the small artistic leeway.

Laura Rollins has always loved a heart-melting happily ever after. It didn't matter if the story took place in Regency England, or in a cobbler's shop, if there was a sweet romance, she would read it.

Life has given her many of her own adventures. Currently she lives in the Rocky Mountains with her best-friend, who is also her husband, and their four beautiful children. She still loves to read books and more books; her favorite types of music are classical, Broadway, and country; she loves hiking in the mountains near her home; and she's been known to debate with her oldest son about whether Infinity is better categorized as a number or an idea.

Sign up for her newsletter on her website to get a free novella! www.laurarollins.com

You can connect with her on social media, too.
Instagram: www.instagram.com/author_laura_rollins/
Facebook: www.facebook.com/groups/394530268403144

Mr. Dowling's Remedy

By Annette Lyon

*For Viivi,
who inspired this story*

Sul on erinomainen sisua. Jaksat jatkaa!

Chapter One

THE CARRIAGE RATTLED ALONG THE winding drive, past trees half-dressed with fiery-colored branches, half-naked after having lost many of their leaves. The tops of some trees were like bony fingers reaching skyward as if in supplication of heaven.

Beverly Stanton adjusted the heavy quilt around her legs, though doing so didn't help; the dank air would not be kept out, slithering as it did through any possible crack and crevice. She felt the chill down to her bones.

"Stop fussing," Mr. Pyke, her stepfather, said. "We're almost there."

Beverly quieted her movements and returned her gaze out the window, where thick trees passed by. She felt all too much like them—out in the cold autumn morning, feeling half-alive, supplicating for intervention. To no avail. Her stepfather *would* have his way, and no woman in his household could say a word about it.

Why the man thought that having her sent to the Sherville Retreat—rather, asylum—would solve anything remained beyond her comprehension. Then again, so did the idea that she was a lunatic with hysteria so severe that she needed to be sent away under a certificate.

At times she *almost* believed him. If one *was* a hysterical lunatic, one wouldn't know it, would they? How could she be sure of her own sanity? How could anyone?

And yet when she was away from Mr. Pyke, she felt quite sure of herself and his designs against her, and that nothing she said or did—or thought or felt—had any basis in medical lunacy.

It was all an excuse to get rid of her.

"There it is," her mother said beside her, patting Beverly's leg and nodding through the window.

Sure enough, a large estate came into view. Not as grand as many she'd heard of but many times larger than any house she'd personally laid eyes on. It had a central door flanked by five windows in rows along the sides, going up three floors. The exterior was a pale yellow, perhaps an attempt at cheeriness in the midst of what had to be a life of misery and despair for so many.

Beverly swallowed against the tightness in her throat. What would life hold for her behind those walls? Would she be bound in shackles, as she'd heard some lunatics were—men and women deemed less than human? "Mother, I—"

"It's lovely," Mother said, patting her arm and pointing. "They say that many residents are allowed to walk about the grounds freely."

Beverly looked at her mother. "Truly?" she said hopefully. A look out the window once more gave her brief hope; two women walked together along a path in the distance, not far from the main building. As the coach drew nearer, however, something else became visible: a length of cord tied about one woman's waist and the other woman holding the other end.

These weren't two friends on a stroll. This was some poor woman deemed a lunatic, unable to take a turn about the grounds without someone on the staff ensuring that she was restrained like a dog.

She felt a hand go to her neck as if she could feel a dog collar there. Dread pooled in her middle.

The coach stopped, and at last, they alighted. Beverly felt that she was quite sure what seasickness must be like, as her middle continued to roll as the coach had over the road despite now being on solid ground.

A group of three—two men and a woman—greeted them. One of the men appeared to be in charge. The other man wore livery, and the woman wore a black dress with a white apron. Servants.

"Mr. Pyke, I presume?" the man of about fifty said.

"Indeed," came the reply. "This is my wife, Mrs. Pyke, and this here is *her* daughter, Miss Beverly Stanton."

"Welcome. I'm Mr. Sherville, owner of the retreat. We'll take good care of you, Miss Stanton."

Beverly found her mouth and throat as dry as cotton, so she merely nodded. Mr. Sherville seemed nice enough, but she wouldn't allow his demeanor to raise her hopes. It might have if she hadn't seen the woman on a leash, but if the little she'd gleaned from papers and rumor were anywhere near accurate, patients at the asylum weren't treated as if they were merely on a seaside vacation to rest their nerves, as Mother tried to paint it. For Beverly's sake or Mother's own, she could not say. Possibly for both.

This was no seaside hotel. For one thing, Beverly had no idea when she'd ever leave. *If* she'd ever be able to.

The journey had taken several hours. The hour was approaching noon and the air was beginning to warm. They'd left Fairington House in darkness to ensure that Mother and

Mr. Pyke could return the same day. As miserable as the trip had been, Beverly was grateful for one thing: her stepsister Dorothy hadn't been in the coach. Instead one person who loved Beverly—her mother—accompanied her and just one person who despised her—Mr. Pyke— instead of two.

Dorothy did not need to come along, of course, but she'd hinted she might. Beverly knew why: to be a spectator as Beverly was held on certificates and taken away. She'd always hated Beverly and now she had her wish. Beverly would no longer be in her life.

Mr. Pyke had the same wish. After all, Dorothy, at eighteen, deserved to have the limelight of the Season so she could make a good match. Beverly had already had two unsuccessful seasons, so she was incapable of attracting a suitor. Her "hysteria" was blamed for that and a multitude of other sins.

At twenty-three, Beverly was nigh unto a spinster and would, Mr. Pyke put it, cast a pall over dear Dorothy's Season.

If that were the only reason to rid themselves of Beverly, perhaps Mother would have been strong enough to insist that Beverly stay in the home she'd always known. She would be happy to forgo a Season if it meant not being forced into an asylum.

Alas, Mr. Pyke had additional cause for disliking Beverly. She was a constant irritation to him as she prevented him from squandering her late father's fortune. In Mr. Pyke's mind, a woman with an iron will such as her own simply *had* to be mad. After all, she was a woman who not only understood money matters and had opinions about how to run an estate, but she also *shared* those opinions—and loudly—when they were in opposition to those of the man of the house.

Scandalous.

And apparently insane?

Thanks to Dr. Hornby, she was now under certificate and would be stuck living at Sherville Retreat for the foreseeable future.

Mr. Sherville ushered them toward the front door, where the servants waited, flanking the entrance. "Her trunks will be brought up to her room, so you needn't worry on that account. Come inside. We'll complete the intake process, then get her settled in before tea."

Her mother and stepfather nodded and, arms linked, followed Mr. Sherville toward the main door.

Beverly hung back, her attention caught by the sight of a man perhaps two hundred feet away. He appeared to be dressed well, perhaps in his mid-twenties. He was alone—no leash or other restraint that she could see. Yet he gesticulated as if speaking to someone. With his back to her, she couldn't see if he was speaking, but what else could he be doing? He shook his head several times, then grasped it as if in pain, then sat on the ground and let out a cry. With one fist, he hit his forehead again and again.

All of this happened in a matter of seconds, so quickly she wondered if she'd imagined it. He shifted to one knee, then stood and tugged at the cuffs of his sleeves, stopping when he noted her staring.

Their gaze held for a moment, and despite the distance between them, Beverly felt both intrigued and unnerved—he seemed to be seeing into her soul.

"Beverly, come!" Mr. Pyke said, pulling her from her reverie. He stood inside, just beyond the threshold. "We mustn't make Mr. Sherville wait."

"Apologies," Beverly said. She dipped a slight curtsy and hurried inside, but as she followed them into her new home, she couldn't get the image of the man outside from her mind.

He was handsome, with hair that seemed to be composed

of several shades of brown and slightly wavy. He had a strong jaw and brow. She couldn't make out much more from a distance, but she'd never forget his penetrating gaze.

Was he a member of the staff?

Or was he a lunatic?

And why did the answer to those questions matter so much to her?

Chapter Two

CRANDALL DOWLING STOOD ON THE edge of the gardens, watching the front door of the main building until the party that had alighted from a coach had entered. When a deep thud told him the door had closed, he let out a breath, not realizing he'd been holding it.

Almost immediately, his right fist struck his forehead—three times—and his shoulder jerked twice. He was glad that the new arrivals hadn't seen those twitches, movements he had no say over any more than he could decide when and how fast his heart beat.

He felt quite certain that the young woman had seen some of his "tics," as Dr. Pushman called them, and that fact was embarrassing. Crandall didn't feel as if he'd lost his sanity, but the reality remained that he could not always control the movement of his body, and that loss of mastery at times extended to his speech.

His condition had worsened as he studied medicine at Guy's Hospital. In time, the teacher he most admired, the man who had become a mentor to him, Dr. Pushman, pulled him away from an operating theater, where Crandall had been observing a surgery on a man's abdomen.

"Sir?" Crandall said in the corridor, his middle sinking at the saddened expression his mentor wore.

"My dear man," Dr. Pushman said. He paused, then said, "Unfortunately, a life in medicine is not in your future."

Crandall glanced back at the surgical theater. "Wh-why?" His head jerked to one side several times, and a sound like a bird cawing escaped his mouth. Oh, how he hated it when those things happened. At the time, he'd believed them to be signs of fatigue, that the strange movements and verbal outbursts would end when he'd finished his schooling and could rest. Yet he was being informed that he might not be able to complete his studies.

"I've been deeply unsettled by your recent behaviors," Dr. Pushman said. "I've had my suspicions about what might be causing them, so I consulted my bishop."

"Your ... *bishop*?" That was genuinely alarming. "Why?"

"He agrees that you are afflicted—whether insane or possessed, neither of us can say." To the man's credit, he seemed saddened and took no pleasure in the telling.

Nothing would dissuade the man. Two days later, Crandall's father arrived to bring him home. The goodbye with Dr. Pushman was heartfelt, but as the coach rolled away, Crandall could not stop thinking that his mentor truly believed him to either have an evil nature or to be too insane to live among society. His father believed Dr. Pushman, which was how Crandall had come to live at Sherville.

Which was worse? Others believing him insane or evil?

The result was the same either way; a piece of Crandall's soul had died.

No more medical school. He had no future in healing others. Instead he was bound to a hospital against his will, with no hope of a life free from the Sherville Retreat.

His condition had made even this existence that much

worse moments before, when the pretty young woman had arrived to see him in the middle of one of his episodes. Alas, that, as well as so many other things, could not be helped. Crandall tore his gaze from the door and headed along a path that led to the buildings behind the main one, to his dormitory.

No nurse had come to fetch him after his walk, but they usually did by the time he'd walked the circuit around the estate. Better to return early, before tea, and be seen as a cooperative patient. In doing so, he'd be more likely to have the freedom to go on more outings on the grounds alone—a privilege he'd seen withheld from many.

As he walked, his boots crunching gravel under his feet, he wondered how his former roommate, Jasper, was faring. The poor man had gone into convulsions the other night, and after they'd eased, he claimed to see people who were not real. As far as Crandall could see, the poor man posed no threat to anyone, yet he was taken away in shackles, and Crandall hadn't seen him in the fortnight since.

He had a suspicion that Jasper was in the basement, where the dangerous and most seriously insane patients were kept—and treated abominably if even the mildest of rumors could be believed.

Crandall reached his dormitory and went inside and up the wooden staircase to reach his room. He thought of the group he'd seen arriving minutes before, which appeared to consist of parents and a grown daughter.

Were they visiting a patient at the Sherville Retreat? If so, whom did they seek? The answer could be nearly anyone who resided here. He knew only a handful of fellow patients and even less about their families outside the retreat.

He'd been here only a matter of months, since early spring, and now the colors of autumn were in full force. They would be gone soon enough, making way for the cold of winter. As he walked along the hall leading to his quarters, he thought of the patients whose doors he passed and tried to think of anything he knew about their lives or families. He couldn't think of more than a detail or two among a dozen men but nothing that allowed him to hazard a guess which patient the party might be visiting.

The retreat was truly a lonely and isolating place, no matter that it housed over a hundred guests. He ought to attempt to make more friends and to truly get to know some of them—beyond what their diagnoses and outward challenges were.

Having a few true friends would be a balm to his soul, and perhaps he could be a similar comfort to others. That would certainly be the closest thing to healing the sick he might ever do.

He was but steps from his room when a Mr. Wellings, a nurse in this wing, entered the hall and spotted him. "Mr. Dowling," he called. "I was looking for you outside and worried when I couldn't find you."

"I was outside walking about the pond, as promised," Crandall replied.

"You're usually outside longer," Wellings said.

True. Today was different because of that woman who'd looked at him curiously as he'd hit himself in the head.

As if on cue, the tics returned. Crandall smacked his forehead. His shoulder jerked three times in a row, stopped, then jerked three more times. Then, worst of all, this time his tongue decided to have a mind of its own.

"Blast! You're a molrowing collywobble. Dag-blamed—" He tried to clamp his jaw shut, but the effort only made even more colorful language fly.

"Your return came at a fortuitous time," Wellings said.

"Good thing Nurse Buckler wasn't on duty to hear that. Her face would blush fully scarlet, and then she'd collapse from the vapors."

Crandall gave a weak smile, assuming the man was attempting humor, though as the one afflicted with said tics, he found nothing about the situation amusing. Rather to the contrary.

In his room, he crossed to the wingback chair by the window and sat on it, then gazed outdoors at the grounds. From there he could see miles and miles past the retreat.

Sunken walls created the illusion that the landscape was one unbroken, beautiful picture. A casual observer might think a patient could merely walk away from the retreat at will. In reality, the sunken walls around most of the perimeter meant that they might as well have been the cliffs of Moher rather than a nine-foot drop.

At times he almost appreciated the illusion. Sometimes he could pretend, even for a moment, that he wasn't confined anywhere but merely looking out a window at a lovely landscape.

He could not pretend right now. Oh, that he could.

Oh, that he could fly away and escape this place.

Oh, that he could again become the man he'd once been rather than the "dangerous lunatic" who hit himself, whose limbs moved as if with a mind of their own, who yelled things that were shocking and shameful.

Oh, that he could be the man who'd once had the promise of a career ahead of him as a physician.

That was gone. He'd never be a physician. The best he could hope for, if he ever managed to leave the retreat—about as likely as finding a wood nymph—would be to work as an apothecary. If one day he became able to leave the retreat with his tics, he'd need a business partner to interact with customers while he worked in the back room. Not that a man hidden from the public by certificate would ever need to worry about such a thing.

"Would you like to have tea brought to your room?" Mr. Wellings asked, pulling Crandall from his thoughts.

He turned from the window and blinked—then continued to blink and couldn't stop for several seconds. Finally, he managed, "Yes, thank you."

His tics were getting worse today; he didn't wish to have tea in a common room, where others could see him and stare.

When he was left alone, his gaze returned to the window. He wanted to fly away to London, back to his life before the retreat, when he had a future winding before him like a golden ribbon of road.

While losing the dream of becoming a physician had been hard, Crandall's perspective had shifted in the last several months. Being stuck at an asylum did that to a man. And an asylum this was, no matter that Sherville called it a "retreat."

For the moment, if someone could provide him with the hope that one day, he would leave this place a free man and that he'd be able to then have a simple life with a family of his own, that would be more than enough to keep him content.

A home, a wife, and children, and a way to support them, perhaps as an apothecary. That's all he dared ask for, and he didn't think they were unreasonable requests—nay, pleas—of the heavens. Weren't those the kinds of things every man wished for and most achieved?

On the other hand, perhaps it was too much to ask if he was indeed a demon-possessed reprobate with an inborn evil nature. He sighed and rubbed his aching forehead. Whether the pain was from a regular headache or from the abuse it had taken from his fist, he didn't know.

He closed his eyes and let himself imagine a future with a home and wife. He'd done so many times before, but usually, the woman in his mind was vague and shadowy. This time, she looked precisely like the young woman he'd locked eyes with outside.

Little surprised him of late, but *she* had—and the connection he felt to her, as brief as it was, surprised him even more. For a moment, she'd seemed to be an answer to prayer, a door to a new future . . .

Foolish thoughts. Yet they continued to swirl in his mind and imagination nonetheless. Who was she, and might he find a way to meet her?

Chapter Three

THE NEXT SPACE OF TIME—two hours, perhaps? Beverly couldn't be sure—seemed a blur of unreality, as if she were in a horrible dream and would surely wake in her bed at home in York. Mother, Mr. Pyke, and Beverly were all present for the intake meeting in Dr. Hornby's office, where he asked any number of intimate questions about her life, emotional state, childhood, physical ailments, *lady* ailments, and more. He took copious notes.

The entire meeting made her deeply uncomfortable. She'd never spoken of such things in male company before, and here she had not only a man asking such questions and expecting complete answers, but her stepfather was also present. She could hardly bear to speak of sensitive matters before a man who disliked her so much that he'd found two physicians to agree she was plagued with hysteria. *He* was the reason she'd been brought here. He was the last person she wanted present to hear such an interview.

Patients had no right to expect such privacy.

"That will do for now," Dr. Hornby said at last. He placed his notes into a drawer and stood, gesturing to indicate that the others rise as well. "Time to say goodbye to your parents, Miss Stanton."

"Already?" Beverly asked. She'd expected more time with her mother at least, who would help her unpack her trunks and get her settled in her chambers.

Her face must have registered alarm, because Dr. Hornby chuckled and, eying Mr. Pyke, said somewhat under his breath, "If there were any doubt as to her diagnosis . . ." His voice trailed off, and the two men shared quiet amusement.

I am not mad, Beverly wanted to scream. Wasn't it perfectly natural for a young woman to react with nervousness upon arrival at an asylum? For her to be surprised and distressed at having to say farewell to her mother sooner than anticipated? For her to be nervous at the prospect of being left alone in a strange place? If she *hadn't* responded with any emotion, *that* would have been cause for concern, wouldn't it? Cause for a *diagnosis*?

I am not hysterical. I am perfectly sane, she thought defiantly, though she knew that saying as much would only make the men believe her to be precisely what she denied.

Beverly chose the quiet, submissive path for the moment. When she knew Sherville Retreat's expectations, she might speak more, but not when she was so newly arrived. She silently followed behind Dr. Hornby, who in turn led Mother and Mr. Pyke. A nurse who'd been waiting for them in the corridor took up the rear, behind Beverly. Perhaps to ensure that Beverly didn't get lost. Or attempt to run away or race completely mad through the buildings. The woman was likely past thirty, and while not unhandsome, she had lines that pulled down at the corners of her mouth and eyes. What all had this woman witnessed with Sherville patients to have drawn those lines on her face?

At the same door they'd entered, Dr. Hornby said

goodbye to Mother and Mr. Pyke. He stepped to the side just enough for Beverly to wave and call her farewell but not enough for her to step past him and give her mother a final hug. Oh, to have been able to be in Mother's embrace for just one more moment to breathe in her cedar perfume.

Alas, Dr. Hornby ensured she hadn't the opportunity for any of that "emotional nonsense," as he put it.

"The less emotion we stir up inside you, the sooner you'll be recovered and can return home," he told Beverly as he closed—and locked—the door.

Beverly nodded mutely, though not speaking her mind took every ounce of effort she had. How could this man—a doctor of the mind!—not see that refusing to allow her the small comfort of a moment with her mother had brought on *deeper* emotions of sadness and despair? Saying as much would brand her as hysterical, so she had to pretend not to feel anything.

Would that be the trick to "recovering" and being released to go home?

If she did manage to convince Mr. Hornby that she was cured, how long would it be before Mr. Pyke found another excuse—and two more signed doctor certificates—to get her committed yet again?

That thought was enough to truly make her want to cry—yes, hysterically.

Dr. Hornby led her and the nurse up a flight of stairs to a long corridor that led to a separate wing of the building. There he stopped and gestured to the woman. "Nurse Turley here will show you to your room and help you get settled." He withdrew a watch from his pocket and consulted the time. "You may go to the dining room in the main house for tea, if you like."

"Thank you," Beverly said with a nod and a slight curtsy, bobbing oh so slightly from the knee.

"Most residents eat in the large dining hall in wing C," Dr. Hornby said. "It's a privilege to dine in the small dining room in the main building, but at times we allow residents and others an opportunity to eat with the staff. Sometimes it helps one acclimate."

Beverly supposed the words were intended to be a compliment. "That is most kind of you," she said with another bob.

"Very good." He nodded with a half-bow and left Beverly and Nurse Turley behind.

"Come with me," the nurse said, and she led the way through the halls, which eventually connected to other buildings. At last, she stopped before a wall of cupboards. "Here we'll get some linens for you," she said, opening one, removing a towel and a cloth.

She placed the items in Beverly's arms, closed the cupboard door, and opened another. From that one, she withdrew bed linens, which again were placed in Beverly's arms, and then she presented a quilt and a pillow from yet another cupboard. With Beverly's arms filled to the brim, she could hardly see ahead of her.

"Come along," Nurse Turley said. "Your room is just around this corner."

At last, Beverly found herself in what would be her living quarters for the foreseeable future. The space wasn't large, but it was a private room, something she knew her mother had requested and begged of Mr. Pyke because they could afford the additional cost.

"I'm a nurse for several patients, but I understand your family has made arrangements for me to also be your maid. I'll sleep next door, and I'll be the one to help you bathe, dress, fix your hair, and such. We were unaware of the request until Mr. Pyke arrived, so until they can hire another nurse, you'll have to share with a few others. For now, I'll make your bed so you'll have a place to rest, and then I'll show you about."

"Thank you, Nurse Turley."

The woman smiled at that—a simple expression that brightened her face and lifted five years from it at minimum. "Don't tell Dr. Hornby or the others, but you may call me Gini. I've never taken to all of that proper nonsense."

Beverly smiled back. "If you're sure . . ."

"Oh, I'm quite sure," Nurse Turley—rather, Gini—said with a wink as she worked on Beverly's bed. A moment later, after fluffing the pillow, she said, "Now, come. I'll show you to the small dining room in the main house. I'm sure you're ravenous and could use more than a simple tea. The staff is always fed quite well there."

"That would be lovely," Beverly said. "I am rather hungry." As if on cue, her middle rumbled, and Gini laughed.

Soon they entered a beautiful room with one large table, around which were seated various staff members. The table was far longer and more elegantly decorated than any Beverly had ever been seated at before. The room itself felt luxurious, from velvet drapes to the delicate wallpaper and elegant chairs with detailed carvings and cushions embroidered with what looked like gold and silk.

She was admiring the room, as well as the china, goblets, silver, and more when Gini approached the footman to request a meal from the kitchen. "Cold meats, cheese, and bread will be fine, Spencer."

The footman turned to leave and nearly ran headlong into someone else entering—another man. "Pardon," the footman said, stepping to the side and then making his exit.

The other man entered, and as he came into full view, Beverly recognized him at once as the man she'd seen in the gardens. The one who'd been gesticulating and hitting his head. He was here, in the main house-staff's dining room. Was he an employee, then? Or a patient like her, perhaps being rewarded for good behavior?

As soon as a brown-haired nurse noted his arrival, she pushed away from the table and hurried over to him, reaching him just as a male nurse did too.

The woman spoke first in a tense whisper that failed to be quiet enough; Beverly made out every word without trying. Indeed, the room had grown still, so she couldn't have avoided hearing the interchange.

"Is it wise to bring him in here . . . now?" the nurse asked.

"Hornby requested it," the male nurse said.

"He . . . why?"

The man in question had stopped moving, waiting beside the two who were arguing about his presence. Beverly glanced at Gini, wondering what she thought of the matter, but her face was inscrutable.

The male nurse approached the women staff members and lowered his voice. "Hornby wishes to see how our newest resident will react to certain . . . stimuli."

"Oh, for goodness' sake," the female nurse said. She, too, kept her voice low so the man at the door couldn't hear, though Beverly made out every word. The woman glanced at Beverly and went on, clearly aware that the latter was aware of the conversation. "If her hysteria is serious, this could exacerbate her symptoms and lengthen the duration of her illness."

"I'm merely following orders."

"Very well," the woman said, shrugging. "But don't blame me when things go awry."

Whatever were they talking about? The man behind them had waited patiently, and only when they parted did he step into the dining room proper. All seemed entirely normal until he slid a chair out and took a seat.

That's when their eyes met, and he smiled at her—bright blue eyes beneath a shock of dark hair and a smile that could light up the rainiest of days. Beverly smiled in return.

"I'm Crandall Dowling," he said. "Pleased to meet you."

Despite not being properly introduced by someone else, Beverly opened her mouth to reply. She didn't get a single sound out, however, before she was interrupted—and by Mr. Dowling's movements rather than another person's speech. His shoulder jerked violently three times, his fist smacked his forehead at least as many times, and then he yelled, "Bunters and fartleberries. Whore!"

With a look of horror on his face, he clamped a hand over his mouth. His other hand, however, became a fist, and he was hitting himself again.

Alarmed, Beverly turned to Gini, who seemed more amused than surprised as she put butter on a piece of bread. The other two nurses, who'd argued over whether Mr. Dowling should enter at all, both eyed Beverly for her reaction. That fact alone ensured that she schooled her features and did her best to not show shock. Yet how, precisely, was one supposed to behave after such a display?

She took a sip of her tea, keenly aware of how Mr. Dowling's neck and cheeks had flushed. He was avoiding her eye, no doubt terribly embarrassed.

How she reacted to this moment would define much of her stay at Sherville Retreat, she felt sure of it. Had she successfully portrayed outward calm? Should she have shown moral indignation instead?

Only time would tell if she'd chosen correctly.

Chapter Four

I MUST REMAIN CALM, Beverly thought. *No matter what he says, I mustn't show emotion if I am to convince anyone that I'm "cured" of hysteria.*

So even as the man slammed his fist into his forehead and several additional choice phrases and expletives flew from his lips, she daintily cut the meat on her plate and took one small bite at a time. The effort to not even look at Mr. Dowling was tantamount to torture. She didn't know how long she could keep her eyes downcast and demeanor peaceful.

Turned out that she had no need to maintain the charade for long. Mr. Dowling stood and spoke, giving Beverly an excuse to look at him. Through much effort, which included more verbal outbursts with some strange shoulder movements and head jerks, he excused himself.

However, as he turned to depart, a woman at the head of the table spoke. "Will you be returning to your quarters?" She wore a severe bun streaked with gray, though she didn't look much older than forty.

Mr. Dowling turned back reluctantly as if he'd missed escaping a trap. "Mrs. Buckler, if I may go for a turn about the gardens, I'd be much—much—whore!—much obliged." He spoke so quietly it was a near whisper and a wonder Beverly heard it at all.

Before the woman, apparently Mrs. Buckler, replied, his face squinched together suddenly, then relaxed, and he blinked rapidly several times in a row. When the display ended, he blushed an even darker shade of red, if that was possible.

"You may stroll about the gardens," the woman said with a nod. "The fresh air may do you some good. Be sure to be in your quarters by sundown."

"I will, Mrs. Buckler," he promised. "Thank you." Then, with two quick jerks of his head and another twitch of a shoulder, followed by, "Whore!" he left.

Beverly returned to her plate, extremely aware of every pair of eyes in the room on her. Keenly aware that everyone in the room watched her, she could feel her pulse throbbing in her chest. And yes, some of her increased heart rate was likely due to the startling display she'd just seen.

After several breaths of silence, Gini glanced at Beverly a couple of times and then ventured, "Are you well?" Her gaze flitted to Mrs. Buckler and then back to Beverly. The simple act said that the older nurse had authority here, and that, in turn, told Beverly that any behavior on her part that could be construed as *hysterical* mustn't be witnessed by Mrs. Buckler especially.

"I'm quite well, thank you," Beverly said with a smile before taking a bite of asparagus covered in hollandaise sauce. Her words were mostly true, though heat had already climbed into her neck and cheeks. She was likely blushing from nerves and surprise as much as anything.

"He's harmless," Gini said. "Shocking, certainly, and he *sounds* as if he could be violent—"

"Looks it, as well—" Mrs. Buckler interjected.

Gini gave a pained half-smile and nodded in acknowledgment without voicing agreement. "But I've seen him care for an injured bird, take a spider outdoors instead of killing it, and—"

"In essence," a middle-aged man on the other end of the table said, "he may sound scary, but he's a timid dandy at heart." He chuckled and shook his head, then returned to reading a newspaper on the table.

Back home, any kind of reading material was banned from the dining room, so seeing a newspaper laid out and being read while others ate was quite a surprise to Beverly. What other social norms would she learn did not apply at Sherville?

In truth, the rule at Fairington House affected only Beverly. Mother and Dorothy weren't ones to care about reading much besides the society papers, and those only to keep abreast of local events and gossip. Mr. Pyke certainly didn't approve of her reading Dickens's novels or Keats's poetry. Frankly, he objected to all of the books in her father's library.

His disapproval did not affect Beverly's reading habits, however. A fact that helped him convince the doctors that she was unwell. She read too much emotional literature. Her "fragile" mind could not bear such topics, leading to what he called "emotional volatility."

If that'd been what defined one's loyalty to a late parent and stubbornness in the face of selfishness and cruelty, then yes, Beverly qualified. But millions of people read the same things and weren't any more insane than she was.

Had reading those things affected her emotions? Undoubtedly. Yet she believed they'd given her a more expansive mind and a heart with a greater capacity for compassion.

"Tending an injured bird and taking a spider outside sound, to me, like the behaviors of a gentleman," Beverly said. Should she have remained silent? Perhaps her words would be considered an attack of hysteria. Mr. Pyke certainly would have thought so.

But the man with the newspaper hardly reacted. He shook his head and chuckled to himself as if she were but a silly child. He turned the page and took a sip of tea.

She glanced at Gini, who widened her eyes in warning, so she, too, returned to her meal. No more disagreements or "outbursts" from her. She'd stay in control so she could, she prayed, one day leave this place.

"Don't worry, Miss Stanton. We won't allow Mr. Dowling in the dining room again soon," Mrs. Buckler said, as if Beverly had shown evidence of having been disturbed by the incident. And as if she would be invited back any time soon.

I am not disturbed so much as confused and intrigued, she thought.

"Oh, I wouldn't mind if he did return," Beverly said. "He didn't upset me."

The words were true, but that wasn't why she said them. She hoped the staff would see that she was calm as a still pond, not the least bit hysterical.

"His behavior *should* have upset you," the man with the newspaper said. "I've heard stories about him that would give you terrors in your sleep."

"Oh?" Beverly hoped she sounded indifferent. In truth, she was deeply curious, though not afraid as the man seemed to suggest she ought to be.

"Monte," Mrs. Buckler said to him, "I suggest you stop saying things that upset the residents."

The man—Monte, apparently—shrugged and took

another sip from his cup, which had a silver mustache guard, before turning the page.

The older woman directed her attention to Beverly. "I suppose it's only wise to warn you. Suffice it to say that Mr. Dowling was, sadly, born with an inferior mind that allows him to be controlled by evil forces."

Surely, Beverly hadn't heard correctly. "Pardon?"

"Evil forces. The devil." Mrs. Buckler said the words as if they made logical sense instead of being the least-sane thing Beverly had encountered at Sherville thus far.

"I'm not sure I understand," Beverly said through her shock, though a more precise phrasing would have been, *Surely, you jest or are mad yourself.*

"I presume you've read the Bible and know about the legion of spirits and the pigs?" Mrs. Buckler paused after cutting a piece of asparagus and looked up at Beverly.

"Yes," Beverly said warily.

"Then you understand." Mrs. Buckler returned to cutting vegetables. "Sadly, Mr. Dowling has so weak a character that he is easily influenced by demons." The woman placed a bite of asparagus in her mouth as if it were the full stop at the end of her statement.

Was the woman implying that Mr. Dowling was possessed? Beverly didn't believe in things such as demonic possession. *Something* was wrong with Mr. Dowling—that much was clear—but Beverly suspected that *he* suffered far more than Mrs. Buckler or anyone else on staff. No matter what the woman claimed, demons and a weak spiritual constitution had nothing to do with it.

The meal continued, and the staff in the room began talking more to one another. Beverly ate in silence and soon became aware that so long as she didn't draw attention to herself, the staff seemed to forget her existence. That, or they didn't see her as a reason to withhold stories and opinions about patients, anecdotes shared callously.

Except for Gini, they sounded very much as if they viewed the residents of the retreat as infants. In some cases, as little more than animals. Either way, they certainly did not view the residents worthy of decorum or respect and scarcely as humans.

As she pondered the confusing array of things she'd heard and seen in the last hour, her gaze found the window and the colorful autumn gardens beyond.

What stories could they tell of me? she mused. If she were to befriend Mr. Dowling, would she be seen as having a weak character too, one fooled by the devil?

As the thought crossed her mind, Mr. Dowling himself crossed her field of vision through the window. He walked, perhaps fifty paces away, along the edge of a pond. She startled slightly and then hoped she'd hid the reaction. Best to not start a discussion about him again.

She focused on her plate, but she'd eaten as much as she could stand and couldn't bear the thought of eating more. Rather, she wished to go outside and speak with this Mr. Dowling herself. He intrigued her in ways she could not understand—and had since she'd first laid eyes on him. The surprising outburst, followed by his clear embarrassment, made her deeply curious, drawn to him more than ever.

Beverly set her utensils parallel on her plate and cleared her throat. "I'm a bit fatigued after the day's travels. May I return to my quarters to rest?"

Mrs. Buckler narrowed her eyes as if analyzing every inch of Beverly inside and out. "Very well. I can have the kitchen send up a slice of cake later, if you like."

"That would be lovely. Thank you." Beverly stood and moved toward the door, but just as Mr. Dowling had been interrupted by Mrs. Buckler, so was she.

"Should Miss Turley accompany you, so you don't get lost?"

Beverly turned around slowly, just as Mr. Dowling had not long before. She smiled. "It's not far. I'm quite sure I remember how to get there. Thank you for your concern. I'm ever so grateful for it."

That sounded sane enough—and not at all hysterical, right? The faces looking at her—most in the room, though not Monte, who was still engrossed in his paper—seemed pleased enough with her response.

When no one made a move to stop her, Beverly Stanton took the silence as permission and left. In the hall, instead of going to the wing with her quarters, she turned the other direction—toward doors that led outside. She would go find Mr. Dowling. She would talk to him. At the least, she'd ensure that he knew she was not offended by his words.

Perhaps if she earned his trust, she'd learn more about who he was. The look on his face when he'd first spoken those awful words told her that he had a good heart. Deep down, did he still know that about himself? Or had life at Sherville beaten that understanding out of him to the point that even he believed he was morally flawed?

If an intelligent man like Mr. Dowling could be convinced of such a thing, could she, too, be convinced that she was mad? Would she eventually submit to someone else's reality?

She dearly hoped not, but she hadn't any idea what years in an asylum could do to a person. She didn't know of anyone who returned from one saner than they entered. She feared that she'd gradually become insane herself.

She pushed through the heavy door and set out toward the pond to find Mr. Dowling. If she could help one man find his humanity and believe in his sanity again, perhaps she could hope for herself as well.

Chapter Five

CRANDALL WALKED THE GARDENS, GRATEFUL he hadn't been ordered to return to his quarters. Right then, he could not have borne to be within the constraints of walls and a roof. He needed to be outside, where he could freely breathe clean air and think. As he regularly did, he circled the small pond, around and around. Most of the pond's path, save for two small stands of trees and shrubbery, was visible from the main building's windows—especially from Sherville's and Buckler's offices—as well as from the front doors of the main building.

As a result, Crandall had learned that so long as he remained on the path, he was likely to be left alone, undisturbed for decent stretches of the day. No one at Sherville seemed eager to have him present for group activities like crafts or musicales. He could not blame them for that, and he would have stayed away regardless, not wanting to draw attention to himself by interrupting a performance with cursing.

Yet hours and hours alone did take a toll on a man. Solitude was refreshing; loneliness drained one's life energy.

He tried to enjoy his time alone. After all, there were no guarantees of anything here, including assurance of privacy and time for one's thoughts. Outdoor exercise seemed to be something the staff looked upon favorably. Dr. Hornby declared that some patients had cured themselves by spending time out of doors and exercising often.

If walking the path allowed Crandall time to himself—and even the slimmest possibility of regaining his health—he'd wear out a million pairs of boots doing so.

Today, however, the peace he often found outdoors eluded him. He'd made a fool of himself before the young woman he'd seen arriving. With shame, he recalled the disgusting words that had burst from his mouth in her presence. His hands clenched in fists again and again as he relived the moment repeatedly—including, to his humiliation, the amusement of the staff. Nurse Turley was the only one besides the new woman who hadn't laughed or silently smirked at his distress.

His shoulder jerked wildly, his head doing the same to one side, followed by loud cries he could not restrain that sounded like some wounded bird. What had he done in this life or the one before to be cursed so that he behaved like an animal? He seemed to have no free will, to have lost his humanity. Why else would he behave no more intelligently than the wounded bird he sounded like?

Footsteps on gravel sounded somewhere behind him. Likely one of the groundskeepers or another member of the staff fetching one thing or another from a different building. Not eager to be noticed, he lengthened his stride in the hopes of reaching the next stand of trees and then waiting behind it for whoever it was to leave.

"Mr. Dowling?" a voice called.

He'd nearly made it to the trees. So close. He closed his eyes as his step came to a halt, and he waited for the voice to tell him to return to his quarters or perhaps to the staff dining room to apologize.

When he didn't speak, the voice spoke again. "Mr. Dowling," the person said again—a woman, who'd drawn nearer. "May I join you?"

"May—" He whirled around in surprise and found himself but a stone's throw away from the woman he'd embarrassed himself in front of. He felt his cheeks burn with shame.

"I don't want to intrude but..." Her voice trailed off, and she gestured toward the pond as if the grounds were explanation enough.

They most definitely were not, but Crandall did not have the wherewithal to form a coherent query of any kind. "Am I—that is—" He cleared his throat, stared at the gravel path, and tried again. "Are you come to fetch me inside?"

At that, she leaned back slightly in surprise. "No. Not at all."

Then why was she here? "I don't understand," he said.

She gave a half-smile and took a small step forward. "I confess that I, too, am rather unclear on the reason."

Crandall looked over her shoulder toward the drive where he'd first seen her alight from the coach. "You are newly employed at Sherville Retreat, I presume?" he said. "Are you a nurse? I hear we are short-staffed in the laundry and kitchens, but you strike me as an educated woman."

That was the best explanation he could devise for who she was and why she'd followed him. And those were also the most words he'd spoken in a week without a profane one sprinkled among them. Alas, a few punches to his head did punctuate the speech, but he supposed that giving himself bruises was preferable to foul language in front of a lady.

Her smile widened, and she stepped even closer. "I'm a new resident."

"You—you are?" She looked nothing like the men and

women he'd come to know as mentally and emotionally unwell, many of whom had been at the retreat for a decade or longer. Some had withdrawn, becoming hunched over and hardly able to walk—yet another reason Crandall was determined to walk often.

To his shock, she stepped even closer, now with her hand extended. "We weren't properly introduced before, and I'm unsure whether the traditional rules of etiquette apply to patients of an asylum so . . ."

He took her hand and bowed over it. "Crandall Dowling," he said, though he'd already given her his name in the dining room. As he straightened, their eyes met, and a warmth he hadn't felt in ages flooded his veins. He could gaze upon that face forever and never tire of it, he was certain.

For a moment, she didn't speak. Did she, too, feel the hum of . . . something . . . between them? Was it not entirely in his diseased mind? He prayed that it wasn't. He'd pull out this memory often in upcoming weeks to help him through difficult times. The few happy memories he had were becoming worn with how often he relied on them to get through the black nights when his soul felt trapped in a dungeon of despair.

"Miss Beverly Stanton," she said after a deliciously thrilling pause. She curtsied, and he gave her gloved hand a slight squeeze before releasing it, something that, if he wasn't entirely insane to think so, seemed to bring a brightness to her countenance.

"May I join you?" She gestured toward the path ahead.

Crandall looked back at the retreat buildings and the courtyard before them, fully expecting an actual staff member to come out and explain to Miss Stanton that she'd best not spend time with a deranged and potentially dangerous patient. He'd heard himself described thus more than once, and Dr. Hornby had written the words *deranged* and *dangerous* in Crandall's case book, though he'd literally never hurt anyone physically but himself.

When no one came from any of the buildings to fetch him or Miss Stanton, he looked at her. "Are you sure you—" He could feel certain words bubbling up. He tried to hold them down, but like an itch demanding to be scratched or a sneeze that *would* escape, no matter how you try, their escape was only a matter of time. His efforts at holding back the vile words resulted in his fist smacking his forehead three times and then grabbing a fistful of hair and pulling hard.

"Beardsplitter. Dratted strumpet." He covered his face with one hand. The more he tried to resist any of the impulses his condition created, the worse they became.

"I'm—gerry—whore!" He shook his head, blushing. He shook his head. "Whore!" He returned to the path leaving her behind. "I'll leave you in peace. Strumpet!"

She soon caught up to him and walked at his side. Surprise was not an adequate term for what he felt at that moment. Shock came closer, and he quite nearly tripped on a stone, which would have sent him headlong into the pond if he hadn't grasped a branch. Fortune had smiled on him, for five seconds earlier, he wouldn't have been within reach of the trees or their branches.

Miss Stanton gasped as he tripped and helped steady him, but her kind touch—even through gloves, nothing but the steady weight of her hand on his arm—so overcame him that he could hardly think.

"Are you—certain—whore!—you should accompany me?" He cleared his throat again as if that might rid it of any other questionable phrases.

"I'm at an asylum, because I have hysteria, or so my stepfather says." Miss Stanton spoke in the calmest manner imaginable, a fact that belied her words—and her diagnosis—so entirely that both of them laughed aloud. She placed a hand on his forearm again and assured him, "I have no reputation to protect here. Besides, we're in full view of the buildings, are we not? Plenty of patients—or residents, I believe we're called?—and staff members can see us clearly through the windows. Whatever sliver of honor I might yet possess will not be in danger by walking at your side where any passerby could be a witness."

She slipped her hand through his arm, resting it in the crook of his elbow as if he were escorting her into a dining hall or a ballroom. He'd escorted ladies before in such circumstances but likely never would again.

"So you are here for hysteria," Crandall said. "From what I've seen, that term encompasses a large number of vague things that may or may not mean anything."

"Precisely. You must be a physician," Miss Stanton said with a laugh. "With two doctors signing certificates saying I'm hysterical—something they were happy to do on nothing but the word of my stepfather, with promises of a reward—here I am. And here I likely will be, held on certificates based on an imaginary ailment."

"I am so sorry," Crandall said. "Bullocks!" He breathed out heavily, then had to stop walking for a moment as his physical tics returned—not punching this time but jerks and twitches of his head and shoulders. After they subsided a bit, he murmured, "Apologies."

"No need," she said with a smile. "Truly."

Her tone was so clear and genuine, her face so devoid of shock and horror, that he believed her. The moment felt like cool water on a parched throat.

They continued walking, now stepping on autumn leaves that had fallen onto the path, their colors ranging from pale gold to dark orange.

"What brought you to Sherville Retreat, and how long have you been here?"

"Six months on Saturday," he said. Half a year. How many years lay before him? How many times would he walk this path, watching the seasons change from fall to winter to spring to summer and back to autumn again? "As for what ails me... I wish I could say it were something like your imaginary hysteria or even melancholia."

They walked in silence for several steps, and when she didn't press him to speak, gratitude and appreciation for her swelled in his chest.

"Dr. Pushman, my former teacher, believes I may have a condition that a French doctor recently published a paper about. It describes people who are somewhat like me—some worse, some less serious—but without any significant ideas for causes or treatments."

"Science can find answers, I'm certain," Miss Stanton said. "We live in a modern world, don't we? We'll simply have to hope that some of those answers come sooner rather than later. And I have hope that you'll find some answers. Indeed, we live in what is arguably the greatest scientific time in human history. Even Sherville Retreat has electric lights now. Surely, great minds can study souls like yours and find answers to what troubles you."

Crandall shook his head in amazement rather than shame. "You are remarkable, Miss Stanton. My behavior doesn't seem to frighten you as it does for, well, nearly everyone who doesn't find it humorous and worthy of mockery."

Miss Stanton stopped walking and turned to face him. She gazed into his eyes and spoke fervently. "I don't find suffering humorous in the slightest degree. It's certainly nothing to fear, either."

As they rounded the last section of the pond, making one

complete circuit, they heard a door slam, hurried footsteps, and a frantic female voice.

"Miss Stanton! What are you doing out here? And with *him* of all people?"

Their steps came up short, and Crandall cursed under his breath. That time, it wasn't involuntary.

Mrs. Buckler appeared and strode angrily to them, stopping only when she reached Miss Stanton's side and grabbed her arm. She yanked Miss Stanton away from him as if he were a bonfire that could burn and consume any woman who so much as came near him. Miss Stanton pulled her arm from the other woman's grip and rolled her shoulder. The woman had hurt Miss Stanton. Anger flared briefly, but Crandall tamped it down. Nothing good would come of calling out Mrs. Buckler for hurting a patient, especially not a patient like him. She was here to "rescue" Miss Stanton, no doubt.

Mrs. Buckler grabbed her arm again, harder this time, making Beverly wince. "You said you were returning to your quarters. I do not tolerate deceit."

Had she truly lied to see him? Miss Stanton threw Crandall a look of helplessness and a tiny shrug that seemed to confirm Mrs. Buckler's statement. The nurse appeared to not notice as she rambled on, growing more heated by the moment.

"I apologize," Miss Stanton said. "I must have gotten turned around after all, and when I saw Mr. Dowling, I—"

"You were *deliberately* deceitful," Mrs. Buckler said with short, clipped syllables and far more loudly than necessary. "And on your first day. This type of behavior is *not* tolerated at Sherville. Punishments will teach you quickly how to behave." She spoke as if disciplining a school child.

The sound of carriage wheels and horses' hooves briefly

took Mrs. Buckler's attention. Crandall seized the brief opportunity. He rushed to Miss Stanton's side and whispered, "Don't swallow Weston's syrup. Behave as if—"

Before he could finish, Mrs. Buckler yanked Miss Stanton's arm—hard—and, glaring at Crandall, said, "You, Mr. Dowling, would do well to ponder your own behavior, or you, too, will face punishment. I will be making a report to Mr. Sherville and Dr. Hornby."

He quickly stepped backward to create distance between himself and Miss Stanton to separate himself from her in the hopes that it might spare her even a bit of the punishment Mrs. Buckler was inventing.

The head nurse practically dragged her patient toward the main building. Miss Stanton briefly glanced over her shoulder at him, and he raised one hand in farewell, hoping she would feel the warmth of the kindness he felt toward her. He wanted her to feel at least some of the goodness she'd helped him feel in just the few minutes they'd spent together.

Please, God, don't let her punish Miss Stanton harshly. I may be weak and susceptible to evil, but she is all goodness.

Chapter Six

BEVERLY'S MIND SPUN AS MRS. Buckler pulled her back to her building. At times she came close to tripping on a stone or the hem of her skirts or simply from not keeping up. The woman had tremendous strength and speed despite her seemingly advanced age.

"I would have thought that meeting Mr. Dowling in the dining room and seeing his shocking behavior would have been ample warning to dissuade you from socializing with him or any like him. Yet here you are, having lied regarding your whereabouts and then you compounded the offense by seeking out the very thing you'd been warned about. This shows a shocking lack of character."

Despite the pain radiating from her arm where the head nurse held fast—she would have bruises tomorrow, she was quite sure—Beverly was determined to keep her outward behavior calm and unruffled—as *non*hysterical as possible.

"I apologize," she said, though it came out in huffs because she was breathing heavily with the exertion of keeping up with Mrs. Buckler.

Several seconds went by, during which she hoped that a

general apology would suffice rather than one listing specific transgressions. While Beverly was sorry she'd been found and might be punished, she was even sorrier at the prospect of Mr. Dowling being punished as well when blame for the incident lay entirely at her own feet. But she was *not* sorry for going to speak to him when she'd requested permission to return to her quarters.

If pressed, she'd apologize for those things. If angels kept records of one's lies, as her grandmother used to say they did, Beverly would much rather *not* tell overt untruths. Expressing regret for something she had precisely zero regrets for would fall under that description. So would begging for forgiveness from someone who viewed her as barely human.

Mrs. Buckler seemed about to begin a lecture that would, no doubt, have included an insistence on a proper, detailed apology, but Gini appeared in the hall, looking worried. "Gladys is having a fit—far worse than usual."

"Is she not responding to a hyoscine injection?"

"She hasn't received one yet. That's the problem," Gini said and seemed to brace herself for a blow, though Beverly suspected any assault would be verbal. "She's out of control and fighting us. We need more nurses to help restrain her enough to administer the hyoscine."

With a groan of annoyance, Mrs. Buckler shoved Beverly forward so the latter practically fell into Gini's arms. "Here. Take Miss Stanton. I'll handle Gladys's hysteria since you seem incapable of doing so."

Beverly's heart jumped—could she escape punishment after all? Gini held Beverly's arm, though gently, and didn't move, as if awaiting instructions.

Mrs. Buckler walked on a few paces before turning around. "Oh, and Miss Stanton . . ." She said Beverly's name with disdain, as if referring to a disease, "Well, she requires some restraint herself today. She left the building without permission, which could have put her at risk. We mustn't chance that again."

Beverly heard an intake of breath and realized it was her own. *Calm. Stay calm.* She had to stay away from any outward expression that could be deemed *hysterical.* Then she'd be given an injection like Gladys of whatever that medication was.

"I believe that spending her first night at the retreat strapped to her bed should suffice, seeing as she's already had nourishment . . . and exercise." Mrs. Buckler said the last with a tone that almost sounded like a joke. "If she proves to be any trouble at all, give her an injection as well." A few more steps down the corridor, and she turned about again. She eyed Beverly up and down. "*And* perhaps a dose of syrup before bed. Yes, I think that will do quite nicely."

Gini didn't move until Mrs. Buckler had gone down the hall and turned the corner. She seemed to be thinking, trying to puzzle out a solution. Beverly looked out the window beside her and spotted Mr. Dowling. He faced her, and after a moment, he raised a hand in the air as if he'd spotted her and was wishing her a good evening. She waved in return, but then Gini continued down the hall.

When would Beverly get to see him again? Would she ever? Hopefully, he wouldn't face consequences from their meeting.

She followed Gini back to her quarters in building B. The nurse kept her hand on Beverly's arm the entire way but gently, more for show. Beverly never pulled away, and Gini seemed to know that she wouldn't try to flee.

They went down the hall and turned at the same corner Mrs. Buckler had. Moments later, a ruckus sounded, spilling into the hall and vibrating the wood floors. As they passed the room with the cacophony, Beverly spied three men holding down a woman who screamed and kicked as Mrs. Buckler inserted a hypodermic needle into her arm and plunged a substance into her body. The woman quickly went limp. At first she looked dead, making Beverly gasp slightly.

"She'll be fine," Gini whispered, ushering them down the hall. "She'll sleep through the night and forget most of what's happened today."

"Oh." Beverly wasn't sure whether Gini's words were more comforting or disturbing.

"Will you be giving me an injection . . . like that?" The very idea of being held down as a needle pierced her skin and she collapsed into unconsciousness . . .

"That won't be necessary, will it?" Gini said, brows raised, clearly giving Beverly the message that her behavior would be the determining factor.

"It won't be necessary," Beverly said with a shake of her head.

When they reached her room, she stepped inside and only now noted that the bed had leather straps with buckles on the sides. Were those the restraints to keep her in bed tonight? If she protested, would she be deemed to be having a fit of hysteria and find herself in even more restricting circumstances?

She'd heard of lunacy patients wearing jackets that bound their arms around themselves like a restricting, horrific embrace, or being bound to a chair. She'd never heard of restraints on a bed.

Over the years, Mr. Pyke had sometimes toyed with her by coming up behind Beverly and wrapping his arms about her so she could not move. He insisted it was all a game, but he was the only one who found it enjoyable or diverting. Sometimes he squeezed, making breathing difficult. Once,

Beverly had clamped onto his arm with her teeth. That was when talk of her hysteria began.

His ridiculous "game" was reason enough to never want to see him again, and she hadn't thought of it since leaving home that morning. But the sight of the leather straps on the bed brought the sensation of being held tight by him, entirely at his mercy, having lost any agency and control over her limbs.

Standing miles and miles from Fairington House, the sensations rushed back like a wave racing toward the shore. She could feel his arms about her—and she couldn't move her arms. She couldn't breathe.

"Beverly? Miss Stanton?" Gini's voice echoed somewhere in the distance and slowly brought her back to the present moment.

Which, truthfully, was only slightly better than the memory of being held fast by Mr. Pyke.

"Must I be . . . restrained . . . in bed?" she said in a whisper.

Gini glanced toward the door, checking for any staff who might be within hearing. She stepped closer to Beverly and whispered, "She'll likely check on you throughout the night, and she'll be looking for the straps."

"Oh." Would she ever be able to breathe free?

"But . . . I can attach them loosely, if that would help. So long as she sees them from the door—and by the dim light of a candle in her hand, most likely—she probably won't enter your room to check them. She rarely turns on the electric lights at night."

Beverly pulled her gaze from the bed and the straps to look at Gini in wonderment. "You'd do that for me? Wouldn't that put your position at risk? You hardly know me."

Gini gave a quick smile, which vanished as quickly as when it flashed on her face. "Well, we must do what we can that's right, mustn't we? Others with authority greater than hers are watching." She looked upward meaningfully, and Beverly knew she'd found a kindred soul.

"I suppose we must," Beverly said. "Thank you."

"However . . ." Gini grimaced slightly as she turned to a locked cabinet in the corner. "I'm afraid I can't ignore *all* orders."

Unsure what to expect, Beverly tensed and waited. Gini returned a moment later with a bottle and a small glass cup, into which she poured some of the syrup.

Oh no. That medicine was probably the one Mr. Dowling had cautioned her about.

"It's a little bitter-tasting, but you can drink down some juice right after to wash away the taste." Gini held out the little cup. "You will drink it, won't you?" Her voice had taken on a slightly different tenor, one of warning.

The memory of Gladys getting an injection and going limp was plenty to encourage Beverly to simply nod with a weak smile and take the cup.

"I knew you'd cooperate," Gini said agreeably. She went back to the cabinet to return the syrup bottle.

Beverly took advantage of the moment with the nurse's back to her—she'd have but seconds. She spotted a flowerpot on the windowsill and quickly reached for it, dumping the syrup and then bringing the cup to her mouth so she could pretend to have swallowed the contents.

She managed it just before Gini turned from the relocked cupboard. The nurse nodded her approval at the sight of the empty cup. "Let's get you ready for bed."

Beverly remained quiet, unsure how she'd be expected to respond to the syrup that she hadn't actually taken. Perhaps its effects took time or weren't as dramatic as the injection's.

Whatever the reason, Gini took the empty cup, then

helped Beverly into her nightclothes and kindly brushed and braided her hair.

Ready to sleep, at least outwardly, there was nothing for it but to stoically climb into the bed and lay down. So, fighting a racing heart and trying not to show evidence of fear, Beverly got into the bed. With her head on the pillow, she stared at the ceiling.

Think of something calm and happy, she thought. Sometimes doing so helped her through the worst of her nervous attacks. Perhaps doing so would help her remain calm tonight—and keep away thoughts of Mr. Pyke.

Gini began to secure the buckles—as loosely as she dared, though far tighter than Beverly had hoped for—and found one thought that did help distract her. It wasn't about her mother or about home.

No, the one thought that brought Beverly a measure of calm was recalling and reliving, again and again, every moment of her brief time with Mr. Dowling. Despite his verbal outbursts and occasional odd movements, she felt in her bones that he wasn't a danger. He was certainly not the bad man others made him out to be.

Thoughts of his goodness—and, admittedly, his handsome face—helped her fall asleep and have relatively pleasant dreams.

Through her mind's eye, Crandall Dowling's kind face and gentle soul kept her company throughout the night, and when she awoke the next morning, she yearned all the more to see him again.

Chapter Seven

CRANDALL PACED THE COMMON DINING hall. He'd eaten as much breakfast as his digestion could endure when his nerves were buzzing so intensely. They wouldn't stop, he knew, until he found out what had happened to Miss Stanton overnight. He couldn't very well march into her room in the women's wing and demand to see her.

He walked the length of the room, passing tables of residents eating their morning repasts—many eyed him with odd expressions that he tried to ignore. He failed, largely because of the variety of responses; some residents looked amused, others annoyed, and some downright fearful.

The latter were the ones who made his anxiety race and his tics erupt. If he could just go to the frightened residents and tell them that he wasn't a danger, perhaps that might help. Perhaps if he could do so without yelling obscenities or hitting himself or the table or jerking his head, eyes, and shoulders. All things he could not control. All things that would likely serve only to further scare any worried residents.

When he reached the end of the hall, he turned about and intended to pace the length going the other direction. That's when Harold, one of the workers, reached out and stopped him, resting a hand on Crandall's shoulder.

His step came up short, and he turned stiffly to the man, waiting for a reprimand or some other unwelcome thing. Precious few positives entered one's life on a given day when you lived in a "retreat" against your will.

"Are you well?" Harold asked with a tone far kinder than Crandall expected—something that eased his heart rate slightly.

He took a deep breath. Because his pent-up nervous energy wasn't, for the moment, being used in pacing, he had to do something else to stay put. With one hand, he gripped the side of his trousers and rubbed the fabric between his fingers. It was a rather subtle action, something he'd learned that people often didn't notice—or at least didn't fear. But it was also an action that he couldn't maintain for terribly long. He'd need to move his legs and arms soon; the trouser trick would work for only brief moments.

"Mr. Dowling?" Harold asked when Crandall didn't respond verbally. He'd been trying to find words—and hoping he could get the proper ones out. Any staffers who heard "shocking" language from him would likely record it in his case file, and that would mean less of a chance he'd ever get out. Best to hold back such explosions if at all possible.

Which, quite frankly, wasn't possible at all, but he still tried.

"Is Miss Stanton coming to the dining hall?" Crandall asked, not replying to Harold's question directly. "Have you heard of her condition this morning?"

What he wanted to ask was whether Miss Stanton had been punished or mistreated. Had she been restrained with a straitjacket or bound to a chair? Did they withhold food? Did they give her any one of the many medicines that Crandall believed were little better than poisons? Had she been removed to the basement like Jasper?

"I don't rightly know," Harold said, "but if I learn anything I can share, I'll be sure to let you know."

"Th—thank you," Crandall said. "Hellish bloody whore. So sorry. Didn't mean that."

Harold smiled in understanding and moved to a table, where he gathered used dishes onto a tray. Crandall wanted to demand to know something about Miss Stanton, but he knew Harold's hands were tied—figuratively, that was—a distinction necessary at an asylum. The man, who ranked low on the staff, had no authority to share patient information even if he had access to it.

Crandall grabbed his hair with both fists and pulled. The pressure on his scalp provided an odd relief to the pressure in his head. He'd go mad if he didn't learn what had happened to Miss Stanton. Or he'd go *more* mad, as the case might be, though he didn't quite believe he was a "lunatic." Troubled, yes. Insane, no.

But there was no convincing Mr. Sherville, Dr. Hornby, Dr. Pushman, or anyone else of that.

Needing to move, to expel the nervous energy, he stepped forward to continue pacing, smoothing his ruffled hair as he did so. He faced the entrance of the dining hall now, the perfect timing as it turned out, because there, framed in the arched doorway at the far end, he caught a glint of copper hair. Miss Stanton!

He hurried to cross the distance, and as he drew closer with each step, he felt a loosening of the tension in his chest, for she looked well. Granted, she appeared slightly pale, which he found made her countenance alabaster-like and even more beautiful. He could see no obvious evidence of bruising or other harm. And she was *here*, about to eat in the main dining hall, so her punishment, whatever it had been, must be over.

She spotted him, and her face slowly broke into a smile. He might have imagined the next part, but he fancied that her cheeks had pinked slightly when she'd noticed him. He smiled back and waved, then hurried to the table her nurse had found for her to sit at—one that fortunately had space across from her for him to sit. Suddenly he felt as if he could eat a proper meal after all. All he'd managed to choke down so far was dry toast and tea. He'd been unable to swallow anything else until he knew how Miss Stanton fared.

Her nurse went to fill a plate for Miss Stanton from a sideboard, which left the two of them sitting across from each other in shy silence. Silly, as they'd carried on a lovely dialogue the day before without any effort.

"I am relieved to see you," he said. His shoulder *tic*-ed several times in a row. He smacked the side of his head with an open palm three times. Oh, how he hated his condition.

"I'm relieved to be here and not much worse for the wear." She smiled, and this time her cheeks most definitely had a faint blush, a fact that sent a thrilling buzz up Crandall's neck and nestled in his chest. "I must have behaved calmly enough to save myself from any particularly harsh treatments."

"I'm so glad," Crandall replied, which might have been the greatest understatement of his life. He knew all too well what kinds of punishments and treatments she could have been forced to endure. He hadn't warned her about electrical treatments, something he hadn't experienced himself but had heard far too much about. "Were you given the syrup?"

She grinned, but before answering, leaned to the side to see where her nurse was, and after judging her to be at a great enough distance, Miss Stanton leaned forward and said, "I was given it, but thanks to you, I knew not to drink it."

"Impressive. How were you able to avoid doing so?"

She shrugged with one shoulder. "When her back was turned, I poured it into a flowerpot on the sill." Her tone indicated that the effort was nothing significant, though he knew quite well that she'd undertaken a feat not far from that of Hercules.

"Weston's syrup is nothing to be trifled with. It's truly horrible stuff—and not just the taste. The ingredients are little better than poison, so the belief that it will help lunatics is a bit insane itself. There are so many other promising treatments being developed all the time."

At that, her head tilted to one side. "How do you know so much about Weston's . . . and about other medicines? Did you read the ingredients or . . . ?"

The nurse returned with Miss Stanton's plate of food, as well as a saucer and teacup, making their conversation come to a halt for a moment. The nurse turned to Crandall. "Have you eaten, or would you like me to fetch you some breakfast?"

He was hungry, but more than that, he was eager to speak with Miss Stanton in relative privacy for as many moments as he could manage. If sending a nurse on an errand for food would provide that, he was happy to play the role of a starving man. "I would very much appreciate a meal like Miss Stanton's. Thank you so much."

"My pleasure," the nurse said and left again.

They both waited for her footfalls on the wood floor to fade, and then they returned to their conversation.

"How *do* you know about the medicine?" Miss Stanton asked again. "You seem to know a good amount regarding what happens here, and I suspect that your knowledge is from more than living here for half a year."

Should he share his medical background with her? Crandall debated for but a moment. As a general rule, he kept silent on his past life, but Miss Stanton, though he hardly knew her, seemed to break all rules, general and otherwise, that he felt bound to. Something about her made him *want* to reveal who he was. Perhaps because she had never recoiled from him, not from the first moment his tics and explosive speech had made themselves known in the private dining room.

"Your suspicion is correct," he said after a moment. "You see..."

He'd never put his story into words, and finding ones to express his past proved harder than he expected. As he searched for words, more tics appeared, and they got worse as the nurse brought his plate to him—he quite nearly knocked it from her hands to the floor. As it was, all that spilled was the tea.

After profuse—though expletive-laden—apologies from Crandall, the nurse—Gini, Miss Stanton called the woman—left to fetch more tea and to get a towel to clean the mess.

"Well done," Miss Stanton said with a chuckle. "We can speak freely again for a few more minutes."

Crandall laughed loudly at that. "I suddenly wish I *had* planned it. That would make me far cleverer than I truly am."

"Now that I doubt," she retorted. "You're clearly intelligent. So tell me. How *do* you know about medicines?"

He licked his lips and took a deep breath. "Before coming here, I was studying at Guy's Hospital in London. I was close to becoming an apothecary and a surgeon, and I had hoped to expand my education to eventually become a physician."

Miss Stanton's reaction was her mouth turning into a slight *O* and her eyes lighting up. "Truly?" she said. "I knew you were intelligent."

"*Were* being the relevant term." He sighed, placing a linen square on his lap and picking up his fork. "It was my mentor, the teacher I was closest to, who first noted my ailment and eventually became the first to sign the certificate to send me here."

"That's . . . terrible." Miss Stanton's shoulders rounded, and her brows drew together as if she were feeling the betrayal that he'd experienced six months ago.

Was *that* hysteria? Feeling deeply and fully to the point of nearly feeling another's pain yourself? If so, it wasn't an ailment of lunacy. If that's what the condition truly meant, then the world could use millions more people with hysteria.

Miss Stanton smoothed marmalade across a piece of toast. "I've always been interested in herbal remedies and the like, and I've wanted to learn about them, but my stepfather—the man who convinced two doctors to sign my own certificate—believes that such things are akin to witchcraft. A stepdaughter who is both a hysterical lunatic *and* a witch?" She clucked her tongue several times. "Oh, that wouldn't do. I avoided mentioning the topic, but I did read what I could, so I know more about plants and herbs than many women . . . not that such knowledge will do me any good here."

What a remarkable woman. Crandall could scarcely believe his fortune to have found someone so intelligent, funny, and kind. He hoped their friendship would continue.

"One day," he said, "when we are both free from this place, perhaps we could set up our own apothecary shop. I'd stay in the back room so as not to scare away customers, of course."

Over the table, their gazes caught, and neither said a word for several seconds.

"Do you . . ." Miss Stanton began. She blinked a few times as if sorting through a multitude of thoughts, then finished. "Do you think we'll ever be free? Is that a real possibility?"

Oh, the weight behind that question. He could not bear to admit that the likelihood of either of them ever walking away from Sherville Retreat as an independent citizen was small. The likelihood that they both would? Minuscule. The odds that they would both get out *and* be able to set up an apothecary shop? *That* was nothing more than a fever dream.

Yet the possibility of freedom, even if it was as distant as a star, existed. Occasionally, a patient recovered and went home. Usually, they were women suffering from melancholia or hysteria. He could imagine several scenarios in which Miss Stanton would be released.

But him? No. If either of them left Sherville in the future, it would be Miss Stanton, not him. He'd never heard of the release of someone like him, a man deemed dangerous, evil, and likely possessed.

Yet the glimmer of hope in her face opened his heart just enough to let in a sliver of her hope, which buoyed his spirits.

A tiny amount, but hope all the same.

"Will we ever be free?" Crandall repeated. He felt his mouth smiling, a sensation he'd felt all too infrequently of late. "God willing, yes, we will."

Miss Stanton reached across the table and placed her hand on his sleeve. The gentle weight of her touch sent a rush of warmth through him as if he'd settled into a hot bath after far too long in the cold.

"Yes," she replied, giving his forearm a slight squeeze of encouragement. "God willing."

Chapter Eight

FROM HER SEAT ON ONE end of a settee in the retreat library, Beverly found her mind wandering from the text in her book. She'd read the same page three times now but could not have said what information it contained if the queen's life depended upon it.

She knew the reason for the distraction—the same thing that had distracted her often across the month she'd been at Sherville Retreat: Mr. Dowling, of course. She'd been reading in relative silence for nearly an hour, a handful of other residents doing the same, scattered about the library.

Mr. Crandall had entered some ten minutes before, as she'd known he would, and sat at the other end of the settee. They weren't near enough to touch, but they were also not far enough apart for another person to sit between them. And, as always, his nearness made the rate of her heartbeat speed up like horses galloping. Usually, he picked up a book to read after reading the latest newspaper, and he'd done the same now, picking up a paper from the table on which they were always provided before taking his seat beside her.

They'd taken to meeting here in the library after supper, ostensibly to read and study topics that interested each of them personally—politics and law for Mr. Dowling, medicine and apothecary science for her. After all, if by some miracle they did manage to leave this place under their own volition, perhaps they really could set up an apothecary shop. And if *that* happened, she'd need to know as much as she could about such matters.

Could women study to become apothecaries? She sincerely had no inkling either way, but she intended to find out. If that path wasn't open to her, any knowledge gained would still be useful as the person helping customers. As Mr. Dowling's . . . business partner. That word was her attempt to avoid the other fanciful dream she had: one day she could be Mrs. Dowling.

She *could* let herself float in flights of fancy, imagining a full life with all her dreams realized, but somehow she could not quite allow herself to do so. Who in this mortal realm ever got everything they wanted? No, better not tempt the fates by dreaming *that* large. Best to keep her fantasies within the realm of *nearly* possible, if one squinted just right and tilted one's head when looking at those hopes.

Though they truly did read together, their time here in the library wasn't entirely due to educational motives. It was also to spend time together in a way that would not raise eyebrows or questions among the staff. Here, they were supervised by a worker who cared for the library and kept an eye on residents spending time there. The man largely kept to himself as *he* read book after book.

Every so often, Mr. Dowling's verbal tics would mean he had to leave the room so as not to disturb the others' reading—and to not distress any ladies, though Beverly was usually the only woman in the room, and *she* was never disturbed by his vocalizations.

Rather, she felt compassion toward Mr. Dowling, who

despised every moment he lost control of his speech. She'd become loyal to him, and when others reacted to him with derision, she felt her anger rise in her chest in response. A wave of anger that she tempered, of course. A woman hoping to leave an asylum could not show such intense emotion.

He hadn't been sent out of the room due to an outburst since Saturday, and today was Thursday. He'd gone nearly a week without trouble. He still blinked rapidly at times. His shoulders and neck often seemed to have minds of their own. But the verbal symptoms of his condition seemed markedly improved. Was he on a new medication or another regimen of some kind? She'd have to ask, for he'd certainly improved.

A resident closed a book with a thump and returned it to the staff member—Mr. Brooks—before leaving the room. The brief interruption was noted by nearly everyone. After Mr. Dowling glanced at the man who'd just left, he looked over at Beverly. His dear brown eyes caught her gaze, and a growing smile warmed her chest—as well as every part of her body.

"What are you reading about today?" he asked, speaking quietly, of course, so as not to disturb the other remaining few residents who were reading.

Beverly glanced at the page before her, the one she'd read and reread without comprehending. Not about to admit to that fact, she noted the text at the top of one page. Ah yes. "This chapter is about the use of various poultices, with recipes for each." She glanced at a recipe on the next page and held it out for him to see. "This one purportedly helps with mumps."

He widened his eyes with mock fascination. "Thrilling."

"I'm sure your reading material is no less thrilling." She tilted her head to see the text on the newspaper. "What world events captivate your attention today? Is an MP embroiled in a new scandal?"

"Nothing so exciting, alas." He smiled a bit wider, then adjusted his position. Had he moved a few inches in her direction? Beverly wasn't entirely sure, but her body seemed certain of it, judging by how gooseflesh broke out on her arms and how she wanted desperately to move toward him and fully close the gap between them. Or even narrow it by a few inches.

For a brief moment, during which she must have surely lost her sanity in earnest, Beverly pretended to read the poultice recipe as she, too, adjusted her position, cleared her throat, and kept "reading." She was now near enough to Mr. Dowling that if they were courting, he could easily have taken her hand in his.

To her amazement, he did precisely that. Her body stilled; she dared not move—hardly dared breathe—for fear that the moment would end. She'd never touched a man's bare hand before. Only gloved ones at balls and other social events. Yet here she sat with her hand practically enveloped in Mr. Dowling's strong, soft hand. He stroked the skin of her hand with his thumb, completely erasing her ability to think at all. All she could do was feel his gentle touch on her hand and relish every second of it.

Thank heavens Sherville didn't abide by all of society's standards—this moment wouldn't have been nearly as pleasant if they'd been wearing gloves.

Oh, how she'd been starved of basic human touch ever since Mother had married Mr. Pyke. He'd frowned upon physical affection of any kind, even a simple embrace between mother and daughter. The effect on Beverly had been a great burden.

Ever since Mr. Pyke's arrival at Fairington House, she'd felt as if she'd been locked inside a bottle—she could see out, and others could see in, but she could not touch or be touched.

Sherville was not much better, though she'd had a few

friendly hugs from Gini and some women residents, but this . . . this was something more. Something stronger. Something different. It wasn't a maternal or friendly touch. This touch communicated something deeper, though Beverly was at a loss of words for precisely what was being said. Perhaps it meant nothing at all besides friendship.

But she could not believe that.

Knowing quite well that further attempts at reading would be futile, she held the spot in her book and shifted her attention to the window to appreciate the view. The early autumn yellows that had graced the gardens when she'd arrived a month ago had darkened into deep oranges and reds. Some leaves had turned brown and fragile. The grass was covered in leaves, though many trees had yet to lose their entire loads. Dark-green firs and pines dotted the landscape, more visible now that fewer leaves blocked them from view through the thin, empty fingers of branches.

It was all so beautiful, and she dearly hoped to have a leisurely walk about the pond with Mr. Dowling again so they could both enjoy the changed landscape together. They'd walk among drying leaves, crunching them with each step and leaving a wake of leaf crumbs behind them. They'd smell the crisp air and smoke in the distance, where people burned leaves and dead branches before winter. They'd breathe out puffs of cold air.

Mr. Dowling suddenly breathed in sharply. He released her hand and held the newspaper with both hands, holding the sides so the paper curled in his grip. His eyes moved along the text, back and forth, again and again.

Beverly didn't know whether he'd found something surprising or shocking. His face went through several emotions, none of which she could fully capture and interpret before he went to another. He seemed to read the same article several times, then shook his head and stood, letting the paper drop to the settee.

"What did you read?" Beverly said, her middle turning queasy. "Whatever is the matter?" She snatched up the discarded paper behind her and stood beside Mr. Dowling, who'd drawn a hand down his face and now held his jaw with one hand, his head shaking back and forth. Beverly looked over the page he'd been reading. None of the article titles seemed to explain his reaction.

He took a few steps forward and then a few more, until he stood before the window she'd been looking out. He still said nothing, just stared out and shook his head again.

Beverly watched, unsure what to do—unsure what he was doing or feeling. "Mr. Dowling, please. What is it?" she asked, desperate to know if he'd found some terrible news indeed.

"Whore. Blazing bootlicker!" He whirled about to face Beverly. Despite the vulgarity he'd just spewed, he was grinning. She'd never seen him so happy.

Mr. Brooks spoke up from the desk he sat at. "Mr. Dowling, you'll need to—"

"Fumbler!" He smacked his forehead with a fist.

"Mr. Dowling . . ." Brooks said with a warning tone.

"I'm going!" Mr. Dowling said. "I'm going! Collywobble on the re-raw. Dratted fumbler!"

Beverly had never heard him use such a . . . colorful . . . amount of swears, let alone in but a few seconds. She felt as if she *should* be horrified but *couldn't* manage it when every syllable was laced with excitement and joy. Not when he looked at her with a spark that she'd never seen in him.

"Come with me, Beverly!" He took her hand and pulled her toward the door. She barely had time to toss the book to Mr. Brooks before practically being pulled out of the library and into the corridor. The entire time Mr. Dowling cursed up a storm, his shoulder twitching and rolling. At the end of the corridor, where no one could sneak up on them, he finally halted his step. He looked around to ensure that no one was around. Then he faced her directly, his breath rapid.

When he didn't speak at first, Beverly could bear ignorance no more. "What *is* it?" she asked again. He looked as if he'd suddenly become ten years younger after having a thousand-pound weight lifted from his back.

"I just read about how an asylum in York is being fined for violating the new Lunacy Act. And . . ." He swallowed. "Goodness, I'm almost afraid to speak the words, as if saying them aloud will make them null and void . . ."

"What?" Beverly reached for him. They stood there, hands clasped and looking into each other's eyes. "What did you read, Crandall?" She used his Christian name because he'd used hers a moment before. Perhaps hearing his name would calm him enough to tell her what he'd read.

She also used his name because she wanted him to know that his use of *her* Christian name was welcome. That she, too, felt a closeness between them. That he could trust her.

"I need to contact a barrister about it, find money to pay him, and convince him to argue the case before a judge, but I believe . . ." He licked his lips, his eyes suddenly glassy.

"Yes?" Beverly said. She squeezed his hands gently to show her encouragement. "You believe that . . . what?"

He squeezed her fingers in return, a solid, strong grip. "I believe that we can get out of here."

Chapter Nine

BEVERLY FELT HER LIPS ROUND into the shape of an *O*. "What? How?"

"We'll need to find the complete text of the law," Crandall said.

For the moment, what he called his "tics" didn't seem to be overwhelming what he was trying to say. They still punctuated his speech here and there but less than before. She'd learned to mostly ignore them; they weren't who he was at heart anyway. While his speech wasn't terribly affected at the moment, the excitement of the moment appeared to be making his physical tics constant. Shoulders rolling, head jerking, eyes blinking, and more.

He'd said that the less he worried about them, the less troublesome they became. And the reverse was true as well; the more he tried to hold back a tic, the more forcefully it insisted on bursting forth. Regardless, none of it bothered Beverly.

"Anyone under certificates in an asylum now has the right to be examined by a judge." He pointed in the direction they'd come, toward the library. "That is, if what I just read is accurate."

Beverly listened closely but understanding didn't dawn on her face. "Is that good or bad? I'm sorry; I don't know matters of law all that well."

"Together, the two previous lunacy acts from 1845 meant that lunatics' cases were to be reviewed by someone from the newly created Lunacy Commission, such as a physician. The goal was to help anyone wrongfully detained. The commission helped to significantly improve asylum conditions."

"That sounds good," Beverly said.

"In theory, yes, and some good changes did come about. But it also made it so anyone deemed a lunatic—like us—had no legal recourse. We were essentially stripped of our rights as human beings." He smiled—and his eyes lit up too. "The new law changes that. Now we can petition our certificates before a judge."

"Ah. I see," Beverly said, nodding. Comprehension and hope slowly spread through her. "Hence the need for a barrister."

"Yes. And there's more. The article also listed various guidelines that asylums are recommended to abide by, and I don't believe that Sherville is following them all. I'll need to read more to discover whether they're laws or merely recommendations, but I believe that if the patients at the retreat knew that things could be different, there would be change."

"What kinds of things do you mean?" Beverly stepped slightly closer, clearly eager to learn more. Yet her nearness made his knees wobble ever so slightly.

"For one thing, there should be a record in a patient's casebook stating whether they agree or disagree with their detainment. Another is locking away a patient's personal belongings so they're safe and able to be returned to them when they're discharged—and being able to *see* that their belongings are sealed away or to at least have their solicitor present when it happens."

"Goodness. Those would be welcome changes."

"There's more," Crandall said. "I'll certainly read as much as I can about the matter, then find someone who can look into whether Mr. Sherville is even qualified to have a license to run an asylum at all. At the very least we can petition to be examined by a judge. In court, one or both of us could be deemed sane enough to be examined by a physician chosen by the court, and after that, we could possibly have our certificates revoked."

Beverly released his hands to wipe away tears. She touched her mouth as if holding back more tears. "I didn't dare hope, but perhaps I can now."

They spent the next week reading as much as they both could about past and present lunacy laws, writing notes on things they'd read and comparing their findings. Neither could entirely keep themselves from sharing some of the information with fellow patients they'd come to know and become friends with.

Which was likely why, after Crandall sent a letter to a barrister in London and they awaited a response, a wave of murmurs slowly but steadily made its way throughout the retreat like water moving in at high tide. It began among the patients, with whispers of how things should be, what they wished for themselves.

Some of the facts got distorted in the retelling, which meant that by the time reports of discontent trickled up to the staff and landed in the ears of Mr. Sherville, Dr. Hornby, and

Mrs. Buckler, a lot had been turned upside down and twisted into inaccurate shapes.

The names of Crandall Dowling and Beverly Stanton, however, remained constant. And that was why on one chilly autumn morning two weeks into waiting for the barrister to reply, a maid came into Beverly's room as she readied herself for breakfast with Gini's help.

"Dr. Sherville has requested to see Miss Stanton right away."

"She'll be right down," Gini said as she pinned Beverly's hair into place.

Beverly turned on the stool to face the maid. "What is this regarding?"

The maid didn't answer Beverly. Instead she looked at Gini and said, "He said it's urgent and to come posthaste."

"I'll deliver her just as soon as her toilette is complete."

The maid left, and Beverly turned to face the mirror again. She'd begun to feel invisible, rarely being talked *to* by the staff unless it was Gini or sometimes Mrs. Buckler, who was usually intent on issuing threats or punishments. Being talked about made Beverly feel little more than a child who must be seen and not heard.

As Gini finished her hair with a few pins, Beverly wondered whether she was only now noticing the strange, belittling behavior, or whether it was new.

Had the staff been discouraged from speaking to her directly? If so, was it because of her and Crandall's discussions?

Or was she becoming paranoid, as Mr. Pyke had always said she was when she expressed concern over how he handled her father's estate?

"There. All done. Let's go," Gini said, patting her shoulders as a signal to stand.

She accompanied Beverly through the halls to the office. With every step, her stomach turned sour. Ever since the day she'd slipped outside to see Crandall by the pond, they'd been particularly careful to abide by rules and to never give anyone a reason to separate them or to restrain or otherwise punish either of them.

So far it had worked, a fact that Beverly was deeply grateful for, because in her time at the retreat—over six weeks now—she'd learned of treatment and punishments that gave her chills and made her skin break out in gooseflesh. Some of the treatments involved water or electricity. Restraints sometimes included chains. They all sounded absolutely barbaric. Aside from her first night, when she'd been buckled onto the bed, she'd avoided any punishments except for an occasional missed meal.

She'd been given other medications, and though she did her best to avoid swallowing them, that wasn't always possible. Especially with medicines that weren't administered orally, like coffee enemas. She didn't mind the mustard baths, which seemed harmless enough.

Was Crandall's letter to the barrister why Mr. Sherville had called for her? Neither she nor Crandall could be held entirely responsible for discontent among the patients. They couldn't be punished for *reading*.

Or could they? Would she find herself with a hypodermic injection and an electrical treatment or taken to the cold basement and chained?

When she reached the office, Gini stayed outside. "I'll wait here for you," she promised.

"Thank you," Beverly said. Gini had become the closest thing she had to a mother or sister here, and knowing that she was only feet away was a comfort. She faced the door and stepped inside, keeping her face impassive with the calm expression she'd mastered since her arrival. She refused to behave in any manner that would give cause for anyone to accuse her of being hysterical and needing new treatments.

Crandall was already inside. He stood when she entered, as did Mr. Sherville, and she took the proffered chair.

Mr. Sherville clasped his meaty hands and placed them on his desk deliberately. "It has come to my attention that you two have been stirring up contentions among residents."

Crandall and Beverly exchanged brief, alarmed glances. He shook his head. "Not at all, sir. Bollocks. *Whore.* Bastard!" He cringed as soon as the last words escaped but tried to sit straight and look, well, sane. Just as Beverly tried to look serene.

"We haven't done anything with the intent to cause trouble," Beverly said. "We spend our days reading in the library, and sometimes we share what we've read. Nothing more." Her stomach jumped a little; they'd done a *bit* more than that. Sending a letter to a barrister in an effort to leave the retreat certainly counted, but they'd done nothing that should be deemed problematic or mutinous.

Sherville looked at her with a flat expression, then slid his eyes over to look at Crandall, clearly unimpressed with their defenses. "If this behavior continues, I will be forced to ensure that you are kept apart at all times, and you will both be banned from the library." He let those words hover in the air and sink in before going on. "I assure you, there are many additional steps we can take to maintain order and an institution free of such ugliness. I do not recommend pressing the point to discover exactly what those things are."

Judging by his cool tone, one would never have thought he was threatening them, but he most certainly was. He sighed and looked at Beverly directly. "I must confess to being rather surprised that you are in this situation. Your family has a reputation of being good, God-fearing people, yet here you are, choosing to spend your time with a fallen creature who is evil at heart." He moved one hand in a dismissive, circular motion toward Crandall.

Beverly wanted to stand and yell that Crandall was *not* evil or possessed or insane. That he had a purer, kinder heart than most men, and he was certainly a better man than anyone at Sherville.

Any attempt at defending Crandall, however, would be seen as the outburst of a histrionic lunatic. She would be seen as under his spell, and they would both be punished. So instead of defending him, she gripped her chair with both hands and clenched her mouth shut. Tears streaked down her face. She shook her head no several times, but that was all she dared do. The tears might have already been too much to avoid an injection and chains.

"I—" Crandall whispered the single word and then cleared his throat. After several seconds of facial tics and a few expletives, he managed, "This is all my doing. Do not punish Miss Stanton. Please. I'll stay away from her on my own accord. Just don't—don't hold her accountable for my actions."

She gaped at Crandall. "No," she said. "Cran—Mr. Dowling—"

But he wouldn't look at her. He stared straight ahead at Dr. Sherville, eyes glassy, swallowing against emotion in his throat. "Please," he repeated.

He was sacrificing his happiness for her well-being.

Dr. Sherville waved at her to stand and leave. "Miss Stanton, you are dismissed. I'll finish here with Mr. Dowling." He looked at the door and called, "Nurse Turley?"

Summoned, Gini appeared in the doorway.

"Take her to her quarters and see that she remains there until further notice—until at least Sunday."

Gini bobbed a curtsy. "Yes, sir."

Beverly wanted to stay, to be with Crandall and defend him and his goodness. But she didn't want *him* to be punished any more than he wanted her to be. He'd put himself on the altar, risking punishment in a bid to prevent the same from falling on her head.

Torn in more directions than she could count, Beverly figured that the best decision for her to make, the one least likely to cause hurt to Crandall, would be to meekly obey and follow Gini out the door.

As they went back to her quarters, tears continued to spill down her cheeks. She couldn't help but worry that she mightn't see Crandall again. Sherville might separate them without further warning, permanently. He could send one of them to another asylum. He could bind one of them in the basement. He could . . . the possibilities were endless and frightening.

In her room, Beverly climbed onto her bed, curled into a ball, and prayed for the man she'd come to love.

She didn't think sleep would be her companion that night, not when so many worries kept her thoughts spinning like a top, but at some point she must have dozed off.

For she was awakened in the dark of night by a shriek outside her room, followed by the distinct smell of smoke.

Chapter Ten

SMOKE POURED INTO CRANDALL'S room, and with it came screams of pain echoing through the wing. Crandall hurriedly worked his arms and torso to remove the long-sleeved jacket he'd been tied and buckled into, an order from Dr. Sherville after their meeting a few hours ago.

He heard cries of "Fire!" coming through the building, and though he could not see flames, the air was quickly darkening with smoke. He coughed and struggled to breathe. He had to get out of the jacket if he were to have any hope of getting out alive.

Thankfully, this wasn't Crandall's first time in the restraint.

Who'd have thought he'd ever be *grateful* for having experienced something so awful before? But here he was, glad he'd had enough experience with the jacket that he might be able to remove it.

He'd never taken the jacket off, but that was precisely what needed to happen now if he hoped to live to see the dawn. He had to shut the cries of pain from his mind so he could think—focus solely on the jacket binding him. He worked on freeing his left arm first.

His first experience in the jacket had been sheer misery. By the time he'd been freed of it, his elbows and hands were swollen, his fingers frozen in position like claws, and the muscles in his arms cramped painfully. Ever since, he'd made sure to breathe in deeply and hold his arms slightly outward while a caretaker secured the buckles. He maintained that stance until they left. Only then did he relax his arms and chest, making the restraint tolerably loose.

That looseness was the only thing that would save him . . . *if* he could get the jacket off at all. His left arm pulled free, which helped get his other arm out as well. With a groan of relief, he pulled the jacket over his head, then tossed it aside.

An instinctive deep breath of relief sent him gagging and sputtering against the thick smoke. He dropped to his knees, where the smoke was thinner, then rubbed his eyes and tried to gain his bearings. Visibility had quickly diminished. Already Crandall could barely see the outlines of his bed. Jasper had been returned to the room, and he appeared to be sleeping through the commotion.

Suddenly he wasn't sure where the door was; he couldn't see so much as the moon through the window. Crandall tried to find the window anyway, then remembered that even if it didn't have bars, it was nailed shut. A jump from the third floor would likely be fatal anyway.

But he had to get out and fast. He hurried in the direction he thought Jasper's bed had to be, reaching with his arms. His fingers met metal—part of Jasper's bed frame. He followed it upward until he reached one of the knobs at the head of Jasper's bed.

"Jasper, wake up!" he said, shaking his roommate.

A moment later, he was helping a groggy, drugged Jasper into the corridor. Smoke billowed toward them from the right like an approaching steam engine. Cries of fear and pain reached him, and staff members seemed to be either running here and there in a panic or standing in place, frozen in terror.

Crandall had no such luxury. He had to hurry. He turned left, away from the worst of the smoke, half running, half pulling Jasper along toward the staircase. Praying with all he had in his soul that the stairs were still sound. They were.

The second floor was chaotic, worse than the third, but he had no time to stop to ponder, observe, or help. Downward he went, practically carrying Jasper now, to the ground floor and finally to the outside air, where Jasper collapsed in a coughing heap on the gravel.

"Can—can you breathe? Are you burnt?" Crandall asked, panting.

"I'm—I'm fine," Jasper managed.

Crandall waved over Wellings, who'd carried another patient out. "Make sure Jasper is cared for," he said, then ran back into the building.

He took the stairs two at a time to the second-floor landing and yelled as loudly as he could through the main entrance of the wing. "Wake up! Fire! Fire! Get out! Now!"

Then he raced to the next floor and the next. On the fourth and final floor, he plunged into the fray. If patients were still there, they needed to get out now. Those lower might be able to save themselves.

He hurried down the hall, yelling and waking people, hardly noting that he'd moved from a men's section to a women's one. He certainly paid no mind to what anyone was wearing at that hour. Nightdresses were plenty modest, but even if they weren't, lives were at risk. All that mattered was getting as many people as possible away from danger as quickly as possible.

The smoke and heat grew worse by the minute. Breathing grew laborious, and without enough fresh air, Crandall lost strength. Though his lungs felt as if they were burning, he didn't stop.

He alerted everyone he could to get out and leave the building, his efforts punctuated by helping the physically old or infirm to get out. He carried an older man—wasted away to nearly the size of a twelve-year-old boy—outside, then another man, followed by four more trips bringing out women, one with gray hair, the others were young, likely younger than he.

Back and forth he went, depositing residents outside and running back in. Each flight of stairs felt longer than the last time he'd climbed them. His heart pounded, and his lungs protested.

After each trip, he considered stopping. He was only one man who was growing weaker by the moment. He couldn't possibly rescue everyone. As he deposited another patient— an elderly man—beneath a tree, a massive pop sounded. Everyone in the area was startled and stared at a huge flame bursting from a window. Drapery had ignited, spreading the fire to the next room and beyond. The gathering throng gasped, but Crandall couldn't allow himself to react; he had to get back inside while he still could.

Crandall headed back in, but his legs felt about as strong as bread pudding. He didn't know whether they'd hold but he had to try. He'd never be able to live with himself if he could have prevented one more person from dying in the fire by going in one more time.

Like Beverly. He hadn't found her, though he'd searched her floor. Smoke muddled his thoughts to the point that in the darkness, through his exhaustion, he couldn't remember which floors he'd checked.

Had she gotten out? Was she trapped? If he didn't find her but he'd done his all to get as many others out as he could, perhaps God would help someone else find her and do the same for her. That became his only hope, his only prayer, throughout the last twenty minutes as he plunged into the fray again and again.

He brought out a woman of perhaps forty and laid her on the grass. He made sure she was still breathing, then gave a cursory check for burns. He waved down a nurse. "She's struggling to breathe. Get a cloth soaked in water for her to breathe through. That might ease the pain." The nurse nodded and hurried toward the pond, the nearest water source that wasn't engulfed in flames.

Crandall turned to head back to the building—but a corner of the roof caved in then with a giant crash. Red embers glowed as they showered like fiery rain.

A middle-aged woman with a quilt wrapped about her pointed to her left. "Building C is on fire!"

"So are A and B," a man said.

"I think they all are." The last from someone who sounded weak.

Crandall shook his head and moved to go back inside, but he took only three steps before his legs stopped protesting and simply gave out beneath him. He collapsed in a heap to the ground. Small stones pressed into his scratched face, yet he was unable to move. He'd spent every last drop of strength he'd had.

All he could see as he lay on the ground was the fire; angry tongues of orange and gold moved along the buildings with shocking speed, consuming window frames like hellish specters dancing in a haunted celebration. Crandall still couldn't move. With his cheek pressed into the ground, he panted, unable to get up, no matter how incessantly his mind yelled at him.

Move, it cried. *Go back inside. Save someone else so Beverly will be saved.*

How many more were still trapped in the black smoke, blockaded by heat, getting smothered by the conflagration?

The night sky glowed with foreboding. Crackling and popping echoed constantly, accompanying the constant roar of burning wood. Until that moment, Crandall had no idea how loud fire could be.

The largest crash so far hit him like a wave, marking the collapse of another roof.

Where is Beverly?

Every time he'd gone inside, he'd hoped to find her and bring her to safety. Every time he brought someone outside to the cool night air, he'd looked about in hopes of finding her face among the growing crowd of residents and staff who'd safely gotten out.

Just then, a voice cut through the darkness. "Fetch any buckets you can from the gardening shed, any basins from the laundry, and fill them at the pond. Hurry!"

Was that . . . Did he dare hope it was *Beverly's* voice?

Someone took hold of Crandall by the shoulder and hip and rolled him onto his back. The star-filled night sky stared down at Crandall, who could no longer see the fire directly, though columns of smoke rose into the sky and orange still flickered in the periphery of his vision.

"Found him!" the man beside him called.

A quick gasp was followed by hurried steps. And then, into Crandall's field of vision, an angel appeared and dropped to her knees beside him. Even in the darkness, even with soot smeared across her cheeks and nose, even with her nighttime braid singed and falling apart, he knew that face.

"Praise God you're alive," Beverly said. She leaned down, pressed her cheek to his, and wept.

Chapter Eleven

BEVERLY CLUNG TO CRANDALL, WETTING his face and hair with her tears. She'd been rushing about, helping as many people as she could. No one else had taken charge, not Mr. Wellings, not Gini, not any of the nurses. They all seemed shocked into immobility until she began giving orders.

All the while, she'd worried about Crandall. When she'd asked Mr. Wellings if he'd seen him, the man had shaken his head. "He was put in restraints this evening. He's likely unable to get out on his own."

He hadn't known how he'd been restrained, which made Beverly's imagination roam in horrifying directions. She'd half hoped that Crandall had been taken to the dank basement in chains simply because he might have escaped the worst of the smoke there.

But she'd found him. He was here on the ground beside her, free from whatever he'd been tied to or with, covered in soot, barely conscious.

"I was so worried," she said, clinging to him, not wanting to let him go for fear that he might vanish like ash in the wind.

"I'll—I'll be fine," Crandall said. He tried to embrace her

in return, but he was too weak to do more than lift an arm and let it fall on her back. He began a coughing fit, making her sit up, worried. "Can you breathe? Are you burned? Otherwise injured?"

He coughed some more, unable to reply in words. His breathing sounded terrible. She prayed the smoke and heat hadn't done permanent damage to his insides. "My . . . leg . . ." he managed.

Sure enough, his right trouser leg had a large tear. An angry wound bled beneath. She tore the cloth open further to get a better look—was it a deep cut, a burn, both? Had he broken a bone? She didn't know what to expect, and she didn't care what she would see; she needed to know how he was injured.

His calf had a gash along one side, and the other had skin that was an angry red, likely burned. She spotted one of the workers she'd sent to fetch water and called to him.

"Staunch the bleeding," she ordered. "And cool the burns with water."

He dropped to his knees and obeyed. "I'll get you taken care of, Mr. Dowling. Don't you worry."

Several voices called for Beverly. She'd largely been the organizing force of the care efforts once people had escaped the fire, and no one else had stepped in. She had no idea where Sherville, Hornby, or Mrs. Buckler were, but *someone* had to get things done, so she'd stepped in.

"Miss Stanton, what do I do?" another voice called from several yards away.

She looked in that direction, then back at Crandall. "I—"

"Go," Crandall said.

She looked back at him, eyes welling with tears. He reached up and cradled her face in one hand. "They need you, Beverly. I'll wait for you right here—and I'll be all right."

Another coughing fit belied his words, but after a moment, she nodded. He was right; she needed to go help others. How a patient who'd merely spent time reading about medicine in the retreat's library knew more—or could remember more in a crisis—than those who'd had formal training, she'd never know, but that seemed to be the case.

She'd already ordered every aloe vera plant from the greenhouse to be fetched so the soothing gel inside could be used on burns. A miniature brigade of sorts brought cool water from the pond. She worried that the water might be foul and lead to inflammation but in the end figured that keeping the injured alive to see morning was her priority.

Perhaps she'd been drawn to spend as much time as she had learning and reading for a purpose. Perhaps for such a time as this.

She leaned down and pressed a kiss to Crandall's forehead. "You had *better* be here when I get back," she said with a put-on sternness.

"I won't go anywhere," Crandall promised in a whisper. "Whatever you say. Forever."

I love you, Crandall Dowling, she thought—and nearly said, but her courage failed her. If she said the words aloud, it might be tempting fate. She couldn't bear the thought of losing him.

She kissed his forehead again, then got to her feet and rushed to those calling for help. If she didn't leave while she had the wherewithal to do so, she'd end up staying with Crandall, unable to leave his side. But she was needed elsewhere.

She was beckoned to an older man lying on the ground in a long nightshirt. "Where are you hurt?" she asked, kneeling beside him. At this rate, her night robe, which she'd tied over her nightdress, would be stained and torn to bits, but that mattered little.

"He brought out at least a dozen," he said.

"Who did?" Beverly asked.

He pointed toward Crandall a few yards away. "He did. The man you kissed a moment ago."

She flushed slightly. She'd forgotten that they weren't alone. Potentially dozens of witnesses had seen her kiss Crandall's forehead—twice.

Then she repeated the man's words in her mind. "Mr. Dowling saved people?" She'd been so grateful to find him outside, alive, that she hadn't wondered how he'd gotten there or what he'd done before collapsing.

The man nodded, then shivered. He was aged perhaps sixty years, with a wild beard and wilder eyes. She had no way of knowing what his lunacy certificates said. A few months prior, if she'd seen him on the streets of a city, she might have been afraid of him.

Perhaps he had a dangerous type of lunacy she should be wary of. She didn't recall seeing him at the retreat in the weeks she'd been there, so perhaps he was kept in solitude for the safety of others. She didn't care, and she didn't fear him. His frantic eyes might well be a result of having escaped a fire.

Reacting with fear to a threat to one's life was entirely within the realm of sanity.

"He carried me out. Others too," the man said. "Went back until he couldn't anymore. If not for him, most of my floor would have died in there."

Beverly's throat tightened. Crandall was a *good* man no matter what the certificates and doctors claimed. She'd known he had a good heart from the moment they'd met. But even she would not have predicted the level of courage and determination the fire had shown in him. All the more reason to love and admire the man.

For hours she worked, bustling from one person to

another, giving instructions, organizing efforts, and a few times holding someone's hand as they took their last breaths.

She had no idea how long she'd been out there, how long ago the fire had ignited and begun this interminable night. But suddenly she was aware of the darkness of night being replaced by the slow incoming crawl of dawn's arrival.

Soon the weighty black of night faded into gray. Pale yellows on the horizon made the ruins of Sherville Retreat appear skeletal. Soot streaked formerly bright-yellow walls as if the clouds had wept tar. Fingers of smoke still curled skyward, looking innocent and weak compared to the flames that had preceded them.

Beverly stood still, staring at the remains in a state of hazy exhaustion. This was the first time since waking to the smell of smoke that she'd stood still for more than a brief moment. The first time she'd been able to think beyond what someone needed of her.

She blinked, her eyes stinging from smoke, then turned to look around her. More workers had found ways to help and were caring for patients and the wounded. No one was calling for her.

But where was Crandall?

Everything looked entirely different in the morning light; she wasn't entirely sure where she'd left him lying the night before. She walked through rows of wounded, searching for him.

Out of the corner of her eye, she spotted several jerking movements that were familiar in their uniqueness to Crandall's condition; shoulder and head tics were unmistakable, even as he lay on the ground. She no longer had the strength to run, but she walked toward him as fast as she could, ready to collapse into his arms and weep.

A stagecoach rumbled along the drive, making her stop

and stare. Who'd come at this hour, and for what purpose? The horses stopped, and a man alighted from the stage. He spotted Beverly and strode in her direction.

"Are you Mrs. Buckler?" he asked.

Unease knotted her middle. Who was this man, and why was he asking? Her eyes flitted toward Crandall. If this man was going to take her away or punish her for taking charge when she wasn't a nurse, she needed to ensure that Crandall wasn't put in danger.

"No." She raised her chin to show confidence rather than the fear threatening to make her voice tremble, and that *did* have her knees knocking beneath her robe. "I haven't seen her since the fire broke out. I don't know where she is."

"Are you a nurse? A maid? How are you in the employ of Sherville Retreat?"

"I'm not." She then tried to turn away, but he spoke again.

"You aren't, by chance, Miss Beverly Stanton, under certificates as suffering hysteria?"

Slowly she turned to face him again, a sliver of fear appearing in her middle, but she wouldn't let him see that. With her shoulders squared, she said, "Who is asking, and for what purpose?"

Proper etiquette would simply have to make way for realities. A day ago, she'd believed that under no other circumstances would she let herself be seen in a night robe, yet here she was.

"Mr. Aiden Leaton, barrister, at your service," he said with a bow.

Beverly felt as if a rush of life jolted her heart into beating again. "You're . . . Are you here because of Mr. Dowling's—" She ran out of breath, and Mr. Leaton finished for her.

"His letter. Yes," he said. "It intrigued me, and I came to

learn more about him, your condition, and the retreat in general." He gestured toward the grounds—the smoldering remains, the people lying about in pain, servants now bringing food out that somehow had escaped the fire.

"You appeared to be in charge, but you're a patient . . ."

Beverly swallowed, unsure where he was going.

"I think this is plenty of evidence that you, Miss Stanton, are not a victim of hysteria. Either the dramatic events from last night cured you, or as I suspect is more likely, you never were hysterical to begin with."

Someone believed her. Someone believed *in* her.

"I believe that getting you before a judge to be examined will be relatively easy, and when you are there, we'll merely relate how you administered care with a level head during an enormous crisis. Determining that you should not have certificates of lunacy against you will be one of the simplest cases I've ever taken on."

So many emotions welled up in Beverly: exhaustion, hope, grief, sadness, relief, and more. It all moved from her toes, up her legs, filling her chest, and then she found the emotion pouring down her cheeks in tears.

"I apologize," she said, swiping at her cheeks. "I shouldn't be crying." He might think her hysterical after all—a woman who seemed serene one moment but then turned into a blubbering fool in a blink.

"If you *didn't* feel something after all you've been through, *that* would make me think you weren't entirely right in the head. Could you show me to Mr. Dowling? I . . . I hope he's well?"

"He is, yes. Follow me." Smiling through her tears, she happily showed the way, now that she knew the visitor wasn't a threat to the man she loved.

Crandall's tics had increased, surely due to fatigue and

worry. He practically writhed. She'd never seen his tics so bad. And that's when a sad but likely inevitability dawned on her.

Mr. Leaton might be able to get me free of this place, but what if Crandall is bound here for life?

Chapter Twelve

THE NEXT SEVERAL DAYS PASSED in a whirl, like a storm swirling about Beverly. Due to the condition of the buildings, many patients with mild cases were immediately released to family members. A good number more were sent to other asylums in the county. And about a third of Sherville Retreat's former population remained, now housed in the two buildings of the original five that had sustained minimal damage.

The place bustled with people coming and going—stagecoaches bringing physicians, relatives, members of the county government, engineers to look over the damage and determine what could and could not be safely rebuilt, and representatives of the new iteration of the Lunacy Commission.

Beverly had been given a private room set apart from the rest of the women patients. It was small, nearly a closet, and wasn't in the staff quarters, a sort of middle place between two worlds. She worked as much as any of those in the retreat's employ but was still held under certificates.

At least her days were filled with purpose. She ministered to patients still recovering from the fire, both in body and mind, as the ordeal had understandably exacerbated several patients' mental conditions. The effects manifested in withdrawn silence for some patients and violence for others. The latter cases were sometimes restrained and given injections—things that Beverly could not prevent. She also could not bear to witness them.

Whenever she kept herself busy caring for other residents, she could largely forget, if but for an hour here or there, that she wasn't a free woman. No matter how kind Gini, Mr. Wellings, or any other staff member was to her, they were free and she was not. Moments of forgetting were a welcome respite.

However, she never for a moment forgot that she hadn't seen Crandall since the night of the fire, and she never stopped thinking about him. Those thoughts tended to fall into two areas: First, she missed him terribly and wished to have another fine afternoon walking around the pond and admiring the greenhouse or sitting beside him as they read for hours in the library. Second, she worried if he had succumbed to his injuries.

She'd begun to learn how insidiously smoke could damage a person's body days afterward, often as bad or worse than the fire itself. Was Crandall alive and well? All she knew was that he'd been taken to a hospital in the county. Would he return to what remained of Sherville, or would he be sent to another asylum? How would she ever find him?

She wasn't a relation, which was likely a primary reason they told her nothing. Added to that, no matter how much respect the staff gave her, no matter how often she worked beside them and gave them suggestions and help, she remained a patient.

The third morning dawned with no one on staff able—or perhaps willing, she didn't know which—to tell her about

Crandall. All they'd say was that the matter was being managed by his barrister. Yet Beverly hadn't seen Mr. Leaton since that first morning when he'd given her hope.

She determined to find Mrs. Buckler and demand answers. Sherville and Hornby hadn't been seen since the night of the fire, and reports said that no one was certain if they'd been on the premises that night at all, or if they had been, whether they'd died that night and hadn't been found yet.

Wherever they were, Mrs. Buckler had taken the reins of leadership, at least temporarily.

After breakfast, Beverly left the makeshift dining hall that was set up in a long corridor of building D and headed for Mrs. Buckler's office, also a makeshift setup in the same building.

When she arrived, someone else stepped out of the office into the hall—none other than the barrister.

"Mr. Leaton," she said with almost as much joy as she would have if Father Christmas himself had appeared. "I was beginning to wonder if I'd ever see you again." She closed the remaining distance to him. "How is Mr. Dowling? No one will tell me anything."

"He is well," Mr. Leaton said. "He is at Withersby Hospital. Assuming Sherville will have a bed for him, he should be released to return in a few days."

Beverly sighed and whispered a prayer of gratitude.

"That is not why I am here," Mr. Leaton went on.

Her head came up at that, and she braced herself for whatever news he was about to tell her. Of late, life had been full of unwelcome surprises, and she'd come to anticipate more of them rather than to expect life to work out smoothly as she used to.

Life was nothing if not unexpected and full of painful twists and turns.

"I'm here for you," Mr. Leaton said. "I've secured a time for you to appear before a judge this very afternoon. Your parents have been notified and will be there so that if you are released from your certificates—something that, in light of recent events, is quite certain to happen—you can depart the courtroom and go home straightaway."

"That's—that's... wonderful." And it was. Truly. Yet the wonder and joy were tempered by an ache. Leaving Sherville today, possibly leaving it for good, would also mean missing Crandall when he returned. She wouldn't be able to say goodbye.

Could she truly leave him behind and create a life for herself, leaving him behind? How could she go forward, knowing that he was stuck here? He would forevermore be treated as demon-possessed and evil, detained for life, unable to leave because his body sometimes insisted on doing things against the wishes of his heart.

"Miss Stanton?" Mr. Leaton asked, looking concerned. "You *do* want to contest your detainment? That wish hasn't changed?"

"Correct. But..." She glanced over her shoulder as if she could see the building where Crandall had once lived.

Mr. Leaton nodded, seeming to understand. "Remember, I am his barrister too. I won't be finished working after only you are free." He gazed into Beverly's eyes with intent and a smile so warm that it reignited the spark of hope he'd brought with him that first day. "Will you come with me to see the judge?"

"Very well," she said, nodding. "Let's go."

Chapter Thirteen

CRANDALL WASN'T ENTIRELY SURE HOW he felt as the stagecoach pulled through the gates of Sherville Retreat. The books he'd read over the last several weeks—reading at dear Beverly's side—had included one on theories of the mind and how one's emotions might be trained to effect change in lunatics. One step was to analyze one's feelings, and while that sounded simple enough in theory, arriving at Sherville again proved that it most certainly was not.

He was grateful to be alive. Grateful to be out of Withersby Hospital and grateful he'd mostly recovered from breathing so much smoke. The gash on his leg was healing. All well and good. He likely appeared to have a happy existence.

But he was far from happy.

For he was returning to a place that felt like a prison, especially without Beverly there to make life worthwhile. Leaton had informed him yesterday that Beverly's appeal for an end to her detention had succeeded. She'd gone immediately home with her parents.

He was happy for her, truly. He wanted her to be at liberty to seek out and experience the fullest life. He simply wished that her full life might include him in some capacity.

The horses' hooves clopped and gradually slowed. Soon he'd alighted from the coach and was walking to building D, which now served as the main building.

His soul felt like the ruinous buildings he now passed: beaten down and burned, a shadow of a former self. He'd never imagined that he'd spend his life in an asylum... unless it was as a physician, not as a lunatic.

Oh, how he hated that word.

To his surprise, Mrs. Buckler awaited him at the door. Even more surprising, she greeted him with a smile.

"What a pleasure to see you, Mr. Dowling," she said. "I am glad to see that you are recovered. I trust your journey was pleasant?"

Confusion bubbled in his head—yet another emotion to add to the cacophony. Why was she acting so friendly? Was Mrs. Buckler going to trick him somehow? He hadn't believed her stern face capable of softening so much, let alone of smiling wide enough to show teeth.

"As pleasant as can be expected," he said. His shoulder and head took on a life of their own, jerking and moving. His eyes blinked again and again. At least he hadn't said anything untoward—yet.

Once more he wished that Beverly were with him. Her presence had sometimes eased his nerves and calmed his tics. When his illness wouldn't be soothed by her touch or voice, having her near was still a great comfort, for she did not think less of him for any of his tics, nor did she think of his condition as who he was. She was the one person who saw the real Crandall Dowling.

He loved her all the more for that.

Soon he found himself in a makeshift office with Mrs. Buckler, who'd escaped the fire by hiding in the trees of the gardens. She was pouring tea for him as if he were a gentleman rather than a possessed lunatic. What did this mean?

After serving them both, Mrs. Buckler took a sip of her tea. He couldn't follow suit. He held the cup and saucer in both hands but stared at Mrs. Buckler, waiting to learn if the sword of Damocles that seemed to be hanging above him was about to fall.

Mrs. Buckler set her cup on the saucer, then clasped her hands and looked right at Crandall. His nerves intensified, and he could feel tics forcing their way to the surface. He quickly set his tea on the table before it would spill all over the floor. No sooner had he released his hold on the saucer than his physical tics poured out one after the other for ten solid seconds. Even then they didn't stop, just slowed to a few times per minute.

Instead of Mrs. Buckler looking disturbed or even uncomfortable, she smiled again and said, "Your conscientiousness is much appreciated, Mr. Dowling."

Had he hit his head? Was he dreaming? "Pardon? I don't understand."

"I've been very wrong about you, Mr. Dowling. I must apologize for that."

A breeze could have knocked him off his seat. "I—how—"

"Matters of the mind are still a great unknown area of medicine, as you surely know considering your education."

"Yes . . ." he said, still wary.

"Many illnesses appear to be the kinds of things we read about in the Gospels, so a natural conclusion for a Christian such as myself is that someone behaving in a particularly strange manner may be possessed by devils, as we read about with Jesus."

He knew all of the justifications for how he'd been treated. Mrs. Buckler had to know he was fully aware. What was the purpose of this interview?

"I am ashamed to say that when you first arrived at Sherville Retreat, I truly did believe that you were weak in morals and in spirit, even evil at heart. However . . ."

His gaze had gradually lowered to his hands holding his knees, but now he lifted his face to the head nurse's and waited for her to finish.

She tilted her head to one side. "'By their fruits ye shall know them.' The night of the fire, you, Mr. Dowling, proved that you may well be one of the greatest of men. You put your life at risk saving the lives of others—many of whom you weren't personally acquainted with, and none of whom you share a familial bond with."

Could she mean what she said? That she no longer believed him to be weak or evil? Perhaps he'd be treated a bit less like a savage, given more privileges and fewer restrictions on his life at the retreat.

"Th-thank you," he said, his throat tightening with emotion.

"Furthermore, I proved myself to be a coward, hiding from the fire." She flushed with shame. "Therefore," she went on, her tone becoming more businesslike, "I have discussed your certification with Dr. Hornby, and with the aid of one Mr. Leaton, we have appealed your detention with a judge. I received his decision this morning."

Crandall waited for the verdict that would decide his future as a convict might wait for a sentence.

"The judge decided that if someone steps forward to sponsor you—ensure that you are fed and housed and properly cared for and that you do not become a burden or danger to anyone, including yourself—then you may be released altogether."

The heights at which Crandall's soul soared at her first words thumped to the ground like a lead ball falling from the sky. The judge's decision was the best someone like him could hope for—someone uncured and incurable.

He *could* be allowed to leave *if* he could find a sponsor to take on all responsibility for him. His father wouldn't do such a thing, and he had no other family. Dr. Pushman had sent him here; he'd be unwilling to sponsor Crandall. The judge's decision, while a victory of sorts, lay out of reach, in the ephemeral world of *if.*

"I have some business to attend to, so I shall leave you here. Mr. Leaton should join you this evening to discuss details."

Crandall stood when she did, gave a half bow. He left the room and the building, heading outside. Needing fresh air and exercise—anything to bring him some modicum of peace and relief—he didn't stop until he reached the gardens and the pond.

When he drew near, he spotted a figure at the bend with the small grove of trees. He stopped and hesitated, unsure whether to return to his room after all. He was loath to interrupt another's escape into nature, but he was just as reluctant to return to his quarters.

"I thought you'd be glad to see me," the figure called. A woman.

Beverly.

Crandall stared toward the trees for just a moment, until he spotted her clearly, and then he ran to her, afraid he was seeing things. For surely Beverly hadn't returned to Sherville.

Yet there she stood, wearing a smart purple silk jacket over a violet skirt, the ensemble topped with a jaunty hat. His pace slowed, and when he reached her, his breath came fast.

Her eyes were bright, her cheeks pink. She looked *happy.* And she'd never looked so beautiful.

"What—what are you doing here?" he asked, panting from the sudden exercise.

"I'm taking a turn about the gardens, of course," Beverly said with a wry smile. "Would you rather I leave you alone?"

"No, of course not." Had he gone mad? He couldn't grasp that she was really here until he took her into his arms and held her close. "Weren't you . . . released?" he murmured into her hair.

"I was." Her lips brushed against his cheek as she pulled back and smiled at him. She stood before him, oh so near, and looked up at him. "Mr. Leaton introduced me to a solicitor who helped me regain my inheritance. My stepfather no longer controls my mother, my home, or my money. All I wanted was independence, but apparently, I'm a lady of means now."

Crandall wasn't sure he'd heard everything correctly, for his heart was pounding hard, and it took every ounce of strength to not kiss her then and there.

"A lady of means, you say?" he said.

"Yes." She moved even closer so their faces nearly touched. He breathed in the scent of lavender soap on her skin. "I've come to sponsor you, if you'll let me. After all, if I'm to have a successful apothecary venture, I'll need a business partner who knows the trade."

Her tone said so much more than *business partner*, a fact that sent warmth throughout Crandall's chest. He reached for her gloved hand.

She covered his hand with her other one, and he did the same with his other one so their hands were layered together. She drew their hands toward her chest, making them stand nose to nose. He leaned in and brushed his lips against her hairline.

"Might I . . ." he said, voice trailing off.

"Yes?" She kissed the spot where his ear met his jaw and then rested her cheek against his. "Might you . . . what?"

"Might I propose an additional partnership? A different kind?"

She gazed into his eyes, and a light seemed to glow there. "Perhaps one of a romantic nature?"

"Yes." Oh, he hardly dared believe she might feel the same. "But we can discuss it more fully in time. There is no need to rush—"

To his surprise, Beverly stopped his words with a kiss on his lips. He kissed her back, hardly believing that this moment was real rather than a dream. When the kiss ended, she looked up at him and said, "Whatever you say, yes. Forever," she said, an echo of his words the night of the fire.

He kissed her soundly once more. "Forever."

Acknowledgments

Thanks to Katariina Raikkonen for publicly sharing her own Tourette's journey, the difficult times as well as the triumphs. Some of Crandall's experience is drawn from hers.

A special thanks also to Meg of *The Asylum Archives* YouTube channel, whose videos and notes about Victorian asylums informed this story in many ways and helped me write it with details and resources I would not have otherwise had.

I also have deep gratitude for the Airbnb with the Finnish sauna that Sarah M. Eden searched doggedly for me so I could be extra productive on our annual retreat. You're the best.

Thanks always go to my long-suffering critique partner, Julie Coulter Bellon, to my accountability partner Luisa Perkins, and to the Naked Mole Rat ladies—Luisa and Sarah—who keep me both functioning *and* productive.

Annette Lyon is a *USA Today* bestseller, Whitney Award winner, and eight-time recipient of Utah's Best of State Medal for fiction, four times each for novel-length and short fiction. She's one of three co-founders—and the original editor—for *The Timeless Romance Anthology* series and its spin-off series, and one of the authors of *The Newport Ladies Book Club* series. Though she's well-known for her editing and word-nerdery skills and appreciated for her cookbook, *Chocolate Never Faileth*, her heart has always belonged to writing fiction. She has four adult children, one grandchild, and a flame-tipped Siamese cat with an attitude. She's represented by Jill Marsal of the Marsal Lyon Literary Agency. Her first suspense novel will be released in the spring of 2023 through Scarlet Books.

Find Annette online:
Website: https://annettelyon.wordpress.com/
Blog: http://blog.AnnetteLyon.com
Twitter: @AnnetteLyon
Facebook: http://Facebook.com/AnnetteLyon
Instagram: https://www.instagram.com/annette.lyon/
Pinterest: http://Pinterest.com/AnnetteLyon
Newsletter: http://bit.ly/1n3I87y

A Railway Through the Roses

By Lisa H. Catmull

To David,
my steady rock who embraces change,
never gets flustered,
and always makes time for me

Chapter One

ADRIAN EVERARD WAS THE LAST man I wanted to see first thing in the morning while carrying a vase of flowers, but I forced my best smile. My baroness smile. I held out a hand and hid my annoyance. "Mr. Everard. To what do I owe this unexpected pleasure?"

"Lady Baxter." He clasped my hand and gave me his most dangerous, adorably sheepish smile. The one that had *almost* convinced me to agree to his preposterous idea. "I apologize for the earliness of my visit. I neglected one detail from our conversation yesterday."

He hadn't let go of my hand yet, and my fingers fit perfectly in his. It was hard to remember that we stood in my entrance hall instead of a ballroom, as we had so many times before.

I shifted the vase to my other arm and tried to pull my hand out of his grip. He startled and dropped my fingers abruptly. I motioned awkwardly toward my library. "Shall we?"

"After you." Adrian rubbed the back of his neck. "The guests arrive any moment for my father's blasted house party."

I stopped abruptly and arched an eyebrow coolly.

Adrian held up his hands. "Don't look at me like that. You're invited to all the events."

He had always been a bit oblivious, so I wondered if it was even worth an effort. "It's not that."

"What?" Adrian shifted from one foot to another. "I called you Lady Baxter instead of Annie. I'm on my best behavior today. I knew you'd be awake, and the early hour really can't be helped."

I sighed and set the vase on the closest sideboard. "Adrian, why is your father hosting this *blasted* house party?"

He grinned. "It's not really swearing if I'm around you."

He was hopeless. "And the party?"

Adrian tugged at his waistcoat. "Father rounded up some heiresses for me to marry."

My temper rose at his casual tone, but I took a deep breath and resumed my walk down the hall. "And will you tell the charming and intelligent heiresses about your *deuced* bad luck or the *blasted* contraptions that pass as train carriages?"

He cleared his throat behind me. "You've never complained before. We talk man-to-man about all our business."

I stopped again. "Man to *man*?"

"You know what I mean, Annie. Business associate to business associate. You own half the countryside around here, so I treat you like an equal. Why should I start watching my language now?"

I shook my head and continued to my library, muttering beneath my breath, "And you wonder why you're still unmarried."

"I heard that," Adrian said. "I don't swear around *women*, just around you."

I picked up my pace. "You may be my closest neighbor and oldest friend, but sometimes I want to strangle you." It didn't matter what I wore or how I did my hair, Adrian never saw me as a woman, just as another business partner.

"What? I won't say one inappropriate thing at the house party, I swear."

I laughed.

"Wrong choice of words," he admitted. That grin was going to be the death of me. I couldn't stay mad when one side of his mouth tilted up and that single dimple appeared.

We both knew I would agree to anything he asked, but I intended to put up a fight first. Adrian put a hand on my arm to stop me at the door of my library. "Promise you'll come to some of the events."

I tried to say *no*. "You can be miserable on your own," I said. "I have no desire to marry at present."

"I know," Adrian said, glancing around. His hand fell off my arm. "Where's Fenton? Is he joining us?"

"He and Aunt are just finishing breakfast."

Adrian's smile didn't reach his eyes. "Good chap."

I nodded. "The kindest and best."

We hovered in the doorway together. His pale green eyes, flecked with auburn, were framed by thick eyelashes. His eyebrows were an odd mixture of rust and brown, almost as dark as his hair.

The clock chimed the hour as my cousin rushed down the hallway. "Didn't know we were starting early today." He looked between us. "What did I miss?"

"Nothing." Adrian rushed past me into the burgundy-wallpapered room. "Morning, Fenton."

I seated myself behind my mother's thick mahogany desk as Adrian slipped into his favorite chair across from me. His gaze caught mine, and my stomach flipped. I steeled myself to refuse the request I knew he had come for. "What matter is so urgent that Nicholas must abandon his sausage and mash yet again?"

Adrian's playful look deepened into something serious. "If I cannot secure the hand of an heiress in the next week, my father cannot build the railway in time. I must marry by Christmas to secure funding from the bank."

Nicholas choked. "Rough luck, old man."

Adrian shrugged. "Can't be helped." He reiterated the finer points of his father's proposal to run a railway line through my estate, through my beloved rose garden, and pushed yet another map toward me. "I found a solution for the orangery."

I stared at the maze of lines in front of me. He spoke so carelessly of these things. Marriage. Blasting open the countryside with dynamite. Years of work. Tens of thousands of pounds. Endangering the lives of hundreds of workers.

And my gardens. My only physical reminder of my parents.

"We already allowed a canal along the edge of our estate," I argued. *Again.* "That must be enough. I cannot give up the rose garden and orangery for the rail line. I spent many of my happiest times there with my parents."

Adrian drew his chair closer to my desk and sketched a line across the map. "Your land is the only way to get a rail line into the area. I can move your orangery and build a new hothouse for the citrus plants anywhere. The canals are overloaded, and railways are the future."

A sinking feeling in the pit of my stomach warned me that he might be right. I turned my gaze to Nicholas.

"I've studied his proposals and talked with other stewards. Everyone agrees that our valley needs this." He pointed at the papers strewn across my desk. "This is the only place for miles where the rail can continue through at a reasonable expense."

I shuffled the papers on my desk. "Sure, take his side."

"That's what friends do." Nicholas thumped Adrian on the back. "Loyal, through and through."

"Traitor," I muttered. "You're my cousin and my steward."

Nicholas thumped him even harder on the back. "He's my *mate*. My best friend. Sorry, Anne."

Adrian continued as though Nicholas hadn't spoken. He got like this at times, so focused that he hardly heard a word anyone else spoke. "Rebuilding the orangery is a small expense compared to the cost of running the line through a mountain."

We locked eyes. My mind raced with all the information he had presented over the last few months. "Surely it can wait a few years. The canals can handle the traffic."

Adrian's gaze pierced mine. "Can you honestly say that the location of your orangery is more important than the economic well-being of your tenants and this community?"

"Low blow," I muttered. He knew that was one of the few remaining obstacles.

But I had other objections. I would hear the loud trains barreling through my private gardens several times a day. It would disrupt my peace and change the entire feel of our quaint village. It might be necessary at some point—eventually—but it meant giving up everything I loved.

The gardens were my sanctuary. My escape. The canal was busy at times, but the boats and the river were quiet and beautiful, sunken below the level of the green, where I couldn't see them. But a train? It would disrupt so much of the countryside and tear apart my parents' rose garden as well.

"Anne, we're all making sacrifices. You're not the only one."

I looked at Adrian and detected a hint of sadness in his face.

I shoved the stack of papers aside. "This is too much."

He sprang from his chair and paced around the confines of my small library. "I'll do what I can. I'll drop the train tracks lower than your grazing fields to hide them. I'll build tunnels to preserve your view. I'll work with the best engineers my new wife's money can buy." His humorless laugh caught in his throat. "The livelihood of so many people depends on you and me and this railway. At least consider it."

I looked at the timepiece pinned to my shirtwaist. "I have another appointment."

Adrian gathered the papers on my desk. He placed the map on top and tapped his finger on the stack of papers. "No more stalling. You always have a solicitor coming or a tenant to visit. I won't get another chance to talk to you all week because of my guests. Time is running out, and the village is dying. Shops on High Street are closing. Men are out of work, and the other factory owners are pressuring my father to cut wages because of transportation costs."

That should have been more important than anything else. As baroness, I knew it had to be the most important thing, no matter the personal cost. I inclined my head ever so slightly. "I'll give it some thought if you secure the funding from another source."

Adrian's eyes widened. "Another source?" He exchanged a glance with Nicholas, who shrugged.

I pushed away from my desk to face him. "Yes."

Adrian ran his fingers through his hair. The tips stood on end, where the curl couldn't be tamed. He stared quizzically at me. "There is no other source. Our funds are tied up in loans for the new factory equipment."

I cracked open the door of the library. "Then the railway must wait until the loans are paid."

Adrian paused in the doorway, his presence uncomfortably close once more. Didn't the man know how to pass *through* without stopping? I breathed in the scent of bergamot and sandalwood soap. His beard was neatly trimmed, and the same flecks of auburn dotted his sideburns.

His brow furrowed. "This blasted house party, Annie. After this, I'll have a wife and a fortune."

I took a deep breath. "Mr. Everard."

The crease of his brow deepened, and I wished I had remained seated. His nearness was distracting. "What?"

"You cannot marry a stranger."

He jammed his hands in his pockets. "Why not? We'll get acquainted over the next week." He grinned with catlike charm, the corner of his mouth lifting on one side. "Then we won't be strangers."

I shook my head and sighed. "Be serious for one moment."

His face fell, and the facade cracked. "What else can I do but joke? My father insists there is no other way to fund it. We need a railway, and a railway costs a fortune."

Blood rose in my cheeks. "A woman is not a fortune. *I* am not a fortune."

He had the grace to look ashamed.

"All these years, you and Nicholas have been scaring the fortune hunters away from me. Every time a penniless man tries to ask me to dance, you or Nicholas appear to fend him off."

Adrian stared miserably at the floor. "Please come to the house party."

"I won't allow you to treat a woman like another transaction in your business dealings." The remark felt a little too personal. How many times had Adrian only seen me as a task and not as a person?

Adrian stiffened. "I'll treat her well."

My temper rose at his response. He was going to dismiss my concerns and walk away.

I stepped back inside the library to control my anger and maintain my calm demeanor.

Adrian's jaw was set. "It's not your choice. It's mine."

I scoffed. "It is *her* choice. You cannot fall in love in a week."

Nicholas laughed, as if to cut the tension. "My cousin doesn't believe you capable of capturing a woman's heart."

"That's not—"

Nicholas gestured toward me. "Show her what you're like in London."

I backed away until my legs hit the wingback chair by the fireplace. "That's not necessary."

"You only dance with Annie once during each ball. She doesn't see what you're like the rest of the time." Nicholas arched his brow suggestively.

I did see. I saw Adrian's behavior, and I resented it. He treated every woman differently than he treated me. He spoke to me like he did to Nicholas, but I saw the way he acted around the debutantes, and it made me feel small and insignificant and unseen, even with all the other men pressing around me, eager to marry my title and estates.

"Really." I moved around the chair to put as much space as possible between myself and Adrian—who hovered in the doorway, one foot out of the library and one foot inside.

"I insist." Nicholas leveled a commanding glare at his best friend. "Otherwise, she'll hound you and run the heiresses off." His tone left no room for argument.

Adrian tossed Nicholas a confused look. My cousin responded with an emphatic nod. "Throw your best at her. Give her a taste of what your future wife will be getting."

Adrian slowly dragged himself back into the library, then locked eyes with me and shoved one of the wingback chairs aside.

I swallowed. I hadn't *really* seen this side of him—now intent on me. He stalked me like a tiger at Regent's Zoo. His green eyes glittered with pent-up energy as he moved slowly toward me. With each step, my breath grew shallower until I could hardly breathe at all.

Adrian closed the remaining distance between us. His intoxicating scent filled my senses as one hand wrapped around my waist, and I gasped. It would have felt normal in a ballroom, but in my crowded library, with no space between us, it was the height of intimacy.

I forced myself to look at him. He leaned closer, taking my other hand in his as if we were dancing, and whispered, "I will take exquisite care of my wife." His gaze raked my face, studying each detail, before slowly dropping to my lips. For one wild moment, I thought he might kiss me right there with my cousin watching us. My panic turned to curiosity as he drew near, and my lips parted ever so slightly. A sigh escaped me.

He blinked and drew back, looking as stunned as I felt. He shook his head and dropped my hands, as if scalded. He stumbled backward, hitting his legs on the out-of-place chair. He doubled over in pain, then straightened, grimacing, and limped to the door. "I'll see you at dinner tonight, then. That's settled." He tore down the hallway without looking back.

Nicholas grinned too. "See, Annie, you have nothing to worry about."

I turned to him, bewildered. "What was that?"

Nicholas gave me a calculating look. "Everard doesn't like to lose an argument."

I collapsed onto the wingback chair behind me and fanned myself. Why was it suddenly so warm in my library?

Nicholas scraped the other chair back into place and settled himself. "You threw down the gauntlet when you said he couldn't make an heiress fall in love with him. He picked up the challenge, and he's determined to win."

"I see." I tried to catch my breath and collect my thoughts.

Nicholas shrugged. "He needs to raise capital quickly. How else can he get it?" He left his chair and set a hand on my shoulder. "I'll have to do the same thing eventually. Men must marry prudently too. It's the way of things." He squeezed my shoulder. "Even *you* will have to marry someday, cousin." He gathered a few papers and left the library.

Something broke loose inside me. Something unsettled. Something shaken and rattled loose by Adrian. A voice in the depths shouted, *If he needs a fortune, I have one.* Nicholas's voice echoed, *You must marry.* I shoved the voices into the blackest corners of my soul. I would never allow myself to be bought.

Not by Adrian. Not by anyone. I would be loved for myself and that alone.

And I would ensure that he didn't trap any of the arriving guests into marriage or trick them with his heady scent and purposeful looks and charming smile. Who fell in love in one week?

It was frightening, though, how easy it was to believe I could fall in love in one moment, when a man truly saw me the way Adrian had.

But he'd been pretending. He was only acting because Nicholas dared him.

I would protect these women. I would save them, and I would save Adrian from himself.

Chapter Two

THE USUAL ACTIVITIES OCCUPIED THE rest of my day: discussing estate matters with Nicholas, looking over Cook's menus for the week, meeting with my solicitor, and handling correspondence.

I trudged upstairs reluctantly to dress for dinner. My maid, Mrs. Green, tutted at me. "It's not an execution. It's a hairdo."

"Same thing," I said under my breath. I'd agreed to go to Adrian's dinner to help the other poor, innocent women, not because I wanted to find a husband for myself.

Every brush stroke was torture for my sensitive head. Mrs. Green tugged and pulled my unruly brunette hair into something sleek and manageable. She plaited a small braid on each side and twisted them back to the tight bun at the back of my head.

"He really owes me a favor," I said.

Mrs. Green responded by digging one last pin into my scalp. "There you go, love. That should hold."

I eyed my reflection in the mirror. "I could sleep in this for a week, and I don't think a hair would move."

"But you won't. You'll come home and tell me all about the party while I brush your hair." She smiled fondly at me.

I groaned. "Don't wait up for me. There'll be nothing to tell."

Mrs. Green rearranged her arsenal of brushes and combs and pins. "When you submit yourself to my ministrations willingly, there's a story somewhere. Who's the lad that caught your eye? One of the beaus from London?"

I shifted on the bench in front of the mirror. Mrs. Green had been like a mother since my parents passed away, but she was the lifeblood of the servants' gossip. I couldn't bear to break her matchmaking heart. *Let her imagine that I'm finally ready to marry.* I'd give her a few breadcrumbs without actually misleading her.

It was a fine line that I was quite practiced in walking.

"I promised Adrian that I'd attend some of his events this week. Two gentlemen have arrived for the house party."

Mrs. Green's eyes widened, as if delighted, and she plopped instantly on the edge of my bed. "Adrian, is it? Bless my heart. For the last three months he's been *Mr. Everard*, and you looked like you were eating a sour lemon every time you said his name."

"He's been hounding me about an estate matter."

Mrs. Green nodded crisply. "But now?"

"Nicholas persuaded me to hear him out."

Mrs. Green cackled. "So, all is forgiven. *Adrian.* You two are either thick as thieves or at each other's throats. So, is this hairstyle for Mr. Fenton or Mr. Everard?"

I swatted her hand, as she reached up to push a pin deeper into my scalp. "Neither."

"Oh! The London gents," Mrs. Green said with glee. She reached for my braids, and I ducked.

"Good night, and don't wait up." I kissed her cheek.

She tutted again. "I *will* be waiting up, so don't disappoint me. I want to hear every detail." She smoothed my hair one last time. "You're as beautiful as your mother ever was, and just as kind."

I hugged her, and she squeezed me tight enough that I gasped for air. "Very well. Flattery works every time. I'll tell you every dish we ate."

"Off you go." Mrs. Green pushed me out the door, rubbing her hands. "There'll be children in the nursery at last."

I had no intention of marrying or hiring a nurse anytime soon. Lord Wetherspoon and Mr. Chelmsford were the only men visiting, and I already knew both of them. I'd known Lord Wetherspoon for years, in fact. Six years. Six Seasons.

If either of us had any intention of marrying, we would have done so long ago. He was a notorious and tiresome flirt, more in love with himself than anyone else, and I was only there to warn the first heiress who had arrived.

I cornered Adrian after dinner. "Did your mother draft these seating arrangements? Lord Wetherspoon? He has as much substance as that meringue we had for dessert."

Adrian laughed.

"And Mrs. Green did my hair."

Adrian inspected it, obviously confused. "Yes. Ravishing. You are exquisite." He stared at me for a long minute, then lowered his voice. "Which one should I marry?"

I glared at him.

Adrian's brow wrinkled. "What am I missing? You want to sit next to someone else tomorrow and . . . your hair is . . . braided?" Adrian shook his head. "Honestly, Annie, I already told you that you look beautiful. I'm doing my best here. What else is a man supposed to say?"

I fought the blush trying to redden my cheeks. Six years of being a baroness had not given me enough experience yet. I should have been able to hide every emotion and every reaction, but Adrian so rarely noticed anything about my appearance.

In fact, I wasn't sure he knew whether I was a man or a woman.

"Only one heiress has arrived," I whispered. "How can I choose? How can you?"

Miss Astbury was watching our whispered conversation, so I spoke directly. "I was not fishing for compliments. I am informing you of the *reasons* you are deeply indebted to me. There are twenty-seven pins currently poking into my scalp."

"Right." Adrian squinted at the back of my hair, then grinned. "It shows your neck to great advantage."

"My neck is beside the point," I said quietly. "My shoes pinch, this dress is stiff, Lord Wetherspoon has mutton breath, and my head hurts."

Adrian wasn't listening. He stared intently at my hair, then mumbled, "You're exaggerating, as usual. I only count fifteen pins."

I opened my mouth to argue that they hurt considerably, regardless of the number, but he still wasn't looking at me. His eyes dropped slowly from the braid pinned near my ear to one side of my neck, then down to my exposed shoulders.

"Mr. Everard?"

His eyes snapped to mine. "The pins. They blend in." His gaze drifted to the ridiculous ruffles adorning my evening gown. "You have shoulders."

"I've always had shoulders, Adge."

He turned abruptly and crossed the room. I watched him,

bemused. I'd worn a hundred different ballgowns in the last six years, and he'd never noticed a single one before. Perhaps that was why I'd let his old nickname slip out. *I shouldn't treat him so informally.*

The heiress approached me. "What did you do to the poor man?" She appeared disinterested, but I also knew her from the last two London Seasons. Her aloof demeanor hid a shy reserve.

"Miss Astbury!" I smiled genuinely. "I'm glad to find a friend among the house party. I could not speak to you across the dinner table."

She barely registered a smile. "Here I am, and there he goes." Miss Astbury nodded toward Adrian. "You've completely unnerved him."

I laughed. "Oh no, we're old friends. He's rather—" I stopped. Instead of defending him, this was my chance to warn her. "Mr. Everard gets completely lost in thought. He's thoroughly absentminded at times."

Miss Astbury inspected the linen beneath the vase on the sideboard. "He seems intent on his purpose."

I fiddled with my locket. "Does he?"

She let the linen slip through her gloved fingers. "Is this from Mr. Everard's factory? It's not from my father's."

I recognized it immediately. The delicate flower embroidery had been done by the new machines, the ones the Everards were still paying off. The ones that had put so many women out of work.

It was the most successful cloth they sold, and the reason Adrian wanted to employ more workers, the reason sales had increased, and the reason the canal couldn't handle the volume of orders.

The reason he needed a railway.

And a wife.

"You'd have to ask Mr. Everard," I hedged. "Tell me, how have you been?"

We began a slow circuit around the drawing room, strolling side by side. Miss Astbury and I walked in silence while she formulated an answer. "I visited my cousins in Cambridgeshire. The Barringtons."

"And how was your stay?"

A ghost of a smile flitted across her face. "Fine."

We'd made it halfway across the room. Adrian stopped talking to his father and nodded at us, flashing an automatic grin.

I shook my head. "He can be quite distractible..."

We arrived at a well-appointed sofa, and Miss Astbury settled herself majestically. "He was quite attentive during dinner." She folded her hands primly in her lap. "Incessant talk about my father's urgent need for a new railway to transport his goods."

My heart sank. But perhaps Adrian could get the money he needed without a marriage of convenience. "Would your father consider investing in the venture?"

"He wants partial ownership, and the elder Mr. Everard wishes to retain full control." She smiled a bit sadly. "The cost is clear."

"The expense of building the rail line is exorbitant," I agreed.

"Papa intends to secure the future for his factories at any cost." Miss Astbury gestured toward herself. "Even if it takes my entire dowry."

I heard the resignation in her tone and wished I could help. As a woman with my own title and three estates, I had perfect freedom, but most women did not. Here was my chance to warn her away from an arranged marriage. "Perhaps Lord Wetherspoon is also respectable?"

Her eyes flitted away, and they softened. "I spent a great deal of time with the Chelmsfords recently. His family resides near my cousins."

"Ah." I understood the resignation I'd heard. Her heart was already set on someone else.

Adrian's father called for a round of parlor games. I made certain that Miss Astbury and Mr. Chelmsford partnered with me and my cousin. Adrian was left with Aunt Fenton and his parents for the rest of the night. Although he hid it from the others, Adrian's frustration clearly simmered below the surface.

He escorted me to the door after saying farewell to the others. As soon as they'd left, he rounded on me. "Why did you monopolize Miss Astbury?" He grabbed my pelisse from his butler and held it out. "Here," he said, clearly exasperated, but ever the gentleman.

I didn't deny what I'd done. "It would be cruel to propose when her heart is engaged elsewhere." I slipped one arm into my warm wool coat, equally exasperated by his kind gesture when I wished to be angry with him.

Adrian froze with his arm halfway around my shoulders. "She is secretly engaged?"

He took my meaning too literally. I slipped my other arm into the pelisse and moved out of his almost embrace. "No, but she cares for someone else."

He tugged absentmindedly at his cuffs. "How do you know?"

I sighed. "Observe her carefully."

He wrenched open the front doors as if his butler were not perfectly capable of operating doorknobs, and I scanned the steps for her.

Below us, Mr. Chelmsford assisted Miss Astbury into her carriage. I nudged Adrian. "Watch."

She paused as she entered her carriage. Even though I

couldn't hear them, their mutual affection was obvious from a distance.

"See the way his arm lingers? The way she gazes at him?" I tipped my head up to explain.

Adrian looked down at me. "What does that signify?" His eyes roamed over my face, searching for an answer. Dim candlelight flickered from the lanterns. The same dangerous glint I'd seen yesterday entered his eyes, as my gaze lingered on the bronze in his beard and the waves in his hair.

What does his gaze mean?

Crunching gravel alerted me that the carriages had left.

"Cousin!" Nicholas hollered from the bottom of the steps, and I glanced down at him. "Our carriage awaits." He held open one arm and smiled widely.

I looked back at Adrian, but his face had slipped into a mask again.

"Miss Astbury's heart already belongs to Mr. Chelmsford. Don't pursue her," I begged. "Her father will force her to accept your proposal."

Nicholas stamped his feet impatiently in the chilly autumn air.

Adrian scanned my face. "You can tell that from the way she looks at him?" His eyes darted down to Nicholas and the carriage. "She loves another, and she would not welcome a proposal?"

I nodded.

He stepped back, suddenly formal and distant. "Thank you for your opinion, Lady Baxter. Miss Astbury can decide for herself."

Nicholas rubbed his arms and shuffled his feet in the loose gravel.

I put my hand on Adrian's arm. "Please listen to me this time, Adge."

He looked pointedly at my hand, and I removed it.

"Good night." He bowed stiffly and retreated into the house. I climbed down the steps toward my waiting cousin, confused by the sudden change in Adrian.

He still doesn't see me. He intended to pursue Miss Astbury with even more enthusiasm because I disagreed with his course of action.

Nicholas helped me into my carriage. As the footman shut the door, Nicholas relaxed against the silk-lined interior. "I don't pity Everard one bit. Miss Astbury is a fine woman with a fine, fat purse."

I turned on him. "Is this how you talk about me when I am not around? Are women nothing but pretty faces and large dowries?"

Nicholas and Aunt Fenton both stared at me.

Aunt spoke first. "Of course not."

Nicholas squirmed in his seat. On the plush, silk-lined seat of *my* carriage.

"Would you rather have him marry an ugly woman?" Nicholas spoke the harsh truth, though kindly.

The dark voice yelled again from the depths of my heart, *Yes! He deserves the most horrible woman he can find!* I didn't expect the heiresses to be graceful and intelligent and friends of mine.

"Don't worry, dear," Aunt said. "You're pretty. The men only speak well of you behind your back."

I stared at Nicholas, who turned his head to gaze out of the carriage window into the black night. He was avoiding me, and that was answer enough.

Would I never find a husband who valued me for my attributes instead of my title or wealth? If no one else would protect me, I would guard myself, my fortune, and especially my heart. I would fight to protect the other arriving heiresses from fortune hunters like my cousin and my old friend.

Chapter Three

AUNT AND I WANDERED INTO town the next day. The other guests would not arrive for several hours, and I yearned for a quiet stroll to clear my head. I was unprepared for the explosion of sound that hit my ears as we rounded the corner, since I had thrown my calendar in the fireplace. *Again.* Why was everyone intent on providing me with visual reminders that time moved too swiftly, and that time would never turn back?

It was market day, and the square was filled with carts, merchants, children running wild, and squawking chickens. The scent of meat pies drew me to Mavis's stall. I told myself that she could use an extra coin, but in fact, I hadn't eaten much that morning.

After I smelled the gingerbread, I decided that Mavis *really* needed extra coins this week. *Several.* I bought two pies and a piece of gingerbread.

Aunt and I crossed to the benches in front of the old stone church to watch the commotion. The street from the Everards' manor home led directly to town, and I glanced toward Adrian's home by instinct.

Adrian's party of house guests headed toward us. I hastily

hid the pies behind my back. *How late is it?* I hadn't pinned my timepiece to my shirtwaist.

The most extravagantly dressed woman kept her eyes trained on Adrian like a hawk, until she tripped over my shoe. She noticed the pie my aunt was eating and shot us a look of disgust. "I thought you had aristocratic neighbors." She sniffed and moved past us.

Mr. Chelmsford smiled kindly. Miss Astbury nodded curtly, and Nicholas shot me an amused glance, one eyebrow raised, as he eyed the gingerbread next to my gloves.

I tucked my feet beneath the stone bench, hid my hands behind my back to cover the pies, and tried to melt invisibly into the wall.

Adrian stopped. "Lady Baxter. A delight, as always. I see you've found Mavis's pies. Who else is hungry? I know I am." He whipped off a glove, slipped his bare fingers in the space between the knobbly flint wall and my back, and slid his fingers down to my ungloved hands.

A shock ran through me, and I let go.

A grin lifted one side of his mouth as he tugged a pie from behind me with a note of triumph. "Ha! Best in the valley." He took an exaggerated bite.

"Will you join us?" Nicholas asked.

Aunt waved him away. "Go ahead."

I shook my head discreetly at Adrian's questioning look.

He relished the last bite of his meat pie, bowed to us, and then led the visitors into the maze of market stalls.

My fingers still tingled where his hand had touched mine. *What is happening? It's just Adge.* As soon as I was sure no one would notice me, I picked up my remaining pie. I slumped against the wall, savoring each bite, then moved on to the gingerbread.

Aunt had finished hers and tapped her foot as she waited.

I struck a casual tone. "I'm ready to return home."

She pulled me up by the arm. "We just arrived."

"I'm exhausted."

"You don't wish to encounter Mr. Everard with a beauty on his arm."

I glared at her.

Aunt sighed. "You're right. She was a plain little thing, bless her, but she tries."

I choked back a laugh. "Aunt, you cannot say things like that out loud."

Aunt Fenton shrugged. "It's market day. No one can hear us. The chickens' squawking covers a multitude of rumors." She winked at me. "You thought so too, but you're too proper to say it."

I wiped my fingers on my handkerchief, drew on my gloves, and we edged across the street toward the pharmaceutical chemist, located next to the china shop. I stopped to examine the willow-patterned ceramics in the crowded display window and gather my wits. "I'm sure she's lovely and kind on the inside," I said.

"That china pattern's lovely," Aunt said. "On the *outside*. It doesn't need to wear makeup. That woman's lips are not a natural color."

"Aunt! Hush!" I bit my lip to keep from laughing.

She threaded her arm through mine as we peered at the display. "Never you mind. Just pretend to shop with me, and you can keep on avoiding her."

I glanced around to make sure no one could hear.

She fanned herself dramatically and raised her voice. "Bless me! Gravy boats and soup tureens and teapots and saucers. I've died and gone to heaven."

But she had a point. If I pretended to shop with her, I didn't have to join Adrian's party. "Our old china does well enough," I said. "It belonged to Great-Grandmother."

"But this one tells a story," Aunt said. "Look at the pictures on every plate."

I made a mental note to ask my housekeeper, Mrs. Flynn, to buy a complete set for Aunt for Christmas. The intricately woven blue and white design was beautiful, and I'd put off replacing the old set for far too long.

A light touch on my elbow startled me. "Lady Baxter?"

I breathed a sigh of relief. It wasn't Adrian. "Miss Winters?" I embraced my friend. "Please call me Anne, as you did in London. Have you met Mr. Fenton's mother?"

A faint blush crept up Miss Winters's cheeks. "It's a pleasure to see you both again. And of course I'm Julia to you. I thought I'd missed the group. I'm so relieved."

The group? I drew back. Julia and her parents were dressed in their best, and she could afford the finest. She had to be one of the heiresses.

But she wasn't awful. She was one of the kindest women I knew. Adrian could be happy with her.

The thought failed to reassure me, as it should have.

I pointed vaguely. "The others are somewhere in the market stalls."

"Shall we look together?"

I couldn't think of an excuse.

Aunt fell back to join Julia's parents while we pressed into the busy throng. Julia continued, "I was pleased to discover that Mr. Everard lives near Langton Abbey, so I could visit you as well."

"And I am delighted to see you." The unsettled feeling from yesterday returned. *Am I truly glad?*

Women haggled with merchants while their precariously balanced baskets of produce dangled on their arms. Julia and I searched through the crowded market with people pressing on every side. The smells and sounds overwhelmed me. "We'll see better from the edge," I said to her parents, and we moved back toward the shops.

I took advantage of the noise. We might never have another opportunity for a private conversation. She'd spent much of the last Season eyeing Nicholas, and I couldn't help wondering whether I could ascertain her true feelings. "My cousin will be delighted to renew your acquaintance," I said quietly.

"I look forward to seeing Mr. Fenton again." Julia tossed a furtive glance over her shoulder at her father. "Very much."

Relief washed over me, but I pushed the feeling away.

"You and your cousin are quite close," Julia said.

I smiled. "Yes. He's a tremendous help to me." *Why do people continually comment on our friendship? Shouldn't cousins get along?*

We walked past the tinker, the cobbler, and the draper. *Still no hint of Adrian.* I peered inside the grocer's shop. An assistant shaved sugar from a cone. Sunlight glinted off the grocer's speckled windowpanes and blinded me momentarily.

"Ah, there you are." Adrian's voice boomed behind me. Honestly, the man moved like a predatory animal, coming out of nowhere to startle me.

Two overdressed women crowded their way around the grocer's display window, pushing me out of the way. Adrian's voice was overly loud and unnaturally polite. "Our party wouldn't be complete without you."

"Without me and Miss Winters," I said. Julia elbowed her way between the women to reach Adrian.

"May I make Miss Blackburn and her parents known to you?" Nicholas indicated the overdressed women. The families sized each other up while Nicholas introduced Aunt and the party members to each other.

Lord Wetherspoon eyed me as if I were a cone of sugar,

and I moved away from him. He clearly believed that being a viscount gave him some sort of irresistible charm. The only thing overwhelming about him was his odor.

Nicholas smiled at the group. "Where shall we continue our promenade? This is the finest High Street around. We have nearly forty shops." He extended his arm toward Julia, who stood closest to him. She shot me a questioning look, and I didn't know how to respond. I wasn't sure what she was asking. Which shop? Whether to continue the promenade? Whether or not to walk with my cousin?

"Look at these toys!" Miss Astbury had left the grocer's window and found Kendrick's. "These rival the displays on Regent Street."

Miss Blackburn joined her. "Do you have an adequate dressmaker? How is your tailor?" She eyed Adrian's attire critically as though deciding whether to purchase a leg of lamb from a market stall.

"We're able to get everything from London. Anderson is the gentleman's tailor here on High Street." Adrian gestured to a whitewashed building with half-timbers. "Lady Baxter, I must refer the dressmaking question to you."

Miss Blackburn ran her gaze up and down my dress, and her lips thinned to a tight line. It gave her the appearance of a shriveled fig.

I never wore my finest dress for a morning walk. "Mrs. Rowntree has always given me the highest level of personal attention."

Miss Blackburn trilled an empty laugh. "If this is the quality of her work, I'm not sure I'm fit for country living."

I met her gaze head on. "I only wear Mrs. Rowntree's gowns for important events."

"Then we shall never see one," Adrian said, laughing. "My little dinners aren't important enough for a Rowntree gown."

Before I could retort, Nicholas edged forward. "Langton is my ideal of country life with a lively High Street if I need..." He flicked a casual glance around the storefronts.

"Confections," Adrian said. "Shall we save our appetite for tea, or can we spoil these ladies with a few of Mrs. Rymer's chocolates?"

The group crowded into the store and exclaimed over the candies, toffees, and fudge. Adrian drew me aside. "About tea..."

I knew that look. "Tell them the abbey is hosting the tea today. I'll warn Cook."

Adrian's gaze warmed something inside me as he edged forward and placed a hand on my arm. "Thank you. My father is trying to spend as little as he can, and he insisted the guests stay at the Red Lion." He smiled ruefully. "It's so unlike him."

I eyed the endless row of chocolate creams. "Nicholas has just invited Mr. Chelmsford to stay, so I'll have house guests while you do not." I glanced over at Mr. Chelmsford, who waited off to one side. "There will be billiards and ale and stale smoke all night long."

"Perhaps *he's* your man." Adrian followed my gaze, then arched a brow. "You make him sound so appealing."

Mr. Chelmsford was several inches shorter than Adrian, about Nicholas's height, quite thickset and muscular. Brown curls exploded all over his head, and his dark eyes were kind, like a loyal, gentle puppy.

"He's handsome enough," I said. "Nicholas thinks well of him."

Adrian considered me. "You believe he's handsome?"

Nicholas pushed his way between us, and Adrian's hand fell off my arm. "Shall we? Shop's not meant to hold this many people." He held up a bag of sweets, and we made our way back onto High Street.

"I'll go ahead to the abbey to make sure tea is ready. Could you show the others the way?" I smiled at Nicholas.

It took him a moment, but he finally realized that Adrian had no intention of hosting his own tea party. "We're close to the jeweler. Or shall we try the bookseller? They have an enchanting staircase. I could get lost in their store for hours."

"Do you read much, Mr. Fenton?" Julia's eyes drifted off to one side, then she peeked at Nicholas from beneath her eyelashes. She darted a nervous glance at me, and her eyes instantly dropped back to the ground. *Odd.*

He grinned at her, though she didn't meet his eyes. "All the time, when I'm not riding or hunting."

"I hope I need the jeweler before I need another book," Miss Blackburn said. She directed a pointed gaze at Adrian.

He coughed. "Ah, Wetherspoon, will you escort Miss Blackburn to the shops? I'll make sure Lady Baxter and her aunt make it back to the abbey." He offered us each an arm.

"What are you doing?" I whispered to Adrian as we left the others and passed the clockmaker.

"Selling my soul."

I laughed despite myself. Adrian didn't.

We walked past the gunsmith and reached the Red Lion Inn. We continued along the street, passing the blacksmith and saddlers. Adrian inclined his head toward me as we neared the abbey. "How well do you know Chelmsford?"

"Only a little, from London."

Aunt leaned across Adrian. "He's one of Nicholas's closest friends. Good family. I thought you knew him too."

Adrian patted her arm. "I do, Mrs. Fenton. No cause for alarm."

"He's young," I said. "Barely returned from his grand tour." *And obviously in love with Miss Astbury.* Adrian was still oblivious, even after our conversation last night.

He shot me a sideways glance. "True."

I sighed sadly. "He does seem to fancy Miss Astbury."

Adrian furrowed his brow. "Does he?"

I sighed even more dramatically. "He's hardly old enough to marry." *Am I trying to make Adge jealous?* I resumed speaking in my normal, cheery voice. "You and Nicholas are barely old enough yourselves."

The side of Adrian's mouth lifted in a shadow of a grin. "I'm twenty-eight, and Nicholas is twenty-nine, in case you lost the last calendar I gave you. Plenty old enough." He seemed to draw me closer, but it might have been the uneven stones we walked across just then.

The stone walls of Langton Abbey came into sight. "I remember how old I am, Mr. Everard, so I remember how old you are." I smiled at him. My nicest smile. "Miss Winters would be a lovely neighbor, but I absolutely forbid Miss Blackburn. I shall remove to my furthest estate if you marry her."

Aunt leaned across Adrian again. "Miss Winters clearly prefers Nicholas." Aunt looked up at Adrian and blinked. "Sorry, Mr. Everard."

I swung my head aside to hide my mortification at Aunt's untoward honesty, then she continued speaking. "Annie, you've got to convince Miss Winters that you aren't marrying Nicholas. She'd be a fine prospect for him."

I blanched. "What?"

Aunt hummed the wedding march played at Princess Victoria's wedding. "You know what happens when cousins marry. It's fine for royalty, but you're no princess."

I felt the color drain from my face then rush to my cheeks. "Adge? Do people think that—Nicholas and I . . .?"

He wouldn't meet my eyes.

"*You* believe it too? Why would anyone—" I bit off my sentence.

We'd reached the abbey. "I'll speak with Cook," Aunt said cheerily and climbed the steps.

Adrian lounged against a stone plinth at the base of the stairs, but I sensed tension coiled inside.

He rested his hands behind his head and crossed his feet at the ankles. "I've been waiting for you to announce your engagement for years."

I blinked as the sun came out from the clouds and blinded me.

He shrugged.

I tugged at my bonnet, drawing it close around my face, even though my voice betrayed me. "I—he—no, he's like a brother."

Adrian jammed his hands into the pockets of his trousers. "You get along so well, and you allow him to run things here."

It was imperative that Adrian understand. "Nicholas irritates me even more than you."

Adrian grinned and pushed off the plinth. "All this time, when you said you didn't want to marry, I thought you were waiting for Fenton to propose." He lifted my bonnet, exposing my fiery complexion, and his fingers skimmed lightly down the side of my cheek. "You're blushing."

Mortification at my reaction to him crashed against my resentment at his comment. Heat swallowed me, and I shook with emotion. "I was waiting for someone to love me for who I am. It's been six years, and I still haven't found anyone who can do that. All I've done is fend off fortune hunters."

Adrian's face fell, and his hand dropped away. "Like me."

The anger ebbed. "You wouldn't. Miss Winters obviously adores Nicholas, and you can see Miss Astbury's devotion to Mr. Chelmsford."

He scrubbed a hand down his face. "I don't see it, and my father requires me to marry, or he will disown me."

"I cannot believe your father would truly do that."

He drew a deep breath. "Tell me that Miss Blackburn will make a wonderful neighbor, and that we'll still be friends when I marry."

I ran my hand restlessly along the smooth stone balustrade. "We're not even friends now." I was only half teasing, and it must have shown on my face.

Adrian gently covered my hand. I marveled again at how perfectly my fingers nestled beneath his palm. His pale green eyes pierced me with an intensity I'd never seen. The moment stilled as his laugh faded on the autumn breeze and our gazes held. "Can you forgive me?" he asked, more serious than I'd ever heard him.

"I don't know," I said honestly. "You're changing everything—"

"—and you hate change," Adge finished for me. His fingers rubbed mine gently. "I am sorry," he said. "Sorrier than you know, especially now that I realize . . . Well, I'm sorry."

His sentence hung suspended between us, and I tried to finish it in my mind. *Now that I realize Miss Astbury cares for Mr. Chelmsford? Now that I realize Miss Winters cares for your cousin?* What had changed in the last few minutes that made his choice more painful?

The sun warmed my back, but the contentment spreading through me came from our hands clasped together. I shook myself, uncertain what to say. I could not honestly put Adrian's mind at ease, not while I despised his actions.

But I clearly did not despise him.

Miss Blackburn's shrill voice pierced the air, high above the murmur of other voices. "Mr. Everard!"

Adrian dropped my fingers and jumped back. His eyes pleaded with mine. "I've suddenly gone deaf." He rushed up the stairs without looking back.

Miss Blackburn's voice went an octave higher, until it could have matched a train's whistle. "Mr. Everaaarrrddd?"

Adrian took the steps two at a time until he reached the door.

I couldn't let him marry her. I had to save him from himself and save Miss Blackburn from a loveless marriage. I also had to help him see that Miss Astbury and Miss Winters loved other men so he would not pursue them.

The group approached rapidly, and I had no time to think. This called for action. Desperate action. I needed a plan.

The only problem was that I didn't have one.

Chapter Four

I USHERED THE PARTY OUTSIDE to the balcony. Sheep wandered in the distance across an expansive grazing green. The situation was idyllic. Romantic, even. I seated myself beside Adrian, who paid studious attention to Miss Astbury.

I considered every conceivable way to change his stubborn mind, but I knew him too well. He'd set his mind to a task, and he would not budge. He was loyal to his father and believed the town needed this railway, and if I disagreed, that convinced him even more.

I also imagined ways to hint to Julia that my cousin and I would not suit, but we would not easily find another time to speak privately.

I sipped my tea and picked at my plum cake while Nicholas carried the conversation. He acted as though he was the host instead of me. Adge was right. It was easy for others to get the wrong impression.

"Shall we try our hand at the labyrinth?" Nicholas asked, after finishing his third slice of cake. His chestnut hair lay in perfect waves on his head, shining in the afternoon sun, and yet . . . I felt nothing for him but sisterly admiration and annoyance.

"Oh yes," Miss Winters exclaimed, and I suspected that she might not mind getting lost with him. She'd been eyeing his chestnut waves too.

Our party descended the stone steps from the terrace. Nicholas led the way across the green and toward the maze. Miss Winters glanced back at me, a crease between her eyes.

Adrian had stubbornly asked Miss Astbury to accompany him, and Lord Wetherspoon had deigned to invite Miss Blackburn. Miss Winters hung back and attracted my cousin's attention.

Mr. Chelmsford gallantly attached himself to my side when no one else was left, and we strolled in awkward silence. I pondered how to convince Adrian that he invited misery by courting the wrong woman. The wrong *women*.

Who would ever be right for Adge?

Symmetrical trees lined the pathway leading from the terrace to the gardens. Mr. Chelmsford gestured toward them and cleared his throat. "I studied mathematics at Cambridge."

I frowned a little in confusion but quickly replaced it with a bland smile. Had I missed part of the conversation? Then I noticed where we were walking. "The rectangular trees?"

He nodded. His eyes were fixed on the boxy trees placed in intervals with mathematical precision.

"Perhaps you'll enjoy the bushes ahead. I've instructed the gardeners to trim them into cones, but they've cut various geometric shapes throughout the gardens. Harris is an orderly man. He keeps his tools under lock and key and keeps my gardens just as precisely."

Mr. Chelmsford seemed relieved that I was talking so he didn't have to. He *would* be the perfect match for Miss Astbury, who also preferred discreet conversations. They were each straightforward, and neither liked embellishment.

That was it.

Adrian needed to see for himself that Miss Astbury preferred Mr. Chelmsford, since the carriage incident last night had been so fleeting.

"Harris designed a most difficult labyrinth. Mr. Everard and I already know the solution." I arched a brow and smiled, then continued, "We have an advantage over the other couples." Mr. Chelmsford's eyes flew to Miss Astbury, then back to me.

Miss Blackburn complained loudly. "That's hardly fair."

Adrian paused. "You're right. The others deserve a sporting chance."

"It's much more fun the first time if you don't know where you're going. I daresay Mr. Chelmsford will win with his mathematical mind."

There. I'd set the bait.

Miss Astbury disentangled her arm from Adrian's. "I do love a contest." She left Adrian and slipped her arm into the crook of Mr. Chelmsford's elbow.

I hid my smile. It couldn't be more obvious.

Miss Blackburn looked around. Lord Wetherspoon grinned widely and offered his arm to her. She took it eagerly. "What shall the forfeit be?" Her smile should have been coy, but her face pinched unattractively, and Adrian shot me a sideways glance, clearly alarmed.

Miss Winters blushed beautifully. "Doesn't Mr. Fenton also know the maze? Perhaps we should give the others a few seconds to begin without us?"

Adrian furrowed his brow. "Go ahead. We'll be right behind you."

The others giggled and ran into the labyrinth. Miss Winters followed with Nicholas a minute later.

Adrian scanned the gardens. "We cannot wait too long without a chaperone."

I smiled at him. "They don't know how close or how far behind we are. Everyone knows the rules can be bent a little in a pleasure garden. Aunt Fenton is wandering around somewhere, as are all the other parents. They seem unconcerned about propriety."

The crease on his brow disappeared. "You're right."

I settled on a stone bench outside the entrance and ran my gloves lightly across the hedgerow behind me. A tendril of ivy threaded through the hazelnut bushes, and moss covered the loose pebbles along the path.

"Miss Astbury really does prefer Mr. Chelmsford." Adrian's voice had a note of melancholy in it. "And Miss Winters picks Fenton for her partner every time."

I tried to cheer him. "Indeed, but the ivy is in bloom." The brilliant yellow-green flowers of the vine appeared at intervals throughout the hedge.

Adrian reached down and selected a deep brown conker from the dirt beneath the chestnut tree. He hefted its weight, then tossed it at me. *Hard.*

I rubbed above my ankle where it stung. "What was that for?"

"Being right. It's already October third. I must marry by Christmas for my father to secure the funding."

"Is it? I wouldn't know. No calendar." I leaned over casually. A pile of conkers had fallen beneath an overhanging branch. I selected a handful of smooth brown spheres and filled my pockets. I could carry more if I didn't pick up the chestnuts encased in spiky protective cases.

Adrian noticed what I was doing. "Oh no."

I straightened. "It's not my fault I'm always right."

He grabbed a handful of conkers and darted toward the maze, peering over his shoulder as if he *wanted* me to catch him.

I gathered my crinoline and skirt and lobbed a conker as hard as I could.

Footsteps stumbled ahead of me. I grinned and ran faster.

A conker came back at me from the corner of the hedge. He missed. I stopped running and tiptoed forward.

"You call yourself nobility?" Adrian snorted.

I edged forward, peeking around the hedge, and aimed.

"Missed again!"

I hadn't. I saw him rubbing the back of his head.

Adrian darted from around one alley of the labyrinth just as I gathered my skirts to dash away. His eyes widened, probably at the sight of my exposed legs. My skirts fell back into place, and my eyes flared with challenge and humiliation. He lobbed a chestnut seed toward my knees as he grinned and disappeared. It stung, even through the fabric.

I had to limp more than run for the next stretch. I crept stealthily, but he evidently grew bored of waiting for my attack.

Adrian's voice drifted back from around the bend. "These ivy flowers are stunning. Look at the hazelnuts. I could admire the hedges all day."

I peeked around the corner, aimed carefully, then threw as hard as I could. Adrian ducked right as Miss Blackburn entered the intersection from the center of the labyrinth. The chestnut seed hit her directly in the arm.

"Ow!" She wheeled around.

I snaked my way into a different recess of the maze and ran directly into Adrian. We collided in a whirl of skirts and crinoline hoop and arms and legs. I steadied myself against his chest as his arms wrapped around me in the private nook.

"Did she see us?" I whispered as I fought to catch my breath. I opened my mouth to ask another question, but he put a finger on my lips and shook his head. I waited for him to let go, but his touch lingered, tracing the outline of my lip as he pulled away.

Time stopped. Sounds faded to silence. Adrian's hand flexed against my back and drew me closer, a question in his eye, as his chest rose and fell beneath my hand. *Is that his heart beating wildly or my own?*

I sucked in a breath. Footsteps crunched on the gravel, and the spell broke.

"Who's there?" Miss Blackburn's high-pitched voice warned us in time. She rounded the corner with Lord Wetherspoon, just as Adrian and I sprang apart. *What was that?*

Miss Blackburn squinted, and her face pinched as she glanced back and forth between us. Lord Wetherspoon arched a brow, as though he'd seen us spring away.

"Squirrel," Adrian managed to pant out. He was heaving lungfuls of breath. At least I'd given a good chase. "He's been dropping acorns." His breath punctuated each word as though it was a sentence. "Did he hit you, too?" He pointed to the top of the hedges and squinted at the animal that wasn't there.

Adrian discreetly released the conkers he held while the others looked away. He tried to pry the chestnut seed out of my hand just as Miss Blackburn swung back to face us. She stared pointedly, as though he were holding my hand instead of trying to convince me to drop the rest of my ammunition.

But I still meant to hit him, so I wouldn't release it.

We stood together, guilt all over our faces, with flushed cheeks. An idea formed instantly. I hadn't planned this, but I certainly meant to take advantage of the situation to scare Miss Blackburn away.

She waited, but I didn't offer any explanation or make any excuses. I let her draw her own incorrect conclusions about what Adrian and I had been doing in the maze, in the hopes that she would think he had already chosen someone else. *Me.*

"You navigated the labyrinth without getting lost," Adrian said lightly. "Congratulations."

Miss Blackburn's eyes narrowed. "We've been waiting." She smiled thinly. "We found the way much faster than you two who have traversed the maze before."

I exchanged a glance with Adrian, who repressed a smile. I had to bite my lip to maintain my demeanor.

Lord Wetherspoon cleared his throat meaningfully, and Miss Blackburn glared back at me, her icy stare full of unspoken accusation.

We followed them to the center of the maze, where the others had discovered the oversized wooden swing.

Adrian marched me off to one side while the gentlemen took turns pushing the ladies. He made it too easy, really, to continue giving the wrong impression—the impression that he was falling in love with me.

"She nearly caught us in a compromising position," Adrian whispered.

He locked eyes with me, and all I could remember was the feeling of his arms steadying me moments before. *Did you mean to do that?*

Adrian ran a hand through his hair, tousling the ends. "We got carried away in the labyrinth."

"You could have let go," I said. Tension crackled between us. I said the only thing I could to defuse it. "I still have one conker, which you deserve. My leg is sore."

He rubbed his neck. "I'm here to get married, Anne. We can't flirt like this."

"I'm not flirting," I replied. "You threw the first one." I dug the last chestnut seed out of my pocket and threw it half-heartedly at his shoulder.

Adrian scowled at me. "I cannot tell when you are serious."

I huffed. "Really, Adge. We are not flirting." *Only because I do not know how.* But it was a great idea. If I could learn to flirt with him, maybe the others would leave.

His eyes blazed. "It feels a lot like flirting, Annie." He glanced over his shoulder, then locked eyes with me again. "Why is Miss Blackburn jealous of your *not flirting* with me?"

"I don't know, but we may as well help Nicholas," I said. "I can put Miss Winters's mind to rest once and for all, and you can help me." I ignored his concerns about Miss Blackburn because she was about to get much, much angrier than she had been before.

If I was lucky.

I'd never flirted with Adrian in my life, and he'd barely noticed that I had shoulders. It wasn't a promising start, but I'd try.

Adrian's brows shot up. "What are you going to do?"

I wrapped my arm around his, as closely as I could without being inappropriate. Adrian heaved a deep breath. "Why would I help you, when I'm trying to marry Miss Winters myself?"

"Because you don't want to be miserable." I took care to walk as closely to him as I could without pushing boundaries too far. I only wished to raise a few eyebrows and run off a few heiresses.

"I won't be miserable." He tried for a smile. "I know how to court a woman."

Adrian never knew what to make of me, and he certainly didn't now. One step he would veer away and another he would sway closer to me. He ran his free hand through his hair, obviously distracted.

We stopped halfway to the swing. I tilted my head up and

met his pale green eyes. His disheveled hair lay in uneven waves, and I yearned to run my fingers through it. I was terrified and bluffing, but I lifted my chin. "You'll be miserable if one of you is in love with someone else."

Adrian searched my face, and time froze once more. A warmth flooded me as though the sun had parted the clouds.

"The swing is a terrible idea."

Part of me agreed with him, but I couldn't admit it. "I only broke my arm once, and I won't jump off the seat again."

Adrian shook his head. "It's not a broken *arm* I'm worried about." His eyes shone with intensity, and I couldn't tear my gaze away.

Miss Blackburn's voice broke the spell. "Mr. Everard? Are you joining us?" She fidgeted on the wooden seat of the swing, tapping her foot on the grass below.

I tightened my grip on his arm as we approached the others. "For Nicholas."

He sighed, then flashed Miss Blackburn a bright smile. "Lady Baxter would like the next turn."

Miss Blackburn clutched the thick rope above the swing's seat and batted her eyelashes. "I haven't finished. I require someone to push me."

I clung to Adrian's arm. "Lord Wetherspoon appears strong enough to manage it."

Miss Blackburn glanced quickly at Lord Wetherspoon's broad shoulders and back to me. I tucked myself into Adrian's side and smiled at her.

Lord Wetherspoon didn't wait but gave her a single push. Miss Blackburn's feet flew off the ground. She grasped both ropes, and he gave another push. Miss Blackburn tucked her skirt down with one hand and tried to wrap her other hand around the rope. Lord Wetherspoon pushed her again, and she nearly fell off the swing. "Oh, that will do. Thank you."

He grabbed the rope and stopped the swing abruptly.

She tumbled off. "Quite refreshing." She appeared seasick and disoriented. Lord Wetherspoon steadied her and led her to one of the benches that ringed the center of the maze.

Adrian gestured toward the swing. "No jumping."

I wrapped one arm around the rope and secured my skirt, then clung to the rope with my other hand. I smiled up at him. "Ready."

Adrian pushed me so lightly that I hardly moved.

"Still ready," I said again.

His hand grazed my upper back, and I barely inched forward.

"Honestly, Adge. Just push me like you used to."

His hands slipped around my waist, and he pushed so hard that I flew toward the clouds.

I gasped, then bit my lip. Air rushed across my face. The swing fell back, and his hands encircled my waist again. "Like that?" he smirked, as he bent down to push me.

I soared through the air, higher, then back again.

"We aren't children anymore," Adrian whispered roughly in my ear.

The swing flew even higher, and I fought to keep my skirt down with everyone watching. Once again, his strong hands encircled my waist, and I barely kept a sigh from escaping my lips.

Cool autumn air brushed my cheeks, and the sun warmed me. I reclined in the swing, anticipating the moment when Adrian's hands would land on my waist again, but he grabbed the ropes above me. I nearly fell off as the seat stopped without warning. Adrian handed me off the swing and walked away without a word.

His touch burned through the layers of clothing. I knew

I could not actually feel him, but the memory of his hands lingered. I stared after him. *Come back.*

Nicholas clapped Adrian on the back. "What do you say to a race back through the maze?" He spoke as if nothing had just happened.

But Miss Winters stared at me with wide eyes. She understood that my cousin wasn't jealous. He should have been. If he'd had any sliver of romantic interest in me, my cousin should have been irate.

Miss Blackburn certainly was.

Chapter Five

My mind raced as I dressed for dinner. The bud of an idea had formed in the garden. It blossomed into a full-blown scheme while Mrs. Green gossiped happily.

I needn't concern myself about Miss Winters or Miss Astbury. My cousin and Mr. Chelmsford attended well enough to them.

Only Miss Blackburn remained.

What if I could run her off? It was for her own sake, and for Adrian's.

And if it saved my garden too, I wouldn't complain. The canal would be sufficient for several more years.

It's not. Factory orders increased daily, but they couldn't hire more workers until they could ship the orders. If they didn't fill the orders, merchants would turn to another factory, and we'd lose even more jobs.

I'll worry about it after everyone leaves.

I allowed Mrs. Green to put extra attention into my toilette again and braced myself to see Adrian. *To flirt.*

But he'd seated me between Nicholas and Mr. Chelmsford, as far away from himself as possible. His mother seemed a bit flustered and kept forgetting the seating arrangements, and he studiously avoided my eye.

He'd changed the arrangements at the last moment to avoid me, and I thought I knew why.

Heat still burned my chest as I remembered the way his touch seared me, and I could hardly attend to the conversation around me. I picked at my trifle while Adrian conversed awkwardly with Miss Blackburn.

Can't she see how forced his attention is? How unlike himself he's acting?

Adrian's false laughs jarred my nerves more than her shrill giggles.

I began to rearrange furniture in my mind to keep my headache at bay. I'd nearly gotten through the ground floor of all three estates before dinner ended.

Then there were parlor games again. I refurnished the guest bedrooms in my mind, wallpaper and all, before the night ended.

It was going to be an expensive evening.

I closeted myself in my library the next day while the others slept late, tracing the designs for new furniture arrangements and preparing wallpaper orders. I shuffled the sheets.

I'd left the cloister rooms untouched. The rooms where I grew up. The rooms where my parents lived after they were first married.

I couldn't leave Langton Abbey partially renovated, but I couldn't bear to finish the project. I tossed the orders in the fireplace.

It could wait.

My scheme could not. Like it or not, I had to learn to flirt. I'd done it accidentally in the labyrinth. Surely, I could do it with more success if I set my mind to it. I emerged from my library with fresh determination.

"Jennings, where is the house party?"

My butler pointed toward the rose garden.

I wavered.

His eyebrows raised a fraction of an inch. "What else do you require, madam?"

I glanced around the empty entryway. *No one.* I whispered, "Courage."

He shook his head. "You already have that."

I debated whether to admit my true dilemma. "I've never pursued this—ambition—before."

Jennings straightened even further, which didn't seem possible. "If you gave me a hint regarding your intention . . ."

I dropped my whisper so low that I almost couldn't hear myself. "I don't know how to flirt."

Jennings sniffed. "You don't need to. You are the baroness."

He was adorably infuriating, like most of the men in my life. He could help me, and he was the only person I dared ask. "What if I *want* to?"

Jennings's mouth twitched ever so slightly. "Mrs. Green stands unusually close at times. Quite inappropriate." His eyes drifted off to one side, and his face softened. "And she has a smile that she only smiles for me." He cleared his throat. "Be yourself, Lady Baxter. If Mr. Everard can't see—"

"Thank you, Jennings. I didn't say who—"

"Of course you didn't." He held open the door for me. "But he's blind, that man. Has been for years."

I picked my way toward the rose garden, through the densest part of the foliage. Beech trees and oaks tangled to form a thick canopy overhead. Sunlight streamed through brilliant crimson and golden leaves, while emerald laurel bushes lined the mossy path beneath.

The stillness and peace mocked me as my trepidation

grew. It was one thing to imagine flirting, but it was quite another to put it into practice.

So, I talked to Mama, as I always did when I was in her rose garden. "Mama, I know you're here." The wind rustled a reply. "You prepared me for my first Season, but you never made it to London."

The wind carried the words away.

"You told me how to avoid the men who would seek my fortune, but you never told me what to do if I fell . . ."

I wasn't in love. I batted at a fiery peach rose nearby, and the petals scattered in the dirt. The last blossoms of autumn were fading, but they still had life in them. Their vivid colors belied their fragile condition.

"What to do when I wanted to marry." How would I ever learn to allow a man near me, when I'd only been warned to keep men away?

But the breeze brought back no response, just a chill that cut through my shawl. I drew it around myself.

I was on my own, with nothing but my butler's ambiguous advice about my maid's flirting. I pinched my cheeks to pink them and bit my lips. That was all I'd learned in six Seasons in London.

"Is that you, Annie?" Nicholas's muffled voice barely made it through the canopy of trees and thick hedges.

I pinched my cheeks once more for good measure and plastered on a pleasant smile. Nicholas and Miss Winters rounded the corner.

Miss Blackburn gripped Adrian's arm possessively. "This area's quite overgrown, isn't it? The roses need pruning or removing altogether." Her shrill, affected laugh was too much for my nerves. Her slights had worn my patience thinner than the gauze overlay on her ostentatious dress.

She shrieked as the gauze caught on a thorny bramble.

No one who walked regularly in gardens would wear such finery outdoors unless they wanted to flaunt their wealth. Her boots shone as though new, without a single scuff.

How could he marry her? They were as different as a landscape painting and a meadow. While one was beautiful but lifeless, the other was vibrant and everchanging. Adge and I both preferred gardens over a library. We met outdoors nearly every day.

Lord Wetherspoon stepped forward, snapped a branch, and disentangled the skirt with a flourish. He looked around as though expecting applause. Miss Astbury clapped half-heartedly, and Miss Blackburn thanked him grudgingly. She shot me an accusatory look as if I'd ordered the roses to attack her. I would never harm my bushes like that.

The mishap had separated Miss Blackburn from Adrian momentarily while Lord Wetherspoon preened in front of the group.

This is my chance. I slipped my hand into the crook of Adrian's elbow, and he startled. "Mr. Everard."

He scuffed his well-worn boots in the dirt and pulled away. "Lady Baxter."

"May I join your party?"

Mr. Chelmsford glanced over, and Adrian was caught. He had to accept my offer.

"Delighted." He was anything *but* delighted. We walked with my fingertips barely touching the threads of his coat.

So much for standing close to him.

Miss Blackburn had noticed. Her voice drifted back in overly loud tones, as if she intended me to hear. "Holly trees are vulgar. A well-trimmed bush is sufficient. Why let them grow wild? If I lived here, I should pull out this entire section of garden."

My tree grew wildly, soaring majestically into the air.

White berries with a tinge of blush dotted the branches. The dirt path below my feet and the trees overhead absorbed every stray sound, until only the warbling of birds penetrated this nook.

I couldn't do it. I couldn't flirt when I wanted to strangle Miss Blackburn.

"You look a little flushed," Adrian said.

I panicked. He knew I'd been pinching my cheeks, and the thought mortified me.

"I'm sure you're angry," he said. "Please understand that she's used to London gardens. They're manicured."

Flirt. Don't be yourself. Flirt. I smiled a Mrs. Green smile.

Adrian recoiled.

That didn't work either.

I held on to his arm and quibbled with him in my mind. My gardens were well tended. I only let one section grow beautifully wild.

But he had defended *her* viewpoint. It was too late. I'd already lost my friend.

Miss Blackburn and Lord Wetherspoon took it in turns to complain while Miss Astbury, Mr. Chelmsford, Miss Winters, and Nicholas drew further and further ahead.

Adrian and I trudged behind the group, while he kept me at an arm's length. His jaw was set, and I didn't even attempt to converse with him.

"Especially that tree." Miss Blackburn's voice cut through our uncomfortable silence. She pointed to the kissing tree. "It's completely unkempt."

"Quite agree," Lord Wetherspoon muttered. "Quite right."

"Go ahead and join the others," I said to Adrian. "I'll rest here."

I left the trail and ducked under the branches of the tree to find my old bench. The interlacing canopy overhead filtered the light. Quiet enveloped me, and I sank my head into my hands. A chill sank into my bones, but I welcomed it. I pressed my cool hands against my cheeks and looked up.

Adrian stood inside the shelter of the tree. I rushed to stand and leave, but he pressed a hand onto my shoulder. "You really do look flushed. The shade will do you some good."

"We cannot be found alone here." *Not while we're at odds.*

Adrian shrugged. "No one will notice. They turned the corner toward the statuary."

I gaped at him. "You were furious with me a minute ago."

He collapsed on the bench beside me. "I've been with Miss Blackburn all day. Her voice has drilled a hole in my head, and I'm furious with the whole world." He tipped his head against the back of the bench. "I need a rest too."

But it wasn't quite that easy. "You'll have to get used to her voice when you marry her."

Adrian groaned. "Not here." He gestured around the domelike interior of the drooping beech tree. "This is our tree."

"There won't be any more hide-and-seek or long walks once you marry."

Adrian snorted. "You've been too proper to play for years." He tipped his head forward and opened his eyes. "It used to be fun." His gaze glittered with intent as he shifted.

The air grew still. Had the bench always been so narrow? Adrian's hip nudged mine, and I tried to scoot away. *No, I'm flirting.* I edged closer.

Adrian's legs bumped mine as he turned toward me. "Do you remember our last game of hide-and-seek?"

Too often. Fear flooded me. I shoved it aside. "Yes."

"I remember everything." Adrian pierced me with a gaze. "Every moment."

The memory of our childhood kiss beneath this tree flooded my mind.

"Every game," he said. For a moment, my longing seemed reflected on his face as his hand lifted slowly toward my cheek.

I never intended the flirting to feel so real.

"Every walk." His eyes searched mine. "Every dance." The tips of his fingers brushed my cheek, and my eyes fluttered closed on their own.

As they almost had a few days ago when Nicholas asked Adrian to demonstrate his skill.

This is an act. He was trying to distract me, just as I'd vowed to distract him.

My eyes flew open, and Adrian stopped. His hand cupped my face gently. Somehow my cheek rested there of its own accord. I drew myself up and brushed off my dress. "It's best if we join the others."

Adrian let go and crossed the small clearing. He held open the branches. "I'm sorry, Annie." His unguarded eyes held some kind of plea, but for what, I did not know. *Forgiveness? Understanding?*

I squeezed past him through the narrow opening, and his open arms called to me, like an unspoken invitation. I paused on the threshold between the shade of the tree and the blazing glare of the sunlight. "Thank you, Adge."

He saw me now.

He knew I was a woman. All these years, I'd felt overlooked.

But I'd never considered *him* as anything but a business partner either, and my whole world had just shifted.

I'd looked deep into his soul and discovered that he was in every corner of my own.

Chapter Six

ADRIAN ESCORTED ME TO FIND the others. Neither of us spoke as we ascended the hill lined with Roman statues in majestic poses. Ordinarily, he would have teased me about the nudes, but he didn't seem to have the heart to do it.

And I didn't have the heart to be teased.

"Why so pensive?" he finally asked.

I don't wish to discuss what almost happened. "It's autumn."

"And?"

You almost kissed me but didn't mean it. "The larches are fading to yellow, the hollies are turning red, and the swallows left last week. An entire flock, hundreds of them, lifted off my reflecting pool at dusk. I haven't seen them since."

Miss Blackburn watched us from the top of the hill.

Adrian stopped by a statue. "I've always admired Janus. He can face the past and the future at once."

I wished for cloud cover to shield my eyes. I turned away from the reflection of the alabaster marble. "I want everything to stay the same, all year. Every year. The swallows leave. I don't want anyone or anything else to change or leave."

Adrian scrutinized me with the same rational gaze he'd given the statue. "The anniversary of your parents' death is approaching."

An ache filled my chest. "I don't use calendars. I don't even know when January is."

Adrian tucked a finger beneath my chin and lifted my gaze to meet his. "You're a terrible liar. November thirtieth?"

I nodded. "The last day of autumn before winter begins." I reached for the locket I wore with my parents' portraits and pressed it to my heart.

Adge dug in his vest pocket, retrieved his handkerchief, and offered it to me.

"Nothing good came of *that* change." I wiped one misty eye, then the other.

Adrian took the handkerchief and wiped a stray tear from my cheek. "As sorry as I am, I cannot completely mourn the change. Now you are the baroness, and I conduct my father's business with you instead of your parents. We see each other nearly every day."

My chin wobbled. *That will change too.* I'd see him less frequently after he married, if I saw him at all.

He tucked the soggy handkerchief back into his pocket and sighed heavily. "Is it such misery to work with me?" I smiled weakly at him, and his mouth split into a wide grin.

We moved up the trail toward the faux temple. I composed myself as we ascended the incline.

Miss Blackburn waited impatiently at the top. While the others exclaimed over the architecture, she squinted at Adrian and me. When we passed the last statue, he muttered under his breath, "You've been sneaking out to see the nudes alone again. Admit it."

A laugh escaped me. We were almost back to our normal footing with each other and our old teasing. Miss Blackburn scowled. "What's the joke? Do enlighten us."

Adrian stepped forward. "I apologize for leaving you so long."

Miss Blackburn's face tightened. "I didn't realize how close you two are."

He dropped my arm.

Miss Blackburn trained her gaze solely on me. "You must be thrilled at the idea of getting a new neighbor."

I stood alone at the top of the hill. *Exposed.* The chatter of happy couples surrounded me, and Miss Blackburn waited for my response.

But I couldn't stomach the idea of her married to Adge. I smiled sweetly. "I haven't heard of anyone new moving into the neighborhood."

She narrowed her eyes. "You do know why Mr. Everard invited me here."

Adrian warned me with a look, which I ignored.

"I know why his *father* invited you here."

Miss Blackburn preened. "Then you should be expecting a new neighbor."

"Unless Mr. Everard's intended already lives here." I smiled politely as her eyes narrowed and her mouth dropped open.

I held my head high and stalked past her. I collapsed on the cool stone bench inside the dim interior of the temple and tipped my head against one wall. I had gone too far.

I had skipped flirting entirely and gone to direct confrontation. It was all I knew as a baroness.

Miss Blackburn could not doubt my intent now.

Neither could Adrian. I heard the frustration in his voice. "Fenton, will you accompany the others into town? I'll meet you at the Red Lion for dinner."

Miss Winters's voice floated into my hiding spot. "I've heard the food is exceptional. My friend insisted I try the sticky toffee pudding."

Miss Blackburn protested. "We can wait for Mr. Everard. I despise toffee pudding. So common."

Gravel crunched as the group departed, and I braced myself.

Adrian stormed into the cramped interior of the temple. His jaw was set, and his eyes blazed. He drew a deep breath. "I need a word with you."

I folded my arms defiantly. "Which word?"

Adrian scowled. "No."

I shrugged. "I have no idea what you mean."

He set a hand on either side of me and bent low. His voice was rough. "What was that?" Anger flashed in his eyes. "And earlier, under the tree? You've made it abundantly clear that you have no intention of marrying a fortune hunter like me."

I struggled to maintain my composure. With Adrian's intoxicating proximity, I could trace the outline of the day's stubble on his jaw. *Why do you want a fortune when I'm right in front of you?*

His voice rose. "Why would you undermine my efforts to save this town?" His eyes traveled over my face, and we studied each other for a long moment. His gaze lingered on my lips, and he pushed away from the bench. He fisted a hand as he swung away from me. "Why?"

He rested his fist against the interior wall of the temple, then dropped his head onto it as his shoulders slumped.

I drew myself up. "No one cares more about Langton than I do. No one worries more or works harder for its people than I do."

Adrian blew out a long breath but did not face me. "My father is desperate for the railway. If I don't marry, we cannot fund it, and I cannot promise what my father will do. Send me to the Caribbean to seek my own fortune. Shut the factory. He's rash, and the livelihood of every factory worker and of this entire town rests in your hands, yet you act as though it's a"—he glanced at me with obvious frustration—"it's a game."

Something heavy pressed on my chest. "You cannot marry Miss Blackburn. She's completely wrong for you, and it's not fair to her."

"She is the only choice I have," Adrian said, turning fully toward me. The cramped nook shrank even further.

"She would never stand up to your bullying." We hovered inches apart, close enough for me to see the vein straining in his neck. I longed to smooth the crease on his brow. "She doesn't like pudding."

"Please, Annie, leave me alone. Let me do this."

I pressed my palms into the cool stone bench. "I'm trying to help you, as a friend."

"A friend?" Adrian advanced until there was only a breath between us. Tension crackled in the air as he searched my face again. "Yesterday? Just now? That wasn't friendship."

My heart hammered in my chest and all my nerves ignited with his presence, begging him to pull me close.

But he drew back. "I have a duty to my father and our town."

I had to hear him say it, but my mouth couldn't form the words. I swallowed. "You're going to marry Miss Blackburn?" I finally asked.

He took another step back as his agonized voice pleaded with me. "I have no choice."

There's always a choice. The cold from the stone seeped into my bones, and I wrapped my arms around my middle. "Then I will not accompany you to the Red Lion tonight," I said. "Go ahead. Enjoy the pudding."

Adrian's shoulders slumped. "Are you certain? It's your favorite."

I nodded, and his eyes lost any spark they'd had. He shuffled outside.

As soon as he was out of sight, I stumbled out of the temple. I pressed a hand to my mouth to contain the sob building in my chest. Each step widened the fissures splitting my heart into jagged pieces. I rushed down the hill and back to the dying rose garden, where I could cry surrounded by memories of my parents.

Chapter Seven

Jennings informed me the next afternoon that the party was on the east lawn with my falcons. The ones I'd just begun to train. The ones that only responded to me and my gamekeeper.

I thanked him, stormed out of my library, and marched down the stone steps. The gamekeeper and the others were specks across the carefully manicured grass.

I scanned the skies, but none of my birds flew in the park area.

Someone noticed me, and the entire group turned around. Miss Blackburn whirled so quickly that my birds fluttered and fought against the cords binding them to the gamekeeper's arm.

Miss Blackburn stared at me accusingly. "Mr. Everard said you twisted your ankle."

Miss Winters glanced around. "No, Mr. Fenton said she fell ill." She lowered her voice and whispered, "One of her headaches."

I glanced at Nicholas. What else had he told her? What did he know about my argument with Adrian?

Nicholas cleared his throat. "Right. Are you recovered now?"

"Quite well." I avoided Adrian's gaze. "Only some business matters to attend to."

Miss Blackburn muttered something about *women* and *business* and *vulgar*, but the birds fluttered again at her shrill laugh.

"If you'll excuse me, my birds aren't accustomed to so much . . . activity. I'd best return them." I nodded to my gamekeeper and made to leave.

Adrian stopped me. "Cook promised me an apple-blackberry pie if we can find the berries. Shall we all search the hedges?"

I stared at him. "*My* cook?"

He pointed to a basket in his hand.

"Pick as many berries as you like." I started forward again, but Adrian stepped in my way.

"Will you join us, Lady Baxter?"

"My birds, Mr. Everard—"

"—will be returned." Adrian waved at my gamekeeper, who glanced at me. I nodded, and he left.

"Fenton only wanted to show them to the ladies."

Nicholas and Mr. Chelmsford had moved toward the hedges with Miss Astbury and Miss Winters. I didn't move but watched the silhouette of the birds as the gamekeeper retreated. Lord Wetherspoon finally convinced Miss Blackburn to join him.

Adrian lowered his voice. "I didn't mean for you to disappear entirely."

I bristled. "You said to leave you alone."

Adrian offered me his basket. "I've missed you."

I accepted it reluctantly. "I don't know why my cook and gamekeeper listen to you."

"There aren't any blackberries at my father's London townhouse or any falcons or hawks or deer."

I hooked the basket on my other arm. "Indeed."

Adrian's voice grew thick. "Will you not ask why I want one last blackberry pie from your garden?"

Miss Blackburn minced her dainty steps ahead of us. "The answer is apparent." But I did not want to hear it from him. *I'm not ready for it.*

Adrian scrubbed a hand down his face. "I need you with me today. Please, Annie."

"Your father gets Miss Blackburn's dowry for his railway, she gets to live in London, and you get a pie?"

He nodded miserably.

"That's a terrible bargain," I said. "Blackberry seeds get stuck in one's teeth and ruin the apple flavor."

Adrian still wouldn't fight with me. If sticky toffee pudding was my year-round favorite, autumn's fleeting apple-blackberry pie was undeniably his.

"Are you even listening?" I asked.

He trudged alongside me in melancholy silence. Miss Blackburn sent a dark look back at us.

"I'm moving to another estate when you marry," I said. "If your father's railway ruins my gardens, it won't be worth staying here."

Adrian kicked a pebble off the path.

"You're rather dull today," I said. His pale green eyes reflected the gray afternoon sky, turning almost colorless. A ripple of wind moved across his hair, lifting the bronze curls.

"What?" Adrian asked.

I shook myself. "I don't know why you needed me here if I cannot get a rise from you." I nudged him, and he smiled weakly.

He grunted. "You haven't agreed to the railway yet. No need for theatrics."

"That's better," I said. "I have not and will not."

He still refused to argue.

We veered away from the gravel walks and back onto the west lawn, where I allowed the thickets to grow. Miss Winters exclaimed, "What a charming view!"

Nicholas gazed at her with obvious admiration. "It is."

A flush crept up her cheeks. Miss Blackburn's face pinched, as though jealous. She flounced her skirt. "The path is too wide, and the raspberries are too close."

"Nature was much at fault when it allowed berries to grow thorns." The sarcasm in Adrian's tone was evident to me, but Miss Blackburn pursed her lips.

"Quite right. Nasty things." She narrowed her gaze at me. "Some people have no regard for others and let their gardens grow wild. If I lived here—"

Miss Winters interrupted, oblivious to Miss Blackburn's increasingly sour mood. "It's positively magical here. The mushrooms look like they're straight out of a children's book." She bent over the red toadstools with white knobbly buttons on top. "When I have my own garden, I shall let a portion of it run wild for the birds."

Nicholas tossed a nervous glance back at me. He didn't have his own estate to offer Miss Winters, but she evidently didn't know that. "Ah, yes, here are the berries." His attempt to redirect the conversation worked. Miss Winters squealed in delight and began filling her basket with ripe raspberries and blackberries.

The few remaining birds that had not left for the winter still warbled in the bushes. Miss Blackburn hugged her skirt. She eyed Adrian and the raspberries more warily than one of my falcons.

Miss Astbury and Mr. Chelmsford walked together, and Lord Wetherspoon headed directly for me.

"I'll check on my birds," I said and ducked into a side row, then turned another corner. I collapsed on a bench and hoped Lord Wetherspoon wouldn't follow me. I could only handle so much, and he was too much.

Footsteps passed my hidden nook, and I breathed a sigh of relief. It was an overcast day with only a slight breeze, and the smell of autumn hung in the air.

Miss Blackburn's tight voice carried distinctly through the hedge. "Lady Baxter recovered quickly from her illness."

Adrian's response penetrated the thicket. "What? Yes, she's fine."

I froze. Leaves rustled behind me. They must not have noticed me through the hedge.

"What did you say she had? A fever?"

"Who?" Adrian's thoughts were clearly as scattered as the leaves falling around me.

Miss Blackburn persisted. "Lady Baxter."

"What? No, she's fine."

More rustling. I shrank, afraid to move, and afraid of what I might hear.

"You said she fell ill." The petulant tone in Miss Blackburn's voice drove it an octave higher.

The rustling stopped. "Did I?"

"Her illness was obviously manufactured."

"I don't believe I have the pleasure of understanding you." Adrian's voice sounded stilted and formal.

As I popped a berry into my mouth, a burst of sour and sweet greeted me. Adrian was like that—vexation and kindness bundled together.

"Let me be clear." Miss Blackburn's voice was low and deadly serious now. "That woman is as false and manipulative as they come, and if you can't see that, Mr. Everard, you're a fool."

Silence.

"If you think I don't see the way she's flirting with you, you're wrong. I have no intention of marrying anyone who carries on with another woman."

I waited for Adrian to defend me, but he remained silent.

"You can choose now. Me or her."

A branch snapped. I sat rooted to my spot, unable to breathe or move.

I heard the dangerous undertone in his voice. "Would you have me cut off a friendship of seventeen years, our daily correspondence, all business communications, and give her the cut direct in this social sphere? She is the baroness and the largest landholder in the area. She's nobility as well as one of my oldest friends."

I held my breath. He would never betray me.

A shrill laugh. "How old *is* she? She couldn't even buy a husband with her title. Lord Wetherspoon says she's been on the shelf for years."

I shrank on the bench and threw away the berry in my hand. Aunt was wrong. *This* was the way people spoke behind my back.

Miss Blackburn's voice returned to an artificially sweet pitch with a distinctly threatening undertone. "You cannot expect me to live in a cramped London townhome forever. If I'll be spending my dowry to purchase her gardens, I may as well buy the abbey, too. Lady Baxter can live alone elsewhere. She doesn't need a vast estate all to herself. It would be selfish of her to keep it when I require it."

I squeezed my eyes shut as tremors shook my body. He would never agree to this. Never.

"Is that clear?" Every word was a shard of ice.

Adrian replied, "Perfectly clear," and my heart shattered.

For the sake of a noisy and unsightly railway, he would sacrifice everything. Himself. Our friendship.

Things that weren't his to give away.
My estate.
My garden.
My memories.
Me.

Chapter Eight

❦

NICHOLAS NOTCHED OPEN THE DOOR of my library. "We're leaving for dinner at Everard's estate. I gave Cook the berries."

I kept my eyes on the papers in front of me and sighed in exasperation. "Enjoy yourself." I tapped the papers meaningfully. "Lots to do."

Nicholas grinned. "He promised us dancing. We'll have enough couples if you come."

"The heiresses' parents can all dance."

"Everard said you'd refuse. Something about avoiding Wetherspoon."

He has no idea who I'm avoiding. "I've had my fill of Miss Blackburn." *And Adge.*

The grin fell from his face. "So have I, truth be told." He shifted on his feet.

I pointed at the door. "I've work to do."

Nicholas bowed ridiculously low. "Your baron-ladyshipness." A hint of sadness lurked behind his playful demeanor.

"Miss Winters leaves tomorrow?"

Nicholas lounged against the door frame. He propped open my library door with his foot. "Aye."

He wouldn't ask me outright. He and Aunt were too aware of their dependence on me. It was up to me, again, to ensure the happiness and tranquility of those around me, no matter the cost to myself.

I shuffled the papers. "I'm in a bind. The steward at Beckingham is growing old. If you ever wished to marry, you could live there as a favor to me."

Nicholas examined his fingernails casually. "If you *really* need me."

"I won't accept any other answer."

Nicholas whooped. The door slammed as he ran down the hall, then it crashed open. "Thank you, cousin." He disappeared in a frantic blur.

Nicholas and Aunt would leave me alone at Langton Abbey. My chest tightened, and I had a sudden need to visit the one place I'd abandoned for years.

I wandered to the entryway. Jennings raised an eyebrow ever so slightly. "It's nearly dusk."

"I'll be in the sunken garden."

He wrapped my mother's scarf around my shoulders and opened the entryway door for me. "Take care. It's grown damp and chill out there."

"You fuss like an old man," I said.

Jennings maintained his soldier-like post by the thick wooden doors. "I *am* an old man."

I patted his arm as I passed him. "You're nearly as bad as Mrs. Green."

"I was here before her," he said, catching my eye. "I'll always be here."

I wrapped the wool scarf tighter around myself. "Thank you, Jennings."

"Come back for dinner," he said. "You haven't eaten all day."

I nodded and started down the steps. A chill shot through me as I reached for the stone balustrade. I picked my way through the overgrown trees of the west lawn until I reached the section, north of the abbey, that led to the sunken garden.

An old cloister formed a square courtyard around the sunken garden's overflowing terraces. I slipped through the abandoned halls until I found the entrance and rested against the stone arches that overlooked the worn steps.

I explored every inch of the old cloister, running my fingers around the intricate arches. Memories of my parents and childhood filled the corridors and reflected back to me in the pond's glassy ripples.

Time escaped me as I stared at the rosemary and lavender, the daisies and wild comfrey. *I can't believe Adrian chose her over me.* Thoughts crashed into each other, overwhelming me. *Could I leave my home? Does my valley need the railway more than it needs me?*

"Anne?" Adrian's voice startled me. I tipped my head against the cool stone without turning to face him.

"Jennings said you'd be here."

I came here to escape you.

He appeared behind me, but I studied the reflection of the plants in the center pool. Rows of herbs and flowers led down to the mossy water. Even the stone arches glittered on the surface of the pool's mirrored images.

Finally, I answered. "I'm here."

"Why?"

A tug in my stomach pulled buried feelings from the depths. "This is the one garden that can never change, enclosed by the cloister's walls."

The fabric of Adrian's coat brushed against the shoulder of my dress. "It's a shame you don't use the rooms in this part of the abbey. They're my favorite."

"Six years," I said. "I haven't stepped foot inside for six years."

Adrian nudged me. "I thought you didn't have a calendar."

"I can still count. I still have birthdays."

The wind rippled the water of the reflecting pool.

"Speaking of birthdays..." Adrian drew something from behind his back. "I brought you a present." An arm wrapped around me as he peeled my hands off the pillar and pressed something into them.

A torrent of emotion overwhelmed me, but a sense of propriety overrode everything else. "We must go inside." I explored the unmistakable outline of his gift.

"Jennings sent a message." Adrian cleared his throat and spoke in an uncanny, nasal impersonation of my old butler. "I can chaperone from here." He grinned, and his voice returned to normal. "I asked Cook to make you apple pudding for dinner tonight."

I hefted the rough wooden birdbox in my gloved hands. "Thank you. Shouldn't you be with your guests?"

"They'll meet me in half an hour. Fenton took them in your carriage."

I hugged the gift to my chest. "You remembered." *Even though you're leaving me.*

"I always remember." Adrian grimaced. "You're going to hate this one." He tapped the box, and it echoed hollowly.

I examined the contours and turned it over. "A train?"

Adrian laughed. "The birds won't know any different."

"I will."

Adrian held out a hand. "Come, let us hang it."

I glanced around. "I cannot be alone with you, not with your recent engagement."

Adrian's hand fell slowly. "I'm not betrothed yet."

I ran a finger lightly over the details of the locomotive as my mind tried to comprehend the idea of him married to Miss Blackburn.

"Let me hang your train with the other boxes, and I'll walk you back."

Our eyes met in the deepening dusk. Streaks of gold and crimson and pink shot through the clouded sky. Adrian drew the pelisse around my shoulders as he gazed down at me.

I thrust my birthday gift at him. The rough edges scraped my skin even through the silk gloves. *I need distance from you.*

He took the birdbox, climbed down into the sunken garden, and hung it on a peg he'd brought. His familiar form stretched, balancing on his right leg, with the nail between his teeth. His tongue stuck out the way it always did when he concentrated.

There they were. A row of birdboxes. *Six.* One for every birthday since my parents had died. *How much more loss can I bear?*

We left the cloister. Adrian didn't complain when I chose the longer, outdoor path instead of walking through the haunted hallways of my childhood. We wound through the thickets toward the abbey as streaks of scarlet and gold deepened in the sky overhead.

A red fox rounded the path, and we stopped. It cocked its head, curious, and considered Adrian, then stared at me, as if it could see into my soul.

The fox was trying to tell me something with its wise eyes. I grasped for the meaning.

"Annie?"

You can't stay here forever. The fox flicked its bushy tail, and its slim body vanished beneath a hedge. I took a deep breath and forced myself forward. Damp air filled my lungs.

The scent of leaves and dirt and autumn hovered around me.

Adrian's hands fisted at his side. "I'm sorry."

"For what?"

He pulled a letter from his pocket. "This is an offer to buy Langton Abbey." He stared at something in the distance. "You don't need all three estates, do you?"

Anger burned in my chest with a tremendous weight of sadness. "The baroness title belongs to the Beckingham estate. That is the only one I must keep."

He flicked a glance up and then away. "I know."

My strength left me, and I fought to stay upright. *You're really going to do it.*

"Are you well?" Adrian jammed the letter back into his coat pocket, wrapped an arm around my waist, and pulled me toward the abbey.

"Miss Blackburn? Live here? Tear out the hedges and my rose garden and—"

Adrian crushed me in a hug. "Stop." His arms wrapped around me, and I could hardly breathe. "I won't let her—I'll take good care of the abbey. I promise. You can visit us."

Us? I wanted to hit him or hate him, but I couldn't. I wrapped my arms around his neck and clung to him.

But I had to let go, for the village, for the factory, for Langton.

What I want doesn't matter.

"I'll sign it," I said. I ran my hand inside his coat to get the letter, and Adrian drew a deep, shuddering breath. My hand rested on his chest for a split second as our eyes met. I withdrew the contract. "Farewell, Adge."

"Happy birthday." He sounded miserable, for a man about to get engaged.

I tried to pull away. "I asked Cook to make a pie for you."

His arms still rested on my waist.

I couldn't bring myself to look up at him. *This is what I want.*

Adrian's voice choked with emotion. "Thank you."

The sun dipped below the horizon as he drew me into another hug. The agreement to sell my childhood home crumpled in my hand as I held on tightly. "Good night, Adge."

We held each other's gaze in the darkening dusk. Emotions raged inside me. Sorrow that I'd lost my friend. Hurt that he'd betrayed me. Anger at Miss Blackburn. Relief that the village would survive and thrive in my absence. Fear of what changes the future would bring. *Loneliness.*

And the pain of losing the only tangible memory of my parents, the home where we'd lived together.

Adrian let out a deep breath. "I really am sorry. I wish things were different." His voice was as raw as the daggers piercing my heart.

"Thank you." A sob threatened to escape, so I turned my back on Adrian and rushed away.

My strength disappeared when I reached the steps. I gathered my crinoline hoop in one hand and dragged myself up, one step at a time, clinging to the balustrade with the other hand. I stopped halfway, certain that Adrian couldn't see me in the dim light, and pressed my locket to my chest. *Mama, Papa, I need you more than ever.* I thought I might collapse and laid my head on the balustrade.

An acorn skimmed the waist of my skirt. I whirled around. Adrian hunched in the cover of the towering holly tree, watching me. I straightened and ascended the stairway slowly, but every step cost me.

I turned back.

He was still there. Still watching me.

The ancient oak door creaked open.

Adge waved.

I couldn't wave back. One hand clutched the contract to sell Langton Abbey, and the other held my parents' locket.

"Close the door, Jennings," I said softly. "That will be all tonight."

Chapter Nine

"Miss Winters wishes to return for another visit as soon as possible," Nicholas said, grinning.

I smiled through the late breakfast. It took all my years of training and every bit of strength I had.

"She credits our engagement to your encouragement. She never would have dreamed it possible without your help."

I smiled again. His raptures had taken the entire morning, and I hadn't managed to get a single sentence into the conversation between my aunt and my cousin.

Miss Winters's fortune was only one of her many virtues. He was not overly concerned with her dowry since I'd promised the use of Beckingham to him. Her kindness, her cheerfulness, her considerate nature, all had to be detailed with numerous examples from the past week and the last Season.

Aunt was thrilled to see her only child so happy, and I was delighted for them both. I could not spoil their day with the news that I'd be moving to my furthest estate, Windmore, and selling the abbey.

I listened to Nicholas's happy chatter and tried not to

reflect on my own misery. Adrian was certainly engaged by now. Miss Blackburn was leaving and would return to become mistress of my childhood home.

I pushed away my teacup.

"Happy birthday, sweets." Aunt kissed me on the cheek. "I forgot in the excitement yesterday." She dimpled a gentle smile at me. "I've ordered you the entire set of willow-patterned china."

I hugged my aunt. "Thank you."

Nicholas hung back. "Thank *you*, cousin."

"Your happiness is my own."

He eyed me shrewdly. How much did he know, as Adrian's closest friend? I hoped Adrian had not had time to talk with him, and kept an artificial smile on my face.

"I'll sleep better knowing that you and Aunt are caring for Beckingham. It has the best dower cottage of any estate."

Nicholas fiddled with his cuff links. "But you'll visit us for Christmas and Easter, and you won't spend holidays alone."

"Go ahead with the marriage settlements, and I'll have my solicitor arrange everything."

Nicholas wrapped me in a brief, but tight, hug.

"You're the only family I have left," I said. "Thank you for helping me out."

Nicholas grinned. "Happy to be of service." He studied me. "You're certain you don't wish to live at Beckingham with us?"

"No," I reassured him. "It's far too grand for my tastes."

But Nicholas continued to study me with a serious air.

I motioned toward the drawing room. "You and Aunt have plenty to discuss."

Nicholas frowned. "Not another headache?"

I pushed away from the table. "No, just tired. Go ahead." His perceptive look unsettled me. Perhaps he *had* spoken with

Adrian about the sale of Langton Abbey, but I refused to intrude and live at Beckingham with Nicholas and his bride.

Jennings watched me as I left the dining room.

"You're still here, old man?"

"Always," he said. "I'm not leaving."

"Thank you."

Would it be selfish to ask him to come to Windmore with me?

I wandered to the library, cleared the papers off my mother's mahogany desk, and tried to find something that required my attention, but nothing could distract me from the sick feeling in the pit of my stomach.

I paced around the room. Even with the extra wood, the rooms felt frigid in the mornings now. I returned to my bedchamber.

Mrs. Green treated my arrival the way Nicholas indulged in Mrs. Rymer's sweet shop. She clapped her hands, then threw open the wardrobe. "Oh my! Let's change your gown." She pulled out a ridiculous confection of ruffles and silk.

"Perhaps something warm? Something wool."

Mrs. Green patted my hair. "We could braid this."

I batted her hand away. "My hair looks well enough for the squirrels who will see it, and those dresses will keep until next Season."

She heaved a deep sigh. "Just as they kept from last Season and the Season before."

"Very well," I said. "If it'll make you feel better, we can order a new dress from Mrs. Rowntree."

She rustled the gowns in my wardrobe. "It'd make me feel better if you'd *wear* one of the new ones you already purchased. You didn't wear a single ruffle or frill this week, even with Lord Wetherspoon here." She pointed at dress after dress until I couldn't stand it.

Mrs. Green looked as though someone had died. I held out my arms. If I could make her happy so easily, it would be worth it today. "Select anything you wish, even though no one will see it."

She slipped the frilly dress over my head in an instant.

"I intend to stain this dress by sitting on a bench in the orchard."

"Hallelujah! I'll have some work to do at last." Mrs. Green had selected my most flattering dress. Mrs. Rowntree had ordered the fabric specifically to match my eyes. The brilliant periwinkle silk had an obscene number of ruffles. Well, two rows on the skirt, but really, that felt excessive, and the sleeves were broad enough to fit two arms in each side, yet the waist cinched my stomach in half.

"The proportions are all wrong on this dress," I complained. "How am I supposed to climb apple trees in this?"

"You're not." Mrs. Green patted my hair one last time. "Bless my soul. You do make me proud."

"If this is all it takes . . ."

Mrs. Green pushed me out the door. "Don't sit on any benches."

"I'm sitting on my favorite bench."

"Och. The nobility are a stubborn lot."

I pinched her cheek. "Thank you, Mrs. Green."

"Get on with you."

Jennings greeted me at the entrance. "Are you coming back for lunch? You didn't touch your breakfast."

"Do you watch everything I eat?"

He sniffed. "Every meal."

I couldn't help smiling. He was right. I hadn't eaten much the last day or two. I couldn't. "I'll eat anything you wish when I return." I patted his arm as I passed him. "Thank you."

His brows shot up. "Then I'll tell Cook to put double portions on your plate." He draped my favorite paisley shawl around my shoulders. My mother's shawl. I traced the design on my shoulders. His face softened. "That's better."

The crisp morning air bit at my cheeks. I blew out a breath, and a cloud of fog formed in front of me. Dew glistened on the grass like a sea of glass. I drew my shawl tighter to keep out the chill. To protect me. Like Mama always had.

I wound my way through the gardens to the pear trees and apple orchard. Mist hung over them like a snowy cloud. We'd only have a few more weeks to harvest the fruit before a true frost arrived.

I wandered through the hazy lines of trees, little soldiers lined up in long rows. The church towered at the other end of my orchard, and the silhouette of Langton Village rose and fell behind it. Somewhere, on the other side, Adrian was working feverishly on plans for the railway. Had he slept terribly too, or had he slept soundly?

I picked an apple and settled on a bench, taking care to tuck a portion of my shawl beneath myself. The shawl was large enough to wrap my entire body, so I certainly had enough to spare for my silk gown.

My mind worked feverishly, trying to imagine ways to delay the inevitable as thoughts swirled in my head like the clouds drifting in front of me. I didn't want to do it. How long could I put off signing the contract? Marriage settlements took months. They didn't have to move into the estate immediately. The railway would need more study before they began work.

Change swirled around me, but I was stuck in the past, unable to conceive of a future different from the life I knew. I wished to live in perpetual summer, but without autumn and winter, the seeds would not fall from the tree to grow in the spring.

The swallows could build new nests. The foxes could find new dens. *Not me.* I clung to memories and hid in an endless stream of duties and obligations without thinking or feeling.

And my village, the workers, the shops, and the poor would all suffer unless I left and sold my home to Adge and his new bride.

I took a bite of the apple. The tart flavor startled me, just as the sting of my parents' death had never lessened. The apples, stored over the winter, would mellow with age, becoming richer and almost sweet.

I'd had six years to accustom myself to the loss of my parents, but the loneliness never dissipated. A few rose bushes couldn't replace my family.

But what if I let go? If I allowed myself to change? What would I find?

Adrian's dimpled smile filled my mind. And I knew—the real reason I opposed Adrian's engagement. I loved him.

I threw the apple across the orchard and fought my way blindly through the trees. That was the reason his marriage upset me.

I *was* jealous.

I pushed my way out of the last tree and stumbled onto the cobblestone street leading into the village. I ran my fingers over the coarse texture of the flint wall and wandered aimlessly down the deserted street. Evidently it wasn't market day.

That was a relief.

A heavy thump rattled the door of the prison cell, a single room along one side street. "Who's there?"

I hesitated. If I walked quickly, I could pretend I hadn't heard.

A voice cried out. "That you, Lady Baxter?"

I sighed, and my shoulders drooped. *I need to be alone. I need to think.* I peeked through the eye-level slit in the door. "Yes."

A familiar figure slumped against the wall. "Out for your usual morning walk?"

"Yes, Mr. Beck. Had a long night at the pub?"

He laughed. "Your cousin put me in here, buying rounds and all. Congrats to him and the grand lady."

I reached for my locket. The cool oval necklace nestled in my palm and gave me strength. "I'm delighted for Mr. Fenton." *Even if I'll be alone again.*

Mr. Beck collapsed on the small bench in the tiny one-room cell. My eyes had adjusted to the dim light of his space. "Fancy misses and their folks came to the pub with him the other night, but you're still my favorite, if I say so."

"How kind." Restlessness propelled me forward. "I'd best return now. Good day."

"You always stop and talk to me, no matter how many times I'm here."

To my horror, he began to cry. I couldn't leave him. Not like this.

"Me and the missus lost our jobs and food is scarce, but you never let us go hungry." He wiped his eyes on his thin shirt. "I always say to my missus, 'The abbey will look after us.'"

"I will." Panic set in. Miss Blackburn wouldn't care for people like the Becks. She wouldn't give to the parish poor. Who would care for my village when I left?

"I tell people, Lady Baxter and I, we're friends. She don't care if she's noble. She talks to me like I'm not dirt."

"We are friends, Mr. Beck." I tried to catch his eye through the narrow slit. "Another factory job will open soon." *As soon as Adge marries.*

"I've been waiting months," he said. "Don't know how much longer we can hold on or where to go. I've lived here me whole life, and my dad before me, and his dad before him. I love Langton, but Mr. Blackburn is offering half-wages to any what will move. Half-wages is better than none."

"Don't move," I said desperately. "Help is coming sooner than you realize. I promise." I winked dramatically. "I know you'll keep our conversation secret and not tell a soul. Big changes are coming."

Mr. Beck closed his eyes. "Bless you." He wiped his eyes again. "The little ones won't go to sleep hungry anymore."

He saluted me, and I rushed home, thinking desperately the entire way. Mr. Beck would certainly tell the entire town of our conversation. Hopefully no workers would leave Mr. Everard's factory to work in cruel conditions for half-wages at Mr. Blackburn's factory.

But I had to do more. *I cannot neglect my responsibilities.* Miss Blackburn would tear out my thorny brambles without seeing the beauty of the rose blossoms. Would she see how much Mr. Beck and others like him were needed, or would she only see their poverty?

I couldn't stop Adge from marrying Miss Blackburn. The railway needed to be built as soon as possible for the sake of the factory and the workers, but I wouldn't sell Langton Abbey.

I would fund the railway myself.

Chapter Ten

I *COULD* FUND THE RAILWAY. I might have to borrow funds from my other estates initially, but it had to be done.

I picked up my skirt and flew toward the abbey, calculating sums the entire time.

I rifled through the papers on my desk as soon as I arrived and found Adrian's proposal. I read every detail, recalculated costs, considered locations, and sketched possible routes. A line running parallel to the canal would be most disruptive to my garden but least expensive.

There was an ancient oak, however, that Adrian disregarded. If I sketched the line slightly lower, the railway could still use my orangery as a depot, avoid uprooting the oak, and only raise the cost slightly.

I got lost in calculations. It was easier than imagining Adrian engaged to Miss Blackburn.

I tried sketching a third line around the far edge of my property, but it quickly became apparent that Adrian was correct. The cost was prohibitive, and the amount of dynamite required to remove the hillside would make the work more dangerous for my men.

The only way to move goods in and out of Langton was through my garden. My grandparents' pleasure garden. The temple would be leveled. The Roman statues could be removed and placed elsewhere. The sheep would graze in other pastures.

My parents' roses and berries would have to be transplanted, but I could keep my apple orchard and the kissing tree.

I collected all the old sketches and figures and walked to the fireplace. I removed Aunt's embroidered screen so I could watch the flames, but I kept a respectable distance. If a cinder melted the silk of my skirt, Mrs. Green would be heartbroken.

Nevertheless, I had to do this. I threw in old sketches and calculations. *Useless.* And the numbers. Page after page curled in the hearth's flames.

And the offer to sell Langton Abbey. I tore it in miniscule pieces, imagining Miss Blackburn's vow to tear out my blackberry hedges and rose garden.

I will decide what happens here.

I watched the edges of the sheets blackening in the fire. The paper disintegrated to ash, and tiny pieces threatened to float out of the fireplace.

I quickly replaced the screen and scrambled to find the ledger with numbers from my other estates. I sank back in my chair. It would cost far more than I realized.

I couldn't fund the railway unless I sold Windmore. I'd have to live here, in the same valley as Adrian, and be Miss Blackburn's neighbor. I'd have to see the man I love married to someone else.

I had a duty to Mr. Beck and the hundreds of other people in this valley that couldn't be measured in neat rows on ledgers. I wanted to be the one to see the children thriving, the families well fed, and the High Street shops alive.

Adge could use Miss Blackburn's dowry to pay off the factory loans, hire more workers, make improvements, and expand his holdings.

Everyone would benefit, except me.

I prepared to have the hardest conversation of my life. I copied the numbers from the ledger, arranged Adge's apple-blackberry pie in a wicker basket, and set out.

I threaded my way through the orchard again, across the gravel path, up the hill, past the Greek statues, around the temple, and over to the canal.

A boat had to come along sometime soon. *Anytime.* It had taken me a couple hours to draw up the plans, so it had to be afternoon by now. I drew my shawl around myself and paced up and down the trail in front of the canal. I could hardly see either way because the fog settled low into the channel.

I grew impatient with waiting and paced to the next stop along the canal route. It must have taken twenty minutes. I did not own a calendar, but I *did* pin on my timepiece today. I still had hours before it grew dark.

The damp air settled into my bones. Silk dresses were not ideal for misty weather. They were meant for ballrooms, not canal trails. I climbed the steps back to the street.

I was barely halfway through the village; perhaps the canal trail was *not* faster. I rushed through Langton as quickly as I could without running. I turned past the church and row houses. Wind whipped my cheeks, and the basket wobbled on my arm. I passed the pub and the stagecoach without caring who saw my wild state.

I was out of breath, but still I walked faster than I ever had. A long meadow stretched on one side, and Adrian's home was at the far end of the lane.

A dark figure moved in the distance. It approached as I

hurried along the cobblestone street. Finally, Adrian's form resolved itself in the fog.

"Anne? What are you doing here?"

I shoved the basket into his hands. "The canal wasn't running."

"It's Sunday."

I stopped. "Oh." I'd have to attend evensong, as usual.

Adrian lifted the basket lid and stared inside. "I could have waited for this." He took in my appearance. "How long have you been walking? You have dew on your lashes." He balanced the basket on one arm and offered a handkerchief with his other hand.

I wiped the moisture from my eyes and drew the letter from the basket. "I must speak with you."

A crease furrowed his brow. "About pie?" His wrinkled, collarless shirt laid open, and dark hollows sunk beneath his eyes.

My sense of urgency intensified, yet I could not formulate a single word. I shivered and drew my shawl tight. "The letter."

"We must get inside quickly, or you'll get a chill. There's nothing but meadow here." Adrian gestured toward the steps down to the canal. "There's a boat docked below."

We advanced along the canal path, with Adrian glancing frequently at me, and stopped at a dust-covered stone bench in front of the gently moving water. The fog and mist had settled on the bench, making the dust into a thick paste.

Adrian took out another handkerchief and wiped the bench. The dust became a layer of mud. He groaned in frustration and led me to a waiting boat, moored to the canal station. The thick rope bobbed with the motion of the river's tide.

"It's dry in here." He opened the door and ducked inside

the small cabin. "Looks safe. Only tobacco stains and stale cigar smoke."

I picked my way across the dock. "You make it sound so appealing."

Adrian grinned and threw back his shoulders. "You're welcome."

I shook my head. *I shouldn't be here with you.* "Be serious for a moment. Please."

"I am." The grin died on his face as I entered the doorway. The canal ship had a tiny cabin, just barely big enough for two men to operate the boat while seated. My wide hoop skirt, his tall frame, and the wide-open door made the space very cramped.

Adrian swallowed and reached around me, still balancing the basket on his arm. "I, uh, cannot close the door to keep the fog and chill out."

I tried to move forward, but there wasn't anywhere to go. "Shall we say that Jennings is chaperoning us?"

Adrian laughed awkwardly as he set the basket on the control panel. "No one comes here on Sunday. It's just for a few minutes. I'd escort you to my estate, but you must warm up first."

We leaned into each other as he reached for the handle, until I was practically hugging Adge. He stretched an arm around my shoulders. "Almost there."

My skirt swayed. "Sorry." I pushed it aside as he lunged for the door. The chill breeze disappeared as the door finally clicked shut, and I sighed with relief.

My skirt swayed again, knocking the precariously balanced basket, and the apple-blackberry pie threatened to slide out. Adrian grabbed the basket, tipping the pie back inside, but his arms also caught me with the basket pressed against my back.

He gingerly set the basket on the floor and dropped onto a stool. "Sorry—I—it's my last pie." Adrian gestured toward the captain's seat. "Please."

I seated myself as daintily as possible, but the control panel was in the way. I swiveled my knees one direction, and Adrian swung his another. My crinoline hoop tried to collapse halfway, as though I were seated on a sofa, and I could only smile and hope he didn't notice.

"Why is your dress lopsided?"

"Honestly, Adge, I ran halfway across the county to find you, and that's the first thing you say?"

"The first thing I said was that it was Sunday."

I blew out an exasperated breath. "Must you be so literal?"

"Must your dress take up half the county?"

We glared at each other, but a laugh escaped me when his glare changed to a smirk.

He huddled on the tiny seat, folding himself nearly double. Clearly the canal company only employed short men.

Adrian closed his eyes and shook his head. "What was so blasted urgent about this pie? You're frozen through, and if you fall ill, I don't think I can take much more after the week I've had."

He was at the edge of his patience, and I had to act. "Will you hear me out?"

He shifted on the stool and grumbled, "I'll be sore tomorrow."

The windows in the cramped cabin had fogged over. I couldn't see outside the boat. I could only see the present. Right here, right now, the man in front of me. *Adrian.*

But how to begin the conversation? I handed the letter to him. "Don't interrupt me for anything."

He shoved it into his coat pocket without looking. "This isn't necessary."

"It's very necessary. Promise you will listen to every word."

He rested his head in his hands but finally answered without looking up. "Yes."

I took a deep breath. "I refuse to sell Langton Abbey to you."

His head shot up. "Then why did you sign the contract?"

"I didn't. Miss Blackburn is awful, and she won't take care of Mr. Beck. I don't care how drunk he is. He's *my* town drunk and my responsibility. And my friend."

Adge's eyes widened.

"I'll sell Windmore, not Langton Abbey, and *I'll* fund the railway. I'll choose which bushes stay and which bushes go, not your blasted Miss Blackburn."

The side of his mouth tilted in a half-grin, which seemed odd.

"The letter is a counterproposal to your father. You and your bride will have to find somewhere else to live because she'll never have my abbey."

His grin widened. "What if I want to live at Langton Abbey with my bride?"

I tried to stand. *My heart cannot take this.* "I've said all I came to say." But my hoop skirt refused to budge.

Adge grabbed my hands and pulled me down. "It's your turn to listen."

I shoved my crinoline hoop to one side. "Mrs. Green insisted I wear this dress."

Adrian eyed my dress from top to bottom. His eyes warmed in obvious appreciation. "It's still my turn, and I've always liked that dress."

Don't start noticing me now. You're engaged to someone else. "I have to leave."

He seemed to brace himself. "You don't need to sell

anything." He drew my counteroffer out of his coat and set it on the boat's control panel beside the pie. I remembered the feel of his strong chest beneath my hands. His shirt hung open at the top where he'd neglected to wear a collar, and his coat hung loosely.

Adge cleared his throat, and my cheeks burned. "You can keep your abbey and Windmore."

"Why?"

He pushed my skirt down and trapped me in the small space. "Promise to hear me out."

"I will not."

"I listened to you."

"No." I could see every eyelash, every speck of gold in his pale green eyes.

"I'm going to make my own fortune—"

There was nowhere to escape. "That's utterly ridiculous."

"My father will disown me. I'll have to leave for the Caribbean, as he threatened."

"He wouldn't. He blusters but never follows through. Besides, you did as he asked."

"I refused to propose to Miss Blackburn. Her father is furious, and so is mine."

I laughed, although I only felt shocked. What about the factory and the village?

"You cannot be serious."

He was.

I closed my eyes as I tried to absorb it all. They fluttered open, but I couldn't form words. "You are not . . . ?"

"Not engaged."

I covered my mouth with a hand, then let go. "Why would you leave?" I sagged against the dusty wall of the boat's cabin. Mrs. Green could wash the scarf later.

A crease furrowed his brow. "I have to live. My father's serious this time. He'll cut me off."

"But I'll fund the railway." I couldn't decide if I felt giddy with relief or ill at the thought of him leaving. Perhaps both. I closed my eyes again.

Something warm enveloped my hands. "Annie?"

"I don't feel well," I whispered. I had to say something. I could never have hoped or dreamed for a chance like this, but the fear of losing Adge paralyzed me. I forced myself to open my eyes. "If you married another heiress who could fund the railway, would your father approve? It doesn't have to be one that he picked."

Adrian stopped wobbling on his stool. His boots landed hard on the cabin floor. "I won't. I tried. I would never—" He hung his head. "I can't."

"I know someone with three estates and more money than any of the other heiresses."

His head whipped up, and he edged forward, a hungry look of disbelief in his eyes. "You said you wouldn't marry me. I'm a fortune hunter."

"I never said that." I tilted my chin up. "I said I wouldn't marry until a man saw me for who I am."

Adrian's voice was gravelly. "I see how lovely you look in that color."

"It's periwinkle," I said breathlessly.

He stripped off his gloves, one finger at a time, then gazed at me in wonderment. "You'd consider me?"

I steadied myself with a hand on either side of the captain's seat. "I can't lose you. You've been the one constant in my life since I was seven."

"A constant nuisance," he said, scooting closer to me. He peeled the gloves off my fingers, slowly, one at a time, letting his bare touch linger on my skin.

"As reliable as rain," I retorted. "I love you, Adge, more than any garden or railway or factory or—"

"I've loved you as long as I've known you. I tried to force myself to forget, but you kept reminding me how superior you are in every way. I couldn't marry anyone else." Adrian wrapped an arm around my waist, and we both wobbled. I crashed into his chest, and he wrapped his other arm around me.

"Are you trying to compromise me?"

"I'll have to propose," he said with a rakish grin as the gloves fell to the floor. "But not yet."

Our lips met as our knees tangled. I slid sideways to keep my balance as Adge pulled me close. The paisley shawl fell to one side, but there was no room for thought. Any distance between us was too far as he surrounded me in a cocoon of warmth.

His desperate kiss gentled as he cupped my face and trailed a feather-light touch down my cheek. "Let's keep the canal."

"What?" I nearly fell backward and wrapped an arm around Adge to catch myself from falling off my stool.

"Keep." A searing kiss. "The." Burning heat flooded every inch of my body. "Canal." The hungry kiss lengthened, and my other hand wrapped around his neck.

Adrian pulled away, and we both drew a breath. "Keep the boats at least, but train cars could be promising too."

I threw my head back with a laugh. "That's not a proposal."

He tightened his embrace. Our eyes locked, and Adrian's reignited with fire. "I remember everything. Every dance. Every Season. I always believed you were beyond my reach."

I looked pointedly at his arms, encircling me. "Clearly not."

Adge fell off his stool. "Ow."

"I'm sorry. Did I knock you down? This skirt."

Then I realized what he was doing. *Kneeling.*

"Annie, will you marry me? I cannot offer anything. The advantage is entirely on your side."

I hugged him around the neck. "You own a calendar."

He kissed me softly on the lips. "One trifling calendar in exchange for your generous dowry. And a pie."

"I don't care about dowries. You remembered my birthday."

He kissed me again, this time slow and tender.

"You have decent aim with acorns. You show up every day, rain or shine. You hear me out. You negotiate fiercely. You truly see me."

He scrambled awkwardly back onto the edge of his stool. "And I love you endlessly." He brushed my hair gently with his hand. "You are beautiful and kind. Generous to your relatives. Loyal to your friends and intelligent—"

"And annoying?"

He shrugged. "Persistent." He kissed me so fiercely that my toes curled inside my boots. "I look forward to our lively conversations."

I planted a swift kiss on his cheek. "Arguments."

"Discussions." He placed a finger on my lips. "You see? I cannot propose without you correcting my language." He traced the line of my lips, and I watched him, mesmerized.

He smirked.

I tapped the counterproposal. "Speaking of which, I've redrawn the railway line to spare the old oak. The cost will nearly be the same."

Adrian groaned. "The canal already has loading stations and roads on the other side. It's far less invasive."

"That oak is one of the oldest in Britain. It's a national treasure. People come from miles to see it."

Adrian sighed. "You want to reroute the entire railway line to spare a tree?"

I ran my hands through his hair—his soft, beautiful, bronze hair. "Yes."

"You cannot accept my proposal without debating business measures?" Adrian leaned forward until his mouth hovered a breath away. "We'll discuss it later." His lips skimmed across mine. "Much later." His hands slid around my waist and tugged me closer to him as a crooked smile broke over his face. "After a slice of blackberry pie."

Epilogue

Two years later

ADRIAN LED ME ALONG THE edge of the orchard.

"This is a roundabout way to walk to the railway ceremony."

"I'm not taking you there."

"We're officiating. They can't start without us." I glanced at the timepiece pinned to my dress. "It's nearly eleven."

"Ah, but are you sure it's today?"

I kissed his cheek. "My husband keeps my calendar now. He makes certain I remember all the important events, and I'm always on time. Why?"

Adge grinned. "He might have told you the wrong starting time in order to steal a few minutes alone together."

I gestured at the pear trees, heavy with fruit, and the full apple trees. "In the orchard?"

He wrapped his fingers around mine. "Not there either."

We wandered along the hedgerow, ripe with berries, until we reached the last remaining portion of my old garden. A lone beech tree, its leaves glistening copper in the autumn sun.

Adge parted the curtain of branches, and we ducked inside. Golden light streamed overhead through the canopy. He curled an arm around my waist. "We saved two trees in your garden. The old oak, but more importantly . . ."

I rested my head on his chest. "The eavesdropping tree."

Adrian tipped my head up to look at him. "The kissing tree." His head dipped down, ready for a full demonstration.

I stopped him with a finger on his lips. "The hide-and-seek tree."

He removed my finger, kissing it slowly. "The kissing tree."

"The shade tree where our children can rest between games."

Adrian bent over me, his intention clear. "I kissed you here first."

"That didn't count. I was twelve. You were sixteen."

His lips moved against mine as he spoke. "It counted."

I pulled back slightly. "If our daughter kisses the neighborhood boys there, that will be well with you?"

Adrian's lips hovered there, tantalizingly near, and I closed the distance. He barely responded. "What daughter?"

I moved his hand to the slight bump of my belly. "It's been enough months that I feel certain this time."

Adrian picked me up and swung me in a circle. I threw my arms around his neck to keep from falling.

"How soon?"

"Late February," I said.

"I'll build a fence around this tree, like the oak, to keep the neighbor boys away."

I laughed as my feet landed back on the ground. "For a moment, I thought you intended to build a fence around our daughter."

"I'll do that as well. But it will be a son, not a daughter."

I waved him off. "You only want to argue in order to kiss afterward."

Adge grinned wickedly. "No, I don't."

"Contradicting me will not earn you a kiss either."

He pulled me close beneath the drooping branches of the beech tree. "Let's skip directly to my apology."

"Apology accepted." I dodged his kiss and shook my timepiece. "When does it actually begin?"

"Noon," he said sheepishly. "We have a full hour to ourselves."

"There are guests to greet."

Adge spun me into a tight hug. "I want two minutes with you beneath the kissing tree."

I breathed in the scent of his sandalwood soap. "Two minutes."

Two minutes grew to ten, and finally we broke apart. Adrian cupped my face between his hands. "I love autumn now. It's our anniversary."

Something had shifted. The changing leaves no longer saddened me. I rested my head on his chest. "I'm at peace now." My life had altered dramatically, but I welcomed the differences.

We wandered down to the new road, where High Street extended almost all the way to Langton Abbey. Window displays glistened in the new store fronts.

"The rent from those stores alone is going to bring in enough income—"

I held up a hand. "Not today, my brilliant husband. Let me enjoy the shops." I peered into Mavis's bakery window. "And a piece of gingerbread. It's like market day every day. I wouldn't mind a pie too."

Adrian looked skeptically at my latest pale pink confection from Mrs. Rowntree.

"Just a piece of gingerbread, then." I stared pointedly at his flowered waistcoat. "You must have five handkerchiefs hidden in there."

He shook his head. "Three."

"Then you'll still have one left."

He ducked into the bakery, coming out with gingerbread for me and a bun for himself. We lingered on High Street, nodding at passing acquaintances, who stared curiously at us. Adrian produced a handkerchief when I finished and slowly caressed nonexistent crumbs from my hand.

I drew a sharp breath. "Mavis won't be able to keep up with business after the ceremony. Did you see the way everyone looked at my gingerbread?"

Adrian leaned in so his breath tickled my ear. "The way I look at you every night."

I was still blushing when we arrived at my old orangery. The gleaming facade and giant clock made the building look brand new.

People crowded around the front, where a Jenny Lind engine waited for the first run of our local line to connect with the Great Western Railway. An official came over. "We're delighted to have your new line connect with ours. Shall we?" He indicated the carriage behind the locomotive.

Adrian whispered in my ear. "11:58. We still have two minutes."

"Thank you," I said to the train official. "I'll be right there." Turning to Adge, I whispered, "We're in public. You already had two minutes."

He adopted his most formal air. "Anything for you, baroness."

Nicholas bumped my shoulder. "She's nobility today, is she?"

His wife, Julia, jostled their newborn child. "Leave her be."

"How are your gardens?" I asked eagerly.

"Wild as ever." Nicholas groaned. "Julia hardly lets the gardener trim anything."

"Thank you for entrusting Windmore to us." Julia thrust the restless child into Nicholas's arms and smoothed the bodice of her dress.

"You made this railway possible by purchasing it." I exchanged a meaningful glance with her. "I cannot thank *you* enough for caring for Windmore the way I would."

"Stop it, or we shall both cry." Julia grabbed her baby back and began rocking side to side. "One wailing infant is enough. No additional tears are required." But I saw her wipe the corner of one eye as she and Nicholas walked away.

I'm finally ready. I waved to the train engineer, who blew his whistle. The crowd quieted, and I began. "We welcome honored government officials, railway investors, guests, those who built the line, and all who came."

A cheer went up from the crowd. I gestured to Adrian's father and the businessmen who had consulted with us to ensure the railway would meet the needs of factories far and wide. "Thank you to those who believed in this project, who worked tirelessly on it, and who made it possible. Today we celebrate a new future for our village and our valley." I stepped onto the first rung of the carriage car with Adrian's hand to support me. "We take our first journey on this new adventure."

A waiting conductor assisted me into the cabin. Adrian followed with his father behind. The local members of Parliament, aristocracy, gentry, and our invited guests filled the cabin. Mr. Beck, now in charge of the railway depot, led the official from the Great Western Railway onto the train.

"They're waiting for your signal, Lady Baxter," Mr. Beck said. He gave me a grateful look. I knew how desperate an edge he'd teetered on before the railway employed him.

I exchanged a glance with Adge, and he reached for my hand. "We're ready to take this journey together."

I leaned out the window and waved my hand. The engineer smiled and waved back. The train gave a small jerk as the first locomotive to pass through Langton left the station.

It cut a path through my former garden. We wound past the newly relocated Roman statues. Adrian lowered his head and whispered, "They're still naked."

I bit my lip and held back a laugh.

A new faux temple, grander than the other, stood atop a rise beside the fenced oak tree. All along the railway, a stone guardrail marked the border between the rail line and the remaining green. It was a public garden now, with walkways leading to the ledges where people leaned over and cheered the train on.

We passed beneath a grand iron bridge. "Here it comes," Adge whispered. A whoosh of air, and we entered a dark tunnel. The others gasped.

The train emerged into daylight again and gathered speed for the stretch ahead.

"We'll go through all the darkness together," he whispered. "I'll bring you back into the light every time."

I wanted to rest my head on his shoulder. I wanted to kiss him. I wanted to wrap my arms around his neck and never let go. Instead, I smiled. My Adrian smile. I squeezed his hand three times. He squeezed back.

"It's dark beneath the beech tree," I said.

One side of his mouth lifted slowly. "I know that tree."

"Until the leaves fall."

"It's dark in the cloister. No one ever goes in the cloister, and the cloister never drops its leaves."

"The music room is rather poorly lit in the afternoon."

Adge considered me, his smile growing. "It grows dark earlier and earlier in autumn. It's getting very dark by late afternoon."

"True. We'll have to stay indoors more often. It gets dark so early now."

"And it's chilly. We may require blankets."

"I'll need you to sit quite close."

We smiled at each other.

"Autumn and winter are definitely my favorite seasons now."

"Are they?"

"It's far too sunny in spring and summer. Nowhere to hide."

The train whistle pierced the air. We passed into another tunnel, and Adge took advantage of the complete darkness to press a kiss on my cheek. The train rattled back into the sunlight. "You don't mind the changes and the leaves dropping and winter coming on?"

"Not if it brings you closer to me."

Adge inched closer on the bench. He cleared his throat. "I'm closer to you."

No one sat in front of us. We occupied the first bench in the carriage, and everyone sat behind. I slipped off a glove, and Adrian explored my hand with a feather-light touch. I shivered.

His brow furrowed. "Are you cold? Is the wind too much?"

I looked into his gentle eyes. I'd given up most of the places where my parents' memories lived. Their rose garden. The statuary. The labyrinth. The orangery.

But Adrian was my family now. With him, I felt valued. I belonged. I wasn't an outsider, watching others and searching for a way to fit. I was everything to him, and he was everything to me.

I gazed up at Adge. "Never better."

He frowned.

"I am a bit cold."

He readjusted my mother's paisley shawl, using the excuse to trail his fingers across my shoulders and down my arms, until he found the sensitive skin around my wrist. He threaded his fingers through mine. "Better?"

"Perfect. Exquisitely perfect."

Acknowledgments

Thanks to my father, who managed a Covid-free trip to England, so I could visit the gardens my characters inhabit. Thanks to Adrian and Jay, who guided us and explored places with us that I never would have found on my own. Thanks to my husband and children for staying alive while I was gone and for thriving in my absence.

Thanks to Michele Paige Holmes, whose writing inspires me and whose editing elevates my thinking and my craft. Thanks to Lorie Humpherys, whose sharp eye catches my typos, my continuity errors, and gaps in common sense. Thanks to Sara Hacken, Meghan Hoesch, Marianne Siegmund, and Judy C. Olsen for their editing help. Thanks to Heather B. Moore for the generous way that she shares her knowledge and mentors other authors.

And thank you to the thousands of unsung gardeners, whose backbreaking efforts create the beauty I so casually enjoy.

Lisa H. Catmull is the author of clean and wholesome romances in the Victorian era and sweet contemporary romances. Her books have been nominated for Swoony, RONE, and Whitney awards. She earned a Bachelor of Art in English from Dartmouth College in New Hampshire and a Master of Education in Elementary Education from Utah State University in Logan, Utah. Lisa taught Middle School English and History for seven years before pursuing screenwriting and writing. She currently lives between a canyon and a lake in Utah with her husband, two cats, and two rambunctious children.

You can find her online at www.lisacatmull.com and on Facebook, Instagram, Twitter, and TikTok.

www.ingramcontent.com/pod-product-compliance
Lightning Source LLC
LaVergne TN
LVHW021803060526
838201LV00058B/3220